APOCALYPSE GIRL DREAMING

EVIL
GIRLFRIEND
MEDIA

Published by Evil Girlfriend Media, P.O. BOX 3856, Federal Way, WA 98063
Copyright © 2015

All rights reserved. Any reproduction or distribution of this book, in part or in whole, or transmission in any form, or by any means, electronic, mechanical, photocopying, recording or otherwise, without the written permission of the publisher or author is theft. Any similarity to persons living or dead is purely coincidental.

Cover art by Fernando Cortes. Cover design by Matt Youngmark.

"Prince of Artemis V" copyright ©2010 by Jennifer Brozek, *Crossed Genres* magazine, Issue 15; "The Priest, the Man, the Gun" copyright ©2011 by Jennifer Brozek, *Tales of the Talisman* magazine, Volume 7, Issue 2; "A Nightmare for Anna" copyright ©2014 by Jennifer Brozek, *By Faerie Light* anthology; "Eulogy for Muffin" copyright ©2010 by Jennifer Brozek, *APEXOLOGY: Horror* anthology; "Honoring the Dead" copyright ©2009 by Jennifer Brozek, *Wily Writers* website; "A Card Given" copyright ©2013 by Jennifer Brozek, *What Fates Impose* anthology; "Iron Achilles Heel" copyright ©2013 by Jennifer Brozek, *The New Hero II* anthology; "Sandcastle Sacrifices" copyright ©2014 by Jennifer Brozek, *Village by the Sea*; "M.O.V.E." copyright ©2011 by Jennifer Brozek, *No Man's Land* anthology; "A Promise Made" copyright ©2011 by Jennifer Brozek, *Showdown at Midnight* anthology; "Ley of the Land" copyright ©2014 by Jennifer Brozek, *Time-Traveled Tales 2* anthology; "An Infestation of Adverts" copyright ©2013 by Jennifer Brozek, *Blue Shift Magazine, Issue #1*; "Discordance" copyright ©2011 by Jennifer Brozek, *Under the Vale and Other Tales of Valdemar* anthology; "Memories Like Crystal Shards" copyright ©2013 by Jennifer Brozek, *HEROES!* anthology; "The Tinker's Music Box" copyright ©2012 by Jennifer Brozek, *Time-Traveled Tales* anthology; "The Bathory Clinic Deal" copyright ©2014 by Jennifer Brozek, *The Future Embodied* anthology; "Showdown at High Moon" copyright ©2012 by Jennifer Brozek, *Westward Weird* anthology; "Found on the Body of a Soldier" copyright ©2014 by Jennifer Brozek; "Dust Angels" copyright ©2013 by Jennifer Brozek, *Beyond the Sun* anthology; "For the Love of a Troll on a Midwinter Night" copyright ©2014 by Jennifer Brozek, *Night Terrors III* anthology, "The Price of Family" copyright © 2013 by Mercedes Lackey. Reprinted by permission of Mercedes Lackey.

ISBN: 978-1-940154-08-4

For Jeff,

*the light of my life and my apocalyptic
partner in crime.*

CONTENTS

Introduction *by Jody Lynn Nye* 6

Foreword 8

Prince of Artemis V 11

The Priest, the Man, the Gun 23

A Nightmare for Anna 33

Eulogy for Muffin 47

Honoring the Dead 57

A Card Given 71

Iron Achilles Heel 85

Sandcastle Sacrifices 99

The Price of Family 109

M.O.V.E. 123

A Promise Made 137

Ley of the Land 147

An Infestation of Adverts 161

Discordance 171

Memories Like Crystal Shards 183

The Tinker's Music Box 197

The Bathory Clinic Deal 209

Showdown at High Moon 229

Found on the Body of a Soldier 245

Dust Angels 253

For the Love of a Troll on a Midwinter Night 263

INTRODUCTION
By Jody Lynn Nye

A good short story is not an easy thing to write. It takes a significant amount of work to put together good world-building, intriguing characterization, not to mention a coherent plot, and all in a word count shorter than it took for your commencement speaker to exhort you to go out and do good in the world. Some people think that it's easier to write a short story than a novel, that those who write them aren't capable of branching out into the longer art form. Quite the opposite is true. It takes a special skill set to put a good tale into such a small space. Many never master the short story. Some do well enough, but not well enough to be memorable.

Within the bounds of these meager pieces of real estate, Jennifer Brozek creates believable worlds. Her work is eminently readable. You'll finish one story, then won't be able to resist moving on to the next. And when you finish that one, they're so good, why not another? Before you know it, it's past midnight, and you're bleary-eyed but content. And they're far less fattening than malted milk balls.

Jenn has honored me by inviting me into some of the anthologies she has edited over the years. She's said that I'm one of her favorite short story writers. Let me return the favor by saying that she's one of my favorite anthology editors. She always comes up with clever, original themes on which her writers are to base their tales. I always look forward to her anthology invitations, because I know I'm going to get a chance to stretch my writing muscles and have a good time.

Within these pages, you and I get to see what Jenn likes to write when she feels like breaking out and busting some literary moves of her own. She shows admirable versatility, ranging from science fiction to fantasy to horror with seeming ease. Fairy tales, before the Brothers Grimm, were moralistic tales meant to frighten a child into proper behavior or tell them unwelcome truths. Jenn chills us with "A Nightmare for Anna," a fairy tale that would have been right at home in an 18th century storybook. Her own take on "The Crucible" is just as horror-filled and just as compelling to read. She drags us into the midst of futuristic riots. She brings us home with a hero who learns what that overused word really means. Her alien cultures are fascinating because they are so resolutely non-human yet comprehendible by our poor human minds. She even writes a good Western ghost story. When you read her work, you walk into well-established, detailed worlds and care about the people in them, even as you know in your deepest heart that their tales probably won't end well.

I know you'll enjoy this collection as much as I have. Jennifer Brozek's writing will glimmer in your memory like the glowing *dusamez* in her Kember Empire tales. Enjoy.

Jody Lynn Nye
Barrington, IL
July 2014

FOREWORD

I love short stories. I love the way they impact my life in just a few words. But I am the practical one. The one who worries about bills, about the feasibility of something, about the realistic problems of the world. Apocalypse Girl is my alter ego. She is the dreamer, the child within who sees the potential in everything, the lover of the macabre, the one who asks "What if?" and runs with it—physics and torpedoes be damned. Most the stories in this collection were written by Apocalypse Girl, fueled by her unquenchable imagination and her undying enthusiasm for what could be.

You will find that many of these short stories were written in a series of common universes. Most of my urban fantasy stories are set in my fictional Pacific Northwest city of Kendrick located on the west side of Discovery Bay between Port Townsend and Port Angeles. The stories are only linked by location. Most of my weird west stories are set in my Mowry universe where magic, mystery, and miracles all live on this side of reality near the town of Mowry, Arizona. They are usually linked by the inclusion of the characters Eric Hamblin and Joseph Lamb. Most of my science fiction stories are set in the far-flung galaxy that houses the Kember Empire based upon a horrific SF novel that will never see the light of day. The universe, though, I did some good world-building there. The stories are linked in chronological order with the vaguest ties between people and alien races.

There are a number of short stories that have nothing to do with the above universes. Stories that reflect my love of the Lovecraft mythos, that are my answer to a challenge to write outside my comfort zone, tie-in stories, and stories specifically written for anthologies I was invited to. Some of my favorite stories fit this last, where I am challenged to write within a very specific set of guidelines. Some of my best work comes from needing to meet a hard writing challenge with an ambitious deadline. Sometimes, I write a short story just to see what will come next.

I hope you enjoy your journey through Apocalypse Girl's dreams. I know I did.

Jennifer Brozek,
September 2014

LIKE MANY OF MY STORIES,
*I wrote this one in response to a call for submissions, specifically for a Crossed Genres YA call in 2010. Many of the young adult stories I read cast siblings in an adversarial role. But, despite sibling squabbles, I find it is usually the opposite: siblings tend to band together to protect each other. I decided to weave a story in which an older brother was willing to give up the world to protect his sister. This is one of my favorite short stories and is the one that has been most reprinted. It is set in my Kember Empire universe.
If I ever have a reason or time to continue
the story, I know what happens next.*

THE PRINCE OF ARTEMIS V
(A Kember Empire Story)

"A princess is a servant to all her people. She's supposed to care for them and never let them down. Ever," Lanteri said.

Hart nodded at his little sister. "What's the first rule of being a princess?"

"Never, ever abandon your people—for they need you more than you know," she said in a tone so serious that it would have indicated satire if it had not come from an eight-year-old's mouth.

"You're a very good princess."

"I'm trying." She smiled at her older brother. "But sometimes, it's hard."

"I know. As Dad says, 'Nothing good…'"

"'…ever comes easy,'" they finished together and grinned.

Lanteri bent over her pixel board and continued to draw her idea of the perfect castle. She drew each line slowly, dragging the pixel pen over the board. Whenever a line was not exactly as she wanted it, she turned the pen over to erase the offending pixels before going back to her masterpiece. She had been working on this particular picture for weeks.

Hart watched her, envying both her ability to manipulate the pixel board and her imagination. He lacked her artistic talent, and had not drawn anything since that night five years ago… since Toor was Taken.

Though only thirteen, Hart felt old. He felt like he thought his parents must feel after a long day in the fields, harvesting the purpuran flower buds; the small purple, yellow, and black flowers used to make a rich, shimmery, dark purple dye. He hoped that Lanteri would never have to feel the way he felt right now… especially as the double moons of Artemis V readied to rise in their annual double-full arc tonight.

The opening and closing of the front door signaled the arrival of their parents. Neither child moved from their respective places in their shared bedroom. The conversation between their parents—or argument as it seemed to be—echoed through the small Company-provided house.

"They all look at me like she's already been Taken," Hart heard his mother say. He imagined the distressed flush of his mother's face. "We've got to do something."

"The Company doesn't give a damn what happens to us. As long as the purpuran flowers are harvested and the royal dye is made, they don't care." In his mind's eye, Hart saw his father's drawn face, and strength failing in his old man's body.

"We've got to do something. Anything. Stop the purpuran shipments. Get their attention." His mother's voice had softened to the whine of a wounded animal. "I can't go through this again."

"Saneri, the last time we tried something, the Company almost starved us to death. The only thing that grows on this mudball is the purpuran flower. The Company doesn't care, I say again. The empire doesn't care. The empress herself can't know of this and even if she did, would she care? No. I don't think so. There are no rescuers. No brave guardsmen. No heroic Hedari. No stranger SLINGing in from another galaxy who'll come roaring to the rescue. We only have us to depend on. That's how it's always been."

"I can't go through this again. I can't lose her."

Hart reached over and closed the bedroom door to shut out their parents' pain and worry, and most of all, their helplessness. He hoped Lanteri had not heard their parents' despair, but as all hopes were dashed on Artemis V, this one was too.

"In my world," Lanteri said without looking up from her pixel drawing of a castle in a beautiful sunny landscape, "there are no Takers, and no one's afraid of losing their children."

"I'm going to Nori's," Lanteri called as she headed out the door.

"Wait!" Saneri said.

Hart, sitting at the kitchen table, heard the panic in his mother's voice and hoped Lanteri would not. He also hoped that their mother would not ground Lanteri on what might be her last day alive.

Lanteri stopped, turned, and gave her mother an impatient look. "What?"

"Uh, don't forget your coat."

"I'm just going next door, Mom."

"Don't you sass me. Go get your coat or you're not going anywhere."

Lanteri sighed and stomped back to the bedroom to get her coat. Hart listened as their mother paced, then fussed with Lanteri's coat. "You be back before dark. You hear me?"

"It's not like it's gonna get all that dark with the double-full moon, Mom."

Hart smiled at the defiance in his little sister's voice.

"Lanteri…" Their mother's tone had a warning in it that promised pain and punishment if she were not obeyed.

Another sigh. "Yes, ma'am. Before dark. Can I go now?"

There was a pause before their mother's reluctant answer came: "Yes. Go."

Hart knew their mother would not make that kind of fuss about him if he wanted to go to a friend's house today. It made him hurt a little more inside. He waited for his mother to come to the kitchen.

Saneri was wiping at her face when she entered. Seeing her son there clearly surprised her. "Hart? What's wrong?"

"You look at her as if she's already been Taken." His voice was flat and full of anger.

Saneri blinked at her eldest in shock and realization. Shock turned to anger in a tightening of her lips. "You don't know what it's like."

"I lost Toor, too. He was my brother. My twin. You act like… like… you're the only one who lost him."

The tightened lips turned into a white line while bright splotches of red shone on Saneri's cheeks. "Don't you dare!"

"No, don't *you* dare!" Hart stood, his chair falling away to clatter on the floor. "We *all* lost him when he was Taken. Now, you act like Lanteri's already gone."

Hart's outrage deflated his mother's anger, and she slumped to the kitchen chair in front of her, calling to Hart's mind the image of a spent windsock. She put her face in her hands and silently wept, her body shaking with her repressed sobs.

It was Hart's turn to be deflated. He watched his mother break down in front of him for a couple of moments before he picked up the kitchen chair, setting it right and sitting across from her. He let the worst of her grief and rage pass before offering her a kitchen towel. For several long minutes, the two of them sat in silence.

"Toor," she said, "was special to me. He promised me he'd never be Taken. He promised me…"

"He was your favorite." There was no accusation in Hart's voice; just a simple, knowing truth. Saneri looked away but did not deny it, murdering the last bit of his child's heart. He swallowed his own grief and pressed on. "Now, Lanteri's your favorite."

"She's the only girl child of age in this harvest zone. She's special."

"What about Nori?"

"Nori's too old. They haven't Taken anyone over the age of fifteen in at least twenty years."

"Then why aren't you worried about me?" The betraying words leaped out of Hart's mouth. Now that the words were on the table between them, he could not snatch them back. At least his mother had the decency to look shocked again.

"What? Of course I'm worried about you! What would make you think… Why? Oh, Hart, I love you. Of course I'm worried you'll be Taken." She paused, waiting for him to respond, but he just continued to look at her, stone-faced. "You're different. You're stronger. Solid. Dependable," she tried to explain.

"Not the prize that Toor was and Lanteri is?"

His mother gave him a look. "Now you're just being sullen. Stop it." She wiped at her face again, but this time it was more of a nervous tic.

This casual maternal admonishment made him smile, though he did not really understand why. Perhaps the admonishment was a sign that she really did care about him.

Saneri took the small smile as a sign of encouragement. "I love you, Hart. You're the one I can depend on. You always have been." She paused, took a breath and then forged onward, "That's why I need you to protect your sister."

"Because you and Dad can't."

She looked away, but not before he saw the flinch of anguish on her face. "Yes. You're closer to her. She idolizes you. You… I think you're her only hope."

Now the truth was out between them—almost all of it anyway. He *was* Lanteri's only hope. He had always known it. "Don't worry, Mom. I'll protect her. I promise." The look of gratitude on his mother's face felt painful. "I know what to do."

Lanteri and Hart sat in their bedroom, watching out the window as the sun set late in the summer evening. Their silence spoke volumes in siblingspeak. They were both worried. She looked to him for comfort, and he gave it in a sudden slap at the button that closed the blinds and signaled the room's automatic sensors to produce a dim light. Then he patted the spot next to him on his bed. She came willingly. She still had enough of a child's need for comfort that she took it when it was offered.

They sat like that on his bed, Lanteri pressed to her brother's side and he with his arm wrapped around her shoulders in a protective embrace. When she finally spoke, her voice was soft. "What was Toor like?" She could not see Hart's frown.

He did not look down at her. "A lot like you. Good with animals. A dreamer. Always forgetting about the time." Hart frowned, "I was always saving him from punishment. Reminding him to do his chores. To come home on time. To remember what Mom and Dad said to do."

"I'm not like that. I remember things."

"You're right. I guess you've got a bit of both me and Toor in you. Part dreamer. Part… not dreamer."

Lanteri offered up a brave smile. "I'm a princess."

"Yes. You are."

The silence settled comfortably between them again and they watched the minutes tick over on the clock. Hart's mind raced. Finally, he shifted, waking Lanteri, who had dozed off.

"What's going on? Are they here?" There was a hint of panic in Lanteri's voice.

"No, silly. We've just got to get ready."

"Oh," she yawned. "How?"

"Like this." Hart reached up to the shelf above his bed and found a small wad of dingy rope. "You're gonna sleep in your clothes tonight and on my bed with me." He tied one end of the rope around his left ankle and then tied the other end of it around her right ankle. "If they come to Take either of us, this will connect us and the pulling should wake one of us up. Then, we have to save the other one. Understand?"

"I'm gonna save you?"

He shrugged. "Maybe. I don't know." He kept his head down so she would not see the look on his face.

Lanteri thrust out her chin. "I'll save you." She curled up next to him, facing the wall while he remained on his back.

"Lan?"

"Yeah?"

"What's the first rule of being a princess?"

"Never, ever abandon your people—for they need you more than you know," she said. There was a smile in her sleepy voice.

"Good. And the second?"

Lanteri's body relaxed in the comfort of the familiar game. "A princess is a servant to all of her people. She's supposed to care for them and never let them down. Ever."

"Yep. What's the third rule?"

"A princess must be kind and generous but firm because she has to make the hard decisions that others cannot."

"Because 'nothing good ever comes easy,'" he quoted.

She let out a breath she'd been holding. "Will you always be my subject?"

"Yes. Always." He closed his eyes and waited.

They came as they had for the past five years, the Takers. They came in light, sound, and beauty. They looked like they could be any one of a dozen humanoid races Hart was familiar with… or none of them. They were all beautiful. Shining. Perfect. Too perfect. But, God, they were *beautiful*.

Hart stood in a field of grass and flowers that could never exist on Artemis V. The sun shone in that bright, cheerful way that made the Harvesters rush to cover the delicate purpuran flowers that could only survive in the shade.

The air smelled cool, clear, and clean, no hint of the musty smell that permeated everything on Artemis V. He knew he was still at home in bed, but at the same time he was also here, in this impossibly ephemeral place of beauty and light. There were several of them in the distance, the Takers, watching him. He wanted to go to them but refused to be moved. They had to come to him.

A boy approached. It was the same boy who had approached him every year for the past five. This boy, with brown hair and blue eyes, grew a year older with each meeting so that he and Hart were always peers. Never one older or younger. "Hart, we're still waiting for you."

Hart ached at the sound of his name. "I can't go with you." He saw the boy's smile falter, and it hurt his soul.

"Please. Hart, why not? You deserve a better life. You deserve to play in the sun and the grass. That world is no place for a child."

Hart shook his head. "You aren't real. You can't prove you're real and that what you say isn't a lie."

The boy sighed with weariness of the familiar argument. He tried something new. "Your brother—"

"Is dead!" Hart interrupted, not willing to listen to anything about Toor. "You killed him five years ago."

The boy tipped his chin up. "No. Far from it. He's here with us and happy. He misses you. He said to tell you to remember the Day of Purple Hands. I don't know what that means, and he wouldn't tell me."

Hart felt his stomach lurch. The Day of Purple Hands was when he and Toor had decided that if they were not allowed to wear the royal purpuran purple color, they would dye their skin with it. It had been Toor's idea; a small act of defiance against the Company and the circumstances that had made their family all but indentured servants to those that employed them. They had gotten in so much trouble, grounded for weeks. But both of them had considered it a victory over the Company. It was something Toor would remind him of.

But he could not leave Lanteri.

"It doesn't matter." Hart turned from the boy, though it was hard to turn from that light.

"Why?" There was a desperate plea in the boy's voice. "Why can't you come with us?"

Hart's answer was a whisper. "Because a prince never abandons his people—for they need him more than he knows."

The boy walked up close behind Hart. "My time runs out. I won't be able to keep coming back. You're my other half. You're the one I was meant to save. If I can't save you, I don't know what I'll do. It might kill me. *Please.*"

The feel of the boy's hand on Hart's shoulder was warm and comforting. It almost unraveled his resolve. The idea that this boy needed him and at the same time needed to save him was almost too much. Then, another sensation distracted Hart. Something tugged at his ankle. He looked down and saw the dingy rope tied around his ankle.

Lanteri.

Lanteri was being Taken… from him, from his mother, from his family. Hart shrugged the boy's hand from his shoulder. "My sister needs me." He closed his eyes and groped for his sister. At first, he thought he was too late. Then he found her curled in a tight ball in the corner of the bed. He grabbed her upper arm and squeezed. "Lanteri, stay with us," he said, praying she could hear him.

When he opened his eyes again he was back on the field of beauty and light. In his hand, he could feel, but not see, Lanteri's arm. "I can't go with you. My family needs me. And I can't let you take Lanteri." He sensed the boy step back. Hart did not turn around, fearing to see the sorrow he knew was etched all over the boy's perfect face.

"I'll go," the boy said. "But I can't wait much longer. We'll meet only one more time, on the next double-full moon. You have one last chance to free yourself of that hellish place and then, all hope is lost. Please…"

Hart squeezed his eyes shut against the temptation of this place and willed that the boy with his promises of light and joy would just go away. Mercifully, the scent of that place disappeared.

◆

"You bruised my arm," Lanteri said as she looked at the finger-shaped marks on her arm in the pale light of the morning. Her voice was subdued as she refused to look at her brother.

"I'm sorry." Hart apologized for more than the bruise, as he bent over to untie the rope from around their ankles. As he wadded up the rope, he could have sworn he smelled that other world on it. He tossed it at the shelf and did not bother to see if he hit his mark. He looked down and saw a bruise around his ankle. "You bruised me, too."

Lanteri turned in a sudden motion, threw her arms around him, and pressed her face into his chest. Her voice came out in choked sobs. "Why didn't you tell me it'd be like that? Why didn't anyone tell me they'd be so pretty?"

He hugged her to him and petted her hair. "Shhhh." He rocked her.

"Shhh, it's fine. You won't remember soon. You won't remember anything about it. It'll be just a dream. No one remembers, really."

"They were so pretty. It was just like my dream, my picture."

"I know, Lan, I know."

She pulled away from him and looked at his face. "Do they come for you every year? Is it like that every year?"

He smoothed away a tear from her cheek and nodded, not wanting to lie to her again.

"How do you not go? Why do you stay?"

Hart closed his eyes and wondered that himself. "I think of you," he said. "I stay because of you. You need me. And so do Mom and Dad."

"But, what if it's not a lie? What if… it's really what they say?"

"You can't think like that. You can't, Lanteri. Think of what it would do to Mom and Dad if you were Taken. If *we* were Taken. It would kill them." Hart shook his head. "Don't think like that ever." He heard the lack of conviction in his voice and was certain she did, too.

She frowned. "I can't remember what she looked like. I can't remember anything but the shining sun."

He turned from her. "Go wash your face, and then wake up Mom and Dad. They'll be glad to know you're still here."

Lanteri walked to the door. She paused, looking back at him. "I want to remember." When he did not answer, she shook her head and left.

He scowled, murmuring "No, you don't." He did not remember most of the time. It was only in the weeks before the next double-full moon that he would remember the field with the flowers and the boy. Last night was the first time the boy had given him proof that Toor was still alive and happy. Last night was the first time the boy had told him how much he needed Hart, and that their next meeting would be their last.

For five years, Hart had resisted for the sake of Lanteri, if not for his parents. Now, he knew for certain the Takers wanted both he and his little sister. Next year, they both could be Taken to that place of wonder, to be reunited with Toor, and to live their lives in the sun instead of the shadows and mud. Could he—should he—keep the beauty at bay one last time?

I WANTED TO WRITE A WEIRD WEST *story. I'd been noodling around with the idea of a blessed gun, a murdered lawman and his host, and how that story would work. This was the first of the Mowry series I wrote, but the third one I sold (even though it came out before the others). I really believe the others worked so well because I had already written this story. Both main characters—Eric Hamblin and Joseph Lamb—were named in a tuckerization. As it turned out, the woman who won the tuckerization came from Arizona, and she chose the names of two of her ancestors who used to live there.*

THE PRIEST, THE MAN, THE GUN
(A Mowry Story)

Joseph felt the man before he saw him; it was the stink of fear and the sweat of desperation that gave him away. He waited until the man picked up the gun before he spoke. "This is a house of God, my son." When the man whirled on him, Joseph said nothing, did nothing, and allowed the panic in the man's eyes to clear in recognition of the priest's traditional black attire.

"The gun… it was here. I didn't bring it." He waved the gun at the altar but did not put it down. The gun was a Colt 1851 Navy revolver, favored of civilians and lawmen alike. This one had a series of intricate flame engravings on the barrel, and a well-worn handle.

"I know, my son. It's my gun." Joseph watched the man. He was dirty, sweaty, and worn-looking from his trek under the Arizona sun. But the care in the making of his shirt said that this was not his usual condition.

"I'm in trouble, Father. I need help."

"What's your name?"

"Eric. Eric Hamblin."

Joseph smiled briefly; a white scar showing brightly against a weather-beaten face. "Joseph Lamb." He offered his open hand for the gun. Eric handed it over after a nervous glance at the door. Joseph took the gun with an air of familiarity, replaced it on the altar, and offered his hand again. "Nice to meet you."

This small act of civility brought Eric's attention back to the here and now. He clasped hands with Joseph in a strong, calloused grip. "Will you help me?"

"How about you start at the beginning, Eric? If you'd like, we can step over into the confessional." He pointed to the left where a small set of dark wood confessional booths stood against the cool brick wall.

"I didn't want to kill him," Eric said, his eyes bright. "I told him to stop. I told him I was gonna shoot. I told him. I swear on it. I didn't kill him in cold blood. You've got to believe me."

Joseph frowned, raising a hand in a 'slow down' gesture. "Whoa, cowboy. Whoa. You've got to start at the beginning before you confess to killing a man."

"It was my sister, Kay. They took her from the ranch. I was gone to town for supplies. When I got back, she was gone. Ma, she was holding her face and crying. They hit my Ma, those bastards, and took my sister. I had to go after her."

"Who took her?" It was an old story in the West. A man had to protect his family from those who would prey on it. Most times, he was either too late or outgunned.

"William Masterson and his brothers. Born bad they say. Been nothing but hell on earth since the day they were whelped."

Joseph stilled. William Masterson was a name he knew well. "Go on."

Eric saw the look in the priest's eyes. "You know them."

"I know them. Go on."

He did not miss the sudden coldness in the priest's voice. "I caught up with them by the river. John was still there with Kay. Will and the rest, they'd gone off hunting I guess. But John, he was… was…" Eric swallowed fear and anger as he controlled himself. "They'd done things to Kay that a man should never see his sister go through. She was crying when I got there. He was throwing pebbles at her. She was in bad shape. When he saw me, he rushed to her with his knife. He was gonna kill her. I told him to stop. I swore I'd shoot, but he raised that knife anyway. I shot him before he could kill her."

Eric stopped; clearly lost in the memory of his raped sister and the man he had slain to protect her.

After Joseph counted to twenty he asked, "And then?"

Eric looked up. "I had to get her out of there. The shot would bring them, the others. I knew it. Kay knew it, but she didn't want me to see her like that. I was as gentle as I could be. I got her out. John wasn't dead then. He promised he and his brothers would come for us both."

He took a seat on the first pew and dragged a hand through his mop of road-dirty hair before looking up at Joseph again. "Father, I've done the best I can. Kay's at the doctor's now. Even the Masterson boys won't mess with the doc on account of he's the only one around for miles and miles. Ma is with them, too. I had to leave. Ma and Kay, they're safe for now. William sent word that his brother died, but not before him telling about me. I overheard it as we fled. They're coming for me now. Can't be that far behind. My horse died. Snake bite. I've been running since high sun."

"What about your pistol? I don't see one on you." There was a rebuke in his voice that Joseph did not like but could not stop.

"I left it behind." Eric hung his head in shame. "I just forgot it when I was getting Kay on my horse. I didn't realize it until we got to the doc's. It's another reason I ran."

Joseph walked to one of the side windows of the small brick church and looked out. The sun hung low, almost touching the horizon. An hour of light left if they were lucky. Less time than that, going by the silhouettes he saw riding toward the church. He turned back to Eric. "What do you want from me?"

"Help."

"Help how? Murder is a sin, my son. I see that you are truly repentant, so I may give you absolution and see your soul to Heaven when the outlaws get here."

Eric looked around, the panic springing forward from the back of his eyes. He heard the distant hoof-beats now. "I don't want to die. I can't. My Ma. My sister… they need me. And how could it be murder, what I done?"

"You will likely die tonight. Only those destined to die find my church."

"How do you know? How—" Eric stopped speaking when his eyes caught sight of the dust motes dancing through the space where Joseph stood. "God in Heaven! What are you?"

"Your only hope for redemption and salvation… or your last chance at life." Joseph looked out at the moving shadows getting closer. "I wasn't always a priest. I was once a man like you, a lawman with a duty to do. I did my job well. But the job, it took a toll on me. I had to bring down a bank robber. He wouldn't stop when I told him to. I gave him warning by shout and by shot. But he kept coming. So, I laid him low. This robber was little more than a boy. Bart Masterson was his name. That must've been fifteen or sixteen years ago."

Eric started at the name.

Joseph's scar of a smile showed itself again, brief as a peck on the cheek. "Yes. One of the Masterson boys, before they all went bad. But after that, I couldn't do the job anymore. Bart hadn't even seen fifteen years. My heart couldn't stand the ugliness of the job. I left. I met up with a preacher man and traveled with him to this place. Neither of us knew Mowry was already a dying town. It was good enough for us." He paused. "Until William Masterson found us and killed us both."

"You're dead." It was a statement, not a question. Eric's confusion warred with the fear he felt. Hope also rose, like the soft bubbling of a warm spring.

"Yes, son. I am. But God gave me a choice. I could take my place in his choir of angels and have the rest I deserved, or I could become his avenging angel. I chose the path of righteous vengeance."

"I don't understand."

Joseph gestured at the pistol on the altar. "William Masterson killed me with my own gun. Now, that gun is who I am."

Eric stood and walked to the altar. He started to reach for the revolver but was halted by Joseph's voice.

"You have a choice, Eric Hamblin. You may die tonight with a clear soul and rise to your rightful place in Heaven, or you may put your trust in the Lord and his righteous vengeance and take the gun… saving your life, but not your soul."

His hand hovered above the Colt pistol. "Not my soul?"

Joseph glided to the altar and stood across from Eric. "Those who carry me in their holsters live a life free from the fear of death for a time, but the corruption of the soul is the price. Power leads a man into temptation. That temptation corrupts the soul until my purpose changes. Then I must become your executioner."

"Is it destined? If I am a good and righteous man, can my soul still be preserved?"

"It's not happened yet."

"How many carriers have you killed?"

"All of them."

Eric looked up from his hovering hand and the gun. He met Joseph's gaze. "Is there a chance that my soul can still be saved, even if I carry you in my holster?"

"There's always a chance, I suppose. But, Eric, you're not the first to ask. I know you won't be the last. It has always ended the same."

"Not this time."

Joseph leaned in. "Always."

"No. Not this time."

From outside, both men heard the sound of hooves pounding the dusty Arizona ground. Joseph looked from Eric to the door and back again. "This is your last chance. I absolve you of all your sins. You may face those men with the knowledge that you *will* join God in Heaven."

"I'm stronger than the others were. I'll save my soul *and* my life," Eric said, and picked up the revolver.

Joseph relaxed and disappeared. Eric still heard him speaking. "*I prayed you'd say that. I have a bone to pick with these men. You've given me the chance.*"

"What happens now?" he spoke to the gun.

"*Put your trust in me. Let me do the talking… and shooting.*"

Eric was startled to discover his body moving on its own toward the door. He was dizzy for a moment; the unexpected movement and swaying reminded him of a rough train ride. His gorge rose then settled again as he heard Joseph say, "Don't fight me." Hearing his own voice speak to him added another level of crazy to the already unreal day.

Joseph stopped in the doorway and holstered the gun. He leaned against the doorframe in a pose of idleness he did not feel. He held that pose for the long minutes it took the riders to come into sight. The man inside Joseph wanted to rail at the approaching men and shout out his vengeance. He did none of these things. The priest, on a mission, simply waited—as did the gun in its holster.

Six men rode, five following a lead. They headed to the small, stone, sun-baked Spanish-style mission that had served Preacher Lamb in life. The man in front, a lanky blond with handsome features, gave a shout when he saw Eric leaning against the doorframe. William spurred his horse forward at the sight. The six horses pounded up to the churchyard and halted in a flurry of stamping hooves and tossed manes.

Joseph never moved. No matter what else Eric felt, he had no fear of these men. He waited, cold-hearted and ready, as they all dismounted. All of them had expensive boots and well-bred horses. His eyes picked out their weapons: six pistols, two rifles, and at least two holdouts.

William must have understood something was different about the man before them. Eric was not the scared rabbit, looking for a place to hide, that he had seen last. William stepped forward with his men at his heels like the curs they were. "You've no place to go, murderer."

"I ain't looking to go nowhere, rapist." Joseph's tone was measured.

"You killed my brother."

"You've done a lot worse, William Masterson. Now, you're going to pay for your sins."

William whipped his hand down and up again, firing a single shot.

It struck Joseph in the left arm, making him grunt in pain. Eric yelped inside his head. "Hush now," Joseph muttered. "Let a man work." Joseph stood up straight instead of keening in pain. He shook his left arm a little before reaching over to pluck the bullet from his flesh. "You still ain't much of a shot, William. Then again, you had to shoot me close up last time. I told you then that I'd come for you."

"What's he babbling about, Will?" David, his younger and even handsomer brother, came forward.

"He ain't bleeding," Peter, the youngest of them, said.

"Shut up both of you," William snarled. His show of anger couldn't cover the man's sudden fear.

"That's right, boys. Let William think. Let him remember the last time he was here at this church. It was nigh on fifteen years ago." Joseph kept his eyes on William, willing him to remember and realize where he was. Just when he was out of patience, William spoke.

"Sheriff Lamb."

"I've been known by that name. Joseph Clyde Lamb to some. Sheriff Lamb to others. Preacher Lamb in the last days of my life."

"You're dead," William said, as if that should send the murdered man back to his grave.

"And yet, here I stand."

"What's he talking about, Will?" David's voice was soft with fear and confusion.

"Hush now," Joseph said. "The grownups are talkin'."

"No we ain't," William said. "Kill him!"

At the bark of the order, every Masterson boy opened fire on the lone man in the church doorway. Through the hail of bullets, Joseph Lamb, Lion of God, walked with the steady step of experience and shot his way through his enemies. He fanned his revolver with deliberate grace, each bullet striking home. He was struck a couple of times, but the bullets did nothing to slow him. While there was pain—there was always pain—Joseph pressed forward, killing every man he set his eyes on. He saved William for last, taking a bullet between the eyes before returning the favor in kind.

Inside his head, Eric, shocked beyond all reason, could do nothing but count the bullets from the gun his body used. He stopped at ten and tried to close his eyes but Joseph would not let him. *This is what you chose. Now watch.* Eric watched the targets of Joseph's vengeance. He watched as their dying eyes saw something he had not yet dared to look at.

When it was all said and done, six men lay dead on the ground. "As soon as I'm done healing, you can have your body back. You don't want it back this way. It hurts." Joseph holstered the revolver and stretched.

"How did you..?"

"When I control the flesh, it's almost impossible to kill, but that don't mean it don't hurt."

Eric watched as his hands pulled three bullets from his arm, one from his chest and felt the one pulled from his forehead. *"When you don't control the flesh?"*

"You can die like any other man."

"The gun. It fired…"

"Twelve times. No reloads. This gun is me and I am God's vengeance." To make his point, he swung the revolver barrel open and showed Eric the empty chambers. "You never need to load me. I fire with God's wrath."

Eric was silent for a long while. He looked around at the six dead men and realized he had control of his body again as he staggered before regaining his feet. He shivered in the dying light. "What now? And what about my soul?"

Joseph appeared to his right, "Now? We get you some dinner. Tomorrow, you take these bodies back to town. No doubt, there's a bounty on every one. You'll have avenged your family and your legend will grow. From then on, people will seek you out to make the wrongs right."

"And we'll do that?"

"Only if *you* choose. The fight for your soul is your own. I'm just your priest… and your executioner… in that matter."

"I won't fail. I'll save myself."

Joseph looked at Eric for a long time. "I hope for your sake you're right." His smile was thin. "C'mon. Let's get you some grub. Tomorrow's gonna be a long day."

THIS IS THE FIRST TIME I'VE
written a story specifically in a fairytale style. Keeping with the grim theme, I wanted it to be as horrific as it was beautiful. The "nightmare" in this tale is based on one of my own nightmares and the feelings I had about the creature while I was experiencing the dream. Its description is as close to memory as I could recall.

A NIGHTMARE FOR ANNA

The Old Forest was dark and Anna was scared. She tried to stay as close to her mother as possible while they walked deeper into the woods. Even though it was morning, the tall trees shut out the light, making it look as if it were the twilight of sunset. As the cries of strange birds called from the canopy overhead, Anna tried to huddle closer, but stopped before her mother's skirt dragged against her. Actually touching mother was forbidden, especially as she sang to her baby boy, Aiden.

"We're almost there," her mother cooed to the sleeping baby. "Almost to the best place to find the best mushrooms."

"I don't see any, Mother."

"Not yet. You will." Her mother looked around. "Here we are." She turned to Anna, who had not yet seen nine summers. "Are you ready?"

Glancing around the dark forest with its giant trees, flickering shadows, and strange noises, Anna nodded, giving her mother her bravest smile. Mother appeared happy, and that was rare. Ever since Aiden was born, Mother had been short-tempered with Anna—even though she tried to be the best big sister she could.

"Do you know what to look for?"

Anna nodded. "The big white mushrooms with the caps, not the bowls."

"Very good."

"We're gonna make Daddy the best mushroom and turnip soup we can." Anna paused, seeing her mother's smile crack and disappear. "When he gets home from the castle, that is." She did her best to make her voice smooth and cheery.

"Mother is tired, Anna." She spoke to the sleeping baby rather than to her daughter. "We're going to rest here. I want you to fill the basket halfway with the mushrooms before you come back."

Anna bowed her head, still not sure what she had done wrong. "Yes, Mother." She picked up the small grass-woven basket and turned to the dark trees. She took several uncertain steps before looking back at her mother who, without looking up from Aiden, waved at her to go on. Anna straightened her back and faced the scary forest. She would find Daddy's favorite mushrooms and all would be well once more.

Anna circled around the small grove again. She hadn't been gone that long. Not long at all. Mother had to be here. But she wasn't, and the third time Anna circled the two trees she'd marked with crossed sticks, she knew either she was lost or Mother had left her here alone in the Old Forest, both of which amounted to the same thing: death. No child came out of the Old Forest once they went in. Not any child alone, that is.

She sat against the tree she was sure her mother had sat against and muttered, "Think, child. Think." She even used the same amused tone of voice Daddy did when the answer was right there in front of her and she couldn't see it. Just the thought of her father made Anna's throat close up. She missed him so much. She hated that he had to take such long trips away to the castle.

After some time had passed, Anna realized she needed to face the fact that her mother had left her behind, and it was up to her to get herself out of this mess. Her child's heart sobbed at the abandonment, while her active mind set upon the task of finding her way home. She was her father's daughter after all, and he would be home soon.

Anna stood and turned in the direction she hoped would take her home. All she needed to do was to follow their own tracks back the way they'd come. Simple. She looked at the ground and saw the trampled grass. She could find her way home. When she did, Mother would be so sorry that she had left her; she'd welcome Anna with open arms.

❦

By the time Anna found the ruins of the manor house, she knew she was well and truly lost. Having lost the trail of footsteps—if there had been any to follow and not just wishful thinking—there was no way to know how to make it out of the Old Forest. The discovery of the stone ruin with its partial roof raised her low spirits only a little. It was something new and interesting. Something more than just endless trees and loamy earth. Even the scent of stone cleared her senses. Best of all, there was a small opening in the treetops that allowed the sunshine in.

Running to the visible shaft of sunlight, Anna could have cried with relief. In the warmth of the sun, feeling it against her chilled skin made it seem like the forest creatures that had followed her could not touch her. In her mind's eye, they were afraid of the sunlight. As she turned back to the forest, she could even see some of them slink away. For the moment, she was safe.

Of course, Anna was too young to wonder what—other than sunlight—might frighten a predator away from an easy meal.

❦

As night fell and the sky morphed from pale blue to deep blue and into black, Anna huddled in the corner of the broken room. She wondered if the night creatures would come or if it would rain. Her tummy rumbled, but the mushrooms she had found were long gone.

The sound of something close by brought Anna to her feet. The following growl had her looking for a weapon. Scrabbling against the broken wall, her hand found a loose stone. She pulled it free and raised it up, ready to throw it at whatever was coming. More stones fell to her side as she watched the large shape prowl the edge of the forest.

It was watching her. That much was certain.

Anna took two steps forward and threw the stone at the monster. "Go away! I'll hit you! Go away!" She snatched three more stones from around her and threw them, too. None of them hit even halfway to the forest line, but the monster came no closer.

Moonlight glinted green and yellow off its eyes. Anna picked up the largest stone near her feet and threw it as far and as hard as she could. The glowing eyes disappeared and Anna felt a surge of pride.

She backed up into the corner again and sat. Still watching where she had last seen the monster, her hand searched out another stone—just one, to keep with her as guard. Her hand found something that felt like stone but was warm. Startled, Anna looked down to see what it was, her eyes struggling to separate the shadows.

Her hand was on a long black stick that was as wide as her wrist and disappeared into the wall. She saw that the wall behind her was actually two walls, with a space in-between. Whatever the black stick was, the rest of it was still hidden. She decided she would figure out what it was in the morning.

Finding a different rock to hold and comfort her, the little girl settled in to sleep.

Anna knew she was dreaming, and that was a strange thing. Not the dreaming. But realizing that what she was seeing wasn't real. Something had just been happening. She frowned. Something awful. Something she could not quite remember. She reached for it...

"Do not do that, little one. I took it away because it would frighten you." The voice was as dark as the shadow it came from. "Do not look for it."

Anna tilted her head, looking up at the humanoid shadow. It was as tall as one of the trees in the forest. Things moved all around it; curiously, she was not afraid. "Was it a nightmare?"

"Yes, little one."

"My name's Anna. Who are you?"

"Sigis. You may call me Sigis." The shadow moved closer and shrank in size.

"Why are you here?"

There was a long pause. "I am old and alone. You are lost and afraid."

Somehow, that answered the question without answering it. Anna looked down at her hands, remembering her mother's abandonment and that she was lost in the Old Forest.

"Will you help me?"

She looked up again. The shadow was closer now and not much taller than her father. "What do you look like? Why are you hiding in shadow?" Anna knew she *should* be afraid but she wasn't. But, more than anything, she wanted to see who she was talking to. It was important.

The shadow shook its head. "I do not wish to frighten you."

"I want to see."

"Will you help me?"

"Show me your face." Anna did not know why it was important, but it was. "Please?"

Sigis nodded. He did not move out of the darkness so much as have the shadows withdraw from him.

Anna saw what she needed to see.

◆

Waking with the first light of day, Anna knew there was something she needed to do. To remember. She sat blinking into the twilight, unafraid at her unusual surroundings. The glade with its broken rocks, rambling vines, and sprouting grasses all glistened with dew. The entire ruin looked like it was covered in little jewels.

Anna stood and stretched, realizing she was not cold. At all. Her little corner had remained warm throughout the chill forest night. She discovered it was only her little corner that was warm when she had to do her necessary. This little bit of magic made her smile. It had to be magic. There was no other explanation.

As she hurried back to her shelter, Anna saw what she needed to remember. There, in the left side of her shelter, part of the fallen wall revealed pieces of a statue. She could not make out the form, but, from her dream, she knew exactly who she was looking at: Sigis… and he was stuck in the wall. She had promised to help him.

Without hesitation, Anna pulled at the crumbling rock. Each stone that came loose showed more of the reddish-black statue beneath. Once the easy rocks were done, the wall seemed unbreakable. No matter what she did, she couldn't shift or move anything more. Only half of Sigis was uncovered.

Anna touched one of the spider-like legs, feeling its warmth, and sighed. "What do I do? The wall won't move." While a ripple of reddish light moved down the leg and over her hand before receding again, there was no answer. She took that as encouragement to try harder. Sigis was trapped, and only she could free him.

After a moment's thought, Anna picked up a large rock and started beating the base of the wall with it. At first, it looked like nothing was happening, then the chips and cracks started. Harder and harder she worked, until she thought her heart would burst, and her hands were bloody with the effort. At last the wall started to crumble.

From that point, it was just a matter of time and diligence… if nothing else, Anna was a diligent child.

Anna was forced to flee when her efforts succeeded in the sudden breaking and tumbling and crumbling of the wall. She barely got out of the way of the ceiling that had once been her shelter as it crashed to the ruined floor. The noise of the falling rock startled all of the nearby forest creatures into silence.

When the dust cleared, she picked herself up and faced the form she had met in her dream. He was taller than her father, made of the reddish-black stone that was smooth to the touch. His fingers and toes were clawed, his head horned, his eyes solid black. The eight spider legs that sprouted from his back, four curling around each of his sides, were the most disturbing thing about him. Even though his face was twisted into a long-tongued leer, it was easier to look at than those legs.

"Sigis?" Anna moved forward and stopped at the sight of something glinting in the rubble. With a bloody, sweaty hand, she picked it up. It was a light blue gem as fair as the summer sky. She looked up and the statue began to move.

"Sigis?" she asked again, this time with a hint of fear in her voice.

The statue shifted down to one knee before her. "Never fear me, little one. By blood and bone, by sweat and toil, we have a pact, you and I. I am yours to command." Sigis bowed his head to her.

Startled, she lifted the jewel up to him. "Is this yours?"

He nodded. "It is. Given in good faith to the wizard I had a pact with."

"What pact?"

"I protected him and his. Those who came to his home with malice in their hearts suffered the guilt of nightmares. Those who were true had no worries for their sleep."

"Oh." Anna thought about this. "Do you want it back?" She offered the jewel to him, her palm up.

Sigis looked at her. "I do. Do you give it to me of your own free will?"

"Yes."

"Then I accept my freedom." His large, clawed hand engulfed hers. When she looked up again, instead of solid black eyes, Sigis now had eyes the color of the summer sky. He smiled at her. "But, I do owe you, child. What do you want?"

"My name is Anna." She smiled at him. "I want to travel with you for a while. I want to know why Mother left me here in the Old Forest."

Sigis looked around. "Is that what they call it?"

She nodded. "How old are you?"

"I was old when this forest was young and the manor house was but a dream." He stared down at her. "I can take you with me. I have tasted your blood. You have tasted my dreams. We will walk the Dreamlands." He offered his hand and she accepted it.

"You'll take me away from here?" Never had she wanted to leave a place so much.

"Wherever you wish to go, Anna. Even in freedom, I am yours to command."

"Why?"

"Because there are rules that were old when I was young. You freed me. Also, I, too, am alone."

Anna understood the fear of being alone in a strange place.

"Are you certain you wish to know? To find out why your mother abandoned you?"

There was concern in his voice. Anna heard it as she stopped to play with a creature that looked like a cross between a caterpillar and a puppy. "I think I'm going to name you Pupapiller," she said, not answering him. She had her own fears as well. "Isn't he cute?"

"Careful." The concern in Sigis's voice morphed into affection. "Here in the Dreamtime, names have power. What was once a passing dream for someone is now a very real creature. What will you do with him now?"

She stood and looked between them—Sigis as still as the statue he once was and Pupapiller cavorting about her feet. "I'll keep him. You want to stay with me, don't you?"

Pupapiller leaped into her arms and licked her face, wagging his whole body. She laughed. "See? Pupapiller wants to stay."

What Anna did not see while holding her new pet was the nightmarish monster that appeared out of the ever-shifting landscape; Sigis, waving a hand at it, forced it away. The human child called to all of the creatures on the Plane of Dreams.

"We need to go. You are certain you wish to see your mother?"

Anna nodded, putting Pupapiller on the ground. "Yes."

Sigis offered his hand once more. "Think of your mother. Think of home."

Trying to keep her heart hidden, Anna smiled bravely. "I will." She closed her eyes and thought of home with her mother and father and baby brother, Aiden. She missed all of them so much her heart ached.

"We have arrived."

Opening her eyes, Anna grinned wide. It *was* her home. The small but snug farmhouse on the edge of the wood. There was a fire in the fireplace and her mother was standing over Aiden's crib, humming the same song she had been singing the last time Anna saw her.

For a moment, she did not know what to do. She looked up at Sigis who nodded and stepped away. Anna stepped forward. "Hello, Mother."

Her mother whirled in surprise and fear. "You shouldn't be here. You can't be here. I've already sent the letter to Niall that you've run away. He's coming home." She put her hand to her breast, looking like she had said too much, and then repeated, "You shouldn't be here."

Anna's nervousness morphed into sudden fury at the accusation of her running away from the home she'd loved all her life. "Why, Mother? Why'd you abandon me? I was lost and alone and scared! I'm a good girl! Why?"

"Stop calling me that! I'm not your mother."

Anna's fury abated and she took another step forward in confusion. "But… you are."

"No. I'm not. I never have been. Your father brought you to me. I wet-nursed you. Your father and I fell in love. I never thought I'd have my own child again. One child died. One mother died. I wanted to die, but Niall needed a wet nurse. I needed a baby. You were it." She glanced at the crib. "It never felt right. You weren't *my* child. But until Aiden, my lovely baby boy, I never knew what a real mother's love for her child was like."

The woman looked at her with something akin to disgust. "You were nothing but a leech to me. One I thought I had to love because of the man I married. I thought I loved you. I tried to love you. Thought maybe something was wrong with *me*. But there wasn't. It was you. Not *my* baby. Not worth the love of a mother. Not like my Aiden." She turned back to the crib. "Not like my Arthur before him. You were a poor substitute. You should not be here."

Tears spilled down Anna's face, her child's heart breaking all over again. She did not understand. She felt a warm, clawed hand on her shoulder. She turned to Sigis, throwing herself into his arms. He picked her up and held her close with both arms and four of his spider limbs as she sobbed on his shoulder.

Anna became aware of her mother's rising voice, panic clear. She turned to see what was happening but held onto Sigis's neck.

"Aiden, honey. Aiden, my love, where are you?" Her mother—for she would always be her mother in Anna's heart—dug through the crib, pulling far too many baby blankets from it. "Where are you?" She turned from the crib and looked through everything in the room that could possibly hold a baby. "Aiden!"

Anna was alarmed. "What's happened to Aiden?"

Sigis stroked her hair with a spider leg. "Nothing. Aiden is safe and sound. I will show you." He turned around and there was Aiden in a floor crib with bright butterflies and flowers floating around him.

Anna wiggled to get down and she hurried to him, kneeling to give him a kiss. Aiden giggled and grabbed for her hair. "He's a good baby."

"He is. It is my experience that those who abandon the innocent do not deserve them. It is your mother's guilt that gave her the nightmare of losing her baby."

She looked up at him. "I've decided what I want."

"What is my command?"

"I want to become like you."

Sigis paused, uncertain. "You wish to become a Nightmare?"

"I want to become like you. I want to stay with you."

"You would have to leave all you love behind."

Anna looked at her mother sitting in the middle of the farmhouse, sobbing for her lost baby. "She doesn't love me. She doesn't want me." The words brought fresh tears to her eyes.

Sigis offered his hand. Anna accepted it and he scooped her up into his arms again. "I know someone who does."

Three steps and three years later, Sigis brought her to a castle with a drawbridge. Sitting on the edge of the drawbridge overlooking the moat was her father. "Daddy!"

Sigis let Anna down and watched as the little girl ran down the bridge to her father, who grabbed her in a huge bear hug.

"Anna, my girl. What are you doing in the city?" He ruffled her hair. "I won't be home for another moon."

"I missed you, Daddy. So much." She hugged him and kissed his cheek.

"I know it's hard. But, when the king calls…" He pulled back from his hug. "What are you doing here? How did you get here? The road to the castle is long and dangerous."

She wriggled out of his arms and then sat next to him on the drawbridge. "My friend, Sigis, brought me." Anna looked between Sigis and her father. "Daddy, why does Mommy say she's not my mother?"

Her father looked like she had slapped him. "Oh, honey. Oh, darling. We were going to wait until you were older…" He looked sad.

"She's really not my mother?"

He shook his head.

"Who is she?"

"Your mother died… it wasn't your fault. Birthing's hard on a woman. You saw that with Aiden."

Anna suddenly understood everything. Her real mother had died in childbirth. The woman she thought of as her mother had been hired as a wet nurse. Wet nurse became a wife and mother. Until… until her own child was born and survived.

"But I love you. We both love you so much. You'll always be our daughter."

She smiled through the pain and nodded. "I know, Daddy. I know." She stood again. "I've got to go. And, I don't think I'll be back. Not for a while. Maybe not ever."

"No, you can't." He stood as well. "Where do you think you are going?"

"Far away, Daddy. But I do love you. I'm going to miss you. I think this is the best thing for you and… and Mommy… and Aiden." Anna stepped back. "I'm going to travel to new places and new dreams. I'll see you sometimes. I'll watch over you and Aiden. I promise." While she spoke, he grew farther and farther away from her.

"No, Anna. Wait! Don't go!" He reached for her, and would keep reaching for her forever. Except for those rare times when she would visit him in dreams.

As he disappeared from sight and sound, Anna turned to Sigis. "I couldn't tell him. I couldn't make him upset. Maybe now he'll think I didn't run away, but that I tried to come to the castle and got lost."

Sigis nodded. "You are certain you wish to be like me?"

The two of them did not walk through the Dreamtime so much as watch it pass them by. Pupapiller showed up again and stayed. The sound and color and sights were a kaleidoscope of dreams, nightmares, and the passing denizens of the realm.

"Yes. Do you promise to stay with me and never leave?"

He was silent for a moment. "Never is a long time. When you become like me, we will have all the time in the universe. I can promise that by blood and bone, by sweat and toil, I will be your Nightmare father for as long as you will have me."

She smiled up at him. "Then, yes, I'm certain."

Sigis leaned down and kissed her on the forehead. Anna felt warmth like a hot bath spread over her, down from her head to her shoulders to her waist, arms, and feet. She watched as her pale, soft skin became hard and smooth and the color of bloodstone. Whole worlds opened up in her mind as her humanity died a quiet death and she was reborn a Nightmare.

Blinking eyes the color of the perfect summer sky, she asked, "What do we do now?"

"Anything you wish, my child." Sigis smiled at her and meant every word.

As they walked deeper into the Dreamlands, Anna's small human form lay curled up in the corner of a broken room, in the ruins of a manor house, deep within the Old Forest. In her hand was a small gem the blue color of a summer sky—a most precious gift of death, and then life.

THIS WAS ORIGINALLY WRITTEN FOR
an anthology about the pig god Moccus. It wasn't selected for that, but I wasn't willing to put it away. The story itself is based on my discovery that there are large, brightly colored pig statues all around Seattle. These were created for the "Pigs on Parade," celebrating a century of Pike Place Market. Each one was made by a different local artist. The story wrote itself.

EULOGY FOR MUFFIN

The five children stood in front of the huge fiberglass pig, with two boxes and one daisy-chained crown in their collective hands. Bundled up against the cold ocean wind, they were somber, even in the face of something as cheerfully yellow as the statue before them. The occasion demanded it. It was time to say goodbye to their pets forever.

Alan looked around and nodded. It was the perfect setting for Muffin's eulogy. The pier was windy and cold, with few tourists around. The Seattle sky was filled with its usual deep gray clouds. The world seemed quiet and respectful of the children's loss. Best yet was the bright yellow Moccus altar with the red writing and the red sun painted on as a necklace. It was like the artist who painted it knew that it would be an altar to Moccus that children would use. This was where Muffin would be laid to rest, at the statue's feet. It was only right. Moccus would make sure that Muffin made it to heaven.

Alan, Eric, and Heather's mother, Sharon, stood off to the side with Emma and Anne's mother, Kathy. The mothers watched with the solemn parental expression of knowing not to laugh at the folly of children and their much-needed rituals. If this was how their children wanted to say goodbye to their dead family pets, there was no harm in it. Though, two very different pets dying so close together made Sharon wonder if the same fox had killed them both. If it had, the neighborhood would have to do something about that.

"Mom! Mom!" Heather called, "I can't reach it." She waved the fragile crown of flowers up toward the top of the pig's head. Heather was the youngest and smallest of the five children, but she was not the weakest. She was braver and bolder than either of the other two girls—even braver than shy Eric. Only Alan was her match when it came to a fierce game of Double-Dog-Dare-Ya.

Sharon hurried over before the crown of daisies came apart and ruined the beginning of this new rite. "Here. Let me, honey." She held out her hand.

"No! I wanna do it." Heather hid the crown of flowers behind her back, mashing one of the buds into loose petals. "I wanna crown Moccus."

"All right, Heather. I'll lift you." Sharon knew she was coddling her daughter, but Heather was the youngest. Coddling her just this once would not hurt anything. After all, the family ferret had just died.

"Okay, Mama," Heather said with angelic innocence, now that she was getting her way. As her mother lifted her, Heather held out the crown to the statue. It was too little to fit around the pig's head, so she hung it off of one ear like a jaunty hat. With her sacred duty of adorning the statue done, Heather squirmed to get down and was obliged by her mother, who then retreated to a safer, more adult corner next to Kathy.

"What a day," Sharon said softly to Kathy, her neighbor of seven years. "What a week. First, we lose Muffin and then you guys lose your cat. It's awful. Just awful." She pulled her coat tight against the wind and wished that the children had chosen a different spot for their ceremony. A warmer spot. But the children had insisted that this was where the ritual had to be.

"I know," Kathy said without looking at her. "But… losing pets… these things happen. It's one of the lessons of life."

"Well, after we get done with this... this... whatever this is—"

"Eulogy," Kathy supplied. She was dressed in the same warm clothing as the rest of them, but seemed unbothered by the cold or the wind.

"Eulogy, memorial, whatever. We need to call a neighborhood meeting to deal with that wild fox. No one else should lose a family pet like this. It's just awful." Sharon gestured to the children. "Look at what they've done to cover their grief."

"Shh," Kathy murmured. "It's time."

Alan glanced at his peers, saw their attentive faces turned to him, and nodded. He turned to the statue. The top of his head did not even reach the bottom of the pig's snout. He bowed his head and began to intone the newly-familiar words. The rest bowed their heads as the words came.

"Our Father, who art in Annwfn, Moccus be thy name. Thy kingdom come. Thy will be done, in the under dark as it is in Annwfn. Give us this day our daily hunt. And forgive us our anger, as we forgive those who anger against us. And lead us into Annwfn when it is our time and deliver us safely. Amen." Alan lifted his head.

"Amen," was murmured around the circle of friends. As their heads rose, the crown of flowers was fluttered by the wind and white daisy petals floated over them: a sign that Moccus had heard their call and was listening.

Alan gestured to Emma. "You can go first, 'cause... you know."

Emma looked down at the box in her hands, her eyes already shiny with unshed tears. Anne put a comforting hand on her big sister's arm. "It's okay. Moccus'll guide Fluffy to heaven."

"Annwfn," Heather corrected.

Anne glanced at her, stubborn anger on her face. "I can say 'heaven' if I want."

Alan broke in before the girls started squabbling. "Annwfn is heaven. Doesn't matter. It's Emma's time to speak. To eu-lo-gy Fluffy." He said the word 'eulogy' very carefully, as one who is not familiar with the sound of the word but likes it nonetheless. He gestured to the box in Emma's hands. "Go on. You should go first."

Emma stepped forward and placed the box at the pig statue's feet. "Moccus, this is Fluffy. She ran hard for you. She caught the prey for you. She fought hard for you. I hope she made you proud. I hope she's happy in Annwfn. Keep her safe." Emma stood and wiped at the tears on her face.

"That's it?" Heather asked, scorn plain in her voice. "That's Fluffy's eu-lo-thingy?"

Eric, Heather's older brother, broke in. "If that's the eu-lo-gy that Emma wants to give, let her." He gave Heather a warning look. They were not supposed to argue in public.

She ignored him, as little sisters often do. "But that's not a proper eulo-thingy! Alan, tell her," Heather demanded.

Alan, the oldest brother, and the oldest of this group of children, nodded. He was the de facto leader after all. He chose his words carefully. "Emma did fine in her way to say goodbye." He paused and thought; his childish face looked older with his concentration. "But, a eu-lo-gy is to honor the dead and through that, honor Moccus. So, it has to tell the story of what happened and why people should be proud. Also, why it honors Moccus."

Sharon glanced at Kathy. "What's this new game? Who's Moccus?"

Kathy appeared to weigh whether the question was idle chit-chat out of boredom or something more. She was surprised to see that Sharon looked honestly confused. How could Sharon have missed Moccus's awakening? Kathy did not want to be distracted from the children's proceedings, but she could not leave her neighbor ignorant.

"Moccus came to the realm of man from the lands of Annwfn. He is known as a great advisor, one who leads the dead to the lands of happiness and the lands of death. He also often leads the Wild Hunt. He's just reawakened and not everyone can hear him—yet. They will. Eventually." She kept her eyes on the ritual before her.

Cold winds whipped around Sharon, making her pull her coat closer to her body. "How do you know all this?"

Kathy was undisturbed by the mercurial wind even as it whipped her hair into and out of her face. "My daughters heard him first. They talked to me about him. Then I heard him. I knew I had been hearing him for a while, but they helped me learn how to listen. The girls told your children, and then they could hear him, too."

"My kids never said anything about Moccus to me." Sharon frowned at the implication that her children had been keeping something from her. She opened her mouth to speak.

Kathy put a finger to her lips to forestall anymore interruptions and pointed towards their collective children. "Listen and learn. This is more than a game. You should already know this."

※

Alan had regained control of the proceedings and separated Heather from the other girls before Heather's grief forced an unnecessary fight. He then allowed Eric to place Muffin's box next to Fluffy's box and smiled reassuringly at his younger brother. Once everyone had settled down again, he began his eulogy for Muffin. He faced the other children with the seriousness of his duty. Not only did he need to honor both Muffin and Moccus, he had to do so in a way that taught Emma what to do in the future.

"When Moccus first talked to us, I didn't hear him," he began. "But Emma and Anne did, and they taught us how to listen." He nodded to the sisters in silent appreciation.

"I heard him already," Heather muttered.

Alan continued, ignoring his baby sister. "We listened. We learned. We understood what Moccus wanted. He wanted the Wild Hunt. He's not strong enough to lead it yet. That's why we have to run it. Why I led it."

At this point Alan paused, looking around at them and through them. "But I won't have to lead it for long, will I?"

There was a soft chorus of noes from the children held rapt by his speech.

"But," he continued, "we ran the Wild Hunt as best we could and it was exciting. Muffin was the prey. Fluffy was the hunter. That's what Moccus chose. We ran with Fluffy in the chase. Not hunters but like hunters. We ran but Fluffy and Muffin ran faster. They were so fast, weren't they?"

"Very fast," Emma said as she looked at the boxes sitting at Moccus's fiberglass hooves.

"When we got there in the garage, Fluffy had Muffin cornered. I'd never seen Muffin so puffed up and hissing like that. I wanted to call it off. I wanted to save my pet. I wanted to but I knew it was wrong. I couldn't. Moccus called for the Wild Hunt. He chose Fluffy and Muffin. I had to let it happen. I had to make the sacrifice." There were tears in the boy's eyes. "We all did, didn't we?"

Anne was the only one with a voice left to agree. "Yes. They were chosen. And they ran just like they were supposed to." Emma and Eric were weeping openly while Heather rubbed at her wet face and kept silent.

"Are they kidding?" Sharon whispered at Kathy. "Did your cat kill my ferret?"

"Hush." Kathy quelled her growing annoyance at Sharon, her interruptions, and her silly questions. It was not her fault that she did not understand what was going on. Was it?

"This game isn't funny. I want to know."

"Shhh," Kathy admonished. "This isn't a game. You'll miss it. Pay attention to the children. This is important." She turned from her neighbor and watched the children with a hint of a smile of pride and love on her face.

Sharon, confused and disturbed, turned back to listen.

"They did. I didn't think they would," Alan agreed. "I didn't know they would run like they were supposed to, but Moccus chose them and they knew it. Animals are smarter than humans sometimes." His eyes flicked to his mother before he returned his full attention to the other children. "Animals know what they need to do."

"But Muffin wasn't gonna go without a fight," Eric said, getting control of his tears and regaining his voice.

"No. Muffin didn't. He was a fighter." Alan agreed.

"So was Fluffy," Emma said in a small voice.

"They both were. They both did what they were supposed to do." Alan smiled. "That's why we're doing eu-lo-gies for them. That's why I'm... I'm doing eu-lo-gies for both of them. That's only fair and right. They were brave and fierce for us and for Moccus. They knew that a Wild Hunt could only end in death. Fluffy had hunted well, but Muffin," he could not keep the pride out of his voice, "wasn't just prey. Muffin could've been a hunter, too. That's why they fought. That's why they died."

"But Moccus is pleased?" Emma asked.

Alan did not have to answer her. Moccus did that for him in another shower of white daisy petals and a certain sense of pleasure. They all grinned at each other and some of the hurt at the loss of their pets floated away on the wind.

Alan nodded. "He is. He saw how they fought. He saw how Fluffy broke Muffin's back and saw how Muffin bit Fluffy's neck until it bled and bled and bled. They fought for him in the Wild Hunt and died for him. They earned their rest and he's taken them safely to heaven."

"Annwfn," Emma said with a small smile.

"Annwfn," Alan agreed.

The five children took each other's hands and stared up into the cheerfully yellow face of Moccus. They listened to what he had to tell them in their time of loss and grief.

"Your cat killed my ferret?" Sharon asked again when the children went silent.

"Moccus's Wild Hunt killed your ferret. But, your ferret killed the hunter in the process. It isn't how these things normally go, you know." Kathy smiled at Emma and Anne holding hands.

"I don't get it. I don't. Our children watched our pets murder each other? I was told that a fox got Muffin." Sharon looked at Kathy's smiling face. "This doesn't disturb you? Our children are worshiping a plastic pig and watched their pets fight to the death because they thought that's what this Moccus wanted."

"Of course it bothers me. Of course it does. No one wants to be chosen as the prey in a Wild Hunt. But when it happens, it's an honor." Kathy turned to her neighbor and frowned. "What bothers me more is the fact that you don't hear Moccus at all. That you don't hear him right now as he speaks to us." Sharon gestured to the pier to include herself, the children, and the gathered strangers. "It bothers me that you don't know what's going on."

Sharon noticed, for the first time, that other adults had joined them on the pier and were watching the children with rapt attention. Anger flared, blotting out her fear and confusion. "What's going on is that your kids have corrupted my kids," she said.

"Seattle, for all its modernization, is still close to the old ways. Haven't you noticed the altars to Moccus all over the city? From the Parade of Pigs to the bronze statues in Pike's Place Market? Many of us have felt his stirrings for years. Now, he's awake and communing with us." Kathy's voice took on a hard edge. "Why don't you know this? Why don't you hear him?"

Sharon did not like Kathy's tone. It made her nervous. "I think it's time for me and my kids to leave."

"Mommy!"

The call of her youngest brought Sharon's attention back to the children. She started to go to them but the way they were looking at her froze her in place. "What is it, baby?"

"Moccus is happy with us. Really happy." Heather's smile was radiant.

"That's good, honey, but it's time to go home."

Heather shook her head. "I didn't tell you the best part yet."

Sharon glanced at Kathy who had not moved. "What's that?"

"There's gonna be another Wild Hunt real soon!" Heather grinned, "And we *all* get to be hunters this time."

Sharon's heart leaped for her throat as she tried to keep calm and rational. She put on her best 'Mommy's-not-messing-around' voice. "That's nice, dear. Come on now. Eric, Alan, you, too. It's time to go home."

None of the children moved. "We can't go yet, Mom," Alan said.

"Why not?" Sharon tried to keep the panic out of her voice.

"Because Moccus is choosing the prey."

"How?" Her questions of 'how do you know and how is he going to do it and this can't possibly be real' were cut off as a huge gust of wind blew over the pier, ruffling hair and chilling skin. It lifted up the battered but still whole crown of daisies and floated it through the air in a haphazard flutter to land on Sharon's head. Sharon flinched, flailing at the flowers in her hair as if they were bees. Daisies fluttered to the ground, circling her. She looked from them to the people around her, terrified.

"You should be honored to be chosen. Especially since you refuse to hear him. Moccus must see something special in you." Kathy paused. "I don't know what. Maybe it's the devotion of your children." She nodded to herself. "That must be it."

Sharon barely heard Kathy. Instead, she watched as the strangers moved closer to her en masse. Some of them stopped to pick up rocks, sticks, and other debris around the pier. "My God. What are you doing?"

"Getting ready to hunt," Kathy said, pulling a small, collapsible steel baton designed for self defense from her purse.

Sharon stared at Kathy, mouth opening and closing in an attempt to find something to say, something rational, something that would stop this madness.

"If I were you, Sharon, I'd run," Kathy said in her mildest voice as she flicked the baton open to its full sixteen inches. "It's the Wild Hunt after all, and we need the hunt before the kill. In the hunt, we honor Moccus. In the kill, we honor you as the chosen one. We'll give you a three minute head start." Kathy gave her watch a significant look.

Sharon looked at the children. All of them, including her own, had stones in their hands except for Heather. She had picked up a dirty glass bottle and was holding it by the neck. "Heather?"

"It's time to run, Mommy. I promise we'll give you a nice eu-lo-gy."

THIS IS MY FIRST KEMBER EMPIRE *short story. I wrote a truly terrible SF space opera novel called* Regresser's Evolution. *There are bones of a good story in there, but I'd have to rewrite the book from scratch to find it. Guard Commander Waithe was one of the secondary characters that all of my beta readers wanted to know more about. In truth, he is one of my favorite Kember Empire characters. This is the story of what happened just before he became the Guard Commander in the novel. The other reason I wanted to write this story is to show the aftermath of war and how much it ripples through the military society and the dependents connected to the soldiers. So many people think war is glorious. Mostly it's paperwork and pain.*

HONORING THE DEAD

BATTLE

The battle was a slaughter. Guard Captain Waithe had known this would happen the moment the kill order had come in. What should have been a simple exercise in quelling a riot had become an example and a message to the Purist Believers everywhere. When the military and the police were rolled into one, all a commanding guardsman could do was obey… and try to do his best for both his fellow guardsmen and the people he was protecting. He also tried to do his worst to those he fought against.

Sometimes, those people were one and the same.

Like now.

The guardsman squad had set up behind protected barriers in front of the walled hospital where the only living survivor of this latest round of Believer attacks against the Hedari explorers was hanging by a thread. A thread these Believers wanted to snap. *Not that I blame them,* he thought. Then the Guard Captain put his own personal feelings aside and looked to his men.

The squad's orders were to put down any attacks against the hospital and bring the leaders of the local cult on this planet to justice. This newest round of attacks had started just over an hour ago. First it had only been a march that had become a stand-off that morphed into the series of rioting charges that battered at the riot barrier the guardsmen had erected. Each one of these charges had been quelled with firepower, and the resulting bodies still lay in the street.

"Why do they keep coming?" Guardsman Kintares asked, his voice breaking with held back tears as he kept his weapon pointed at the chaos of rioters preparing to attack again. "They don't have real weapons. They can't win."

"Stand your ground, Guardsman. Do your duty." It was the only safe answer the Guard Captain could give from his elevated vantage point behind his squad. If he tried to give a real answer, his men would see the rioters as people again and not the enemy. His men would die, and he could not, would not, have that. He stood there, surveying the battlefield with only part of his mind. The other part of it answered his guardsman's question.

They come, he thought, *because it's all they know to do. They come because they have a Cause they won't turn from and that Cause is treason against the empire. For that reason alone, we kill them.* If he could have, he would have wiped the sweat from his head. But, to remove your helmet on the battlefield was to invite death.

Then all time for introspection was done and his earpiece came to life. "We've got another charge and it's huge—funneling in from the three side streets. Biggest one yet, Guard Captain out." The guardsman on the other end of the communication sounded amazed and terrified.

"Received. Out." As Waithe responded, he was already turning to shout orders to his men. They were the same orders he had been shouting off and on for the last hour. "Here they come! Termination ordered! Shoot to kill! Shoot to kill!" He paused and added, "Don't let them cross my line, guardsmen! Not a single one!"

This time, the fighting was fiercer. Though the rioters were not armed with the same high-tech, heavy armament that the guardsmen had, they did have weapons—low-tech, but still deadly—and they had the numbers. A squad of thirty men had been put down to quell the riot of three hundred and bring the cult leaders in for the murder of two Hedari explorers, as well as for the attempted murder of the third. Only, that "three hundred" had been closer to three thousand. The bloodshed was horrific, especially since they were fighting civilians and not professional soldiers.

As all thirty of his men alternated between firing and ducking for cover, Waithe patrolled their backside, shoring up the defenses in the line. He had the overview lay of the land, and this was the dirtiest kind of fighting—in the middle of a city. The collateral damage was overwhelming. Only the walled and protected hospital building behind him was still standing, and some of its walls would need to be rebuilt. He shot two rioters breaking through on the right flank and saw one of his men had fallen.

Jumping down from his higher vantage point, he shouted, "Man down! Right flank, close that hole! Close it!" while he ran to Guardsman Ermath's side. He pulled the man back behind the line of fire and checked for a pulse. The guardsman was dead. Waithe cursed and took the man's ID chit, stuffing it into his pocket.

He got back to his lookout and shot three more rioters as they converged on the line. That, along with the firepower of his center men, drove back the forward middle portion of the charge, breaking it apart. After that, the organized charge became an incoherent riot again. Thirty seconds later, it was a rout. Those who were not running away stayed where they were because they would never move again.

He saw that a man on the left flank was down. It was Guardsman Spiradon, and there was a lot of blood around him. Guardsman Kintares was crouched over him, his hands bloody from trying to keep his friend and squadmate alive. He had his back to the line and while that should have been the death of him with a shot to the back, it was not. Death took a different form.

"Damnit," Waithe muttered. He took one last look and started back down from the high ground toward his downed men. In the seconds it took him to look down, set his feet on the rubble, and look up again, death had reappeared in the form of a teenage girl.

She came out of one of the broken side buildings on the left and sprinted toward him with a homemade bomb in her hands. Kintares turned his head and froze, just staring at the girl as she ran silently with murder in her eyes. By the time Guard Captain Waithe and Guardsman Tascen opened fire on her, she was on top of Kintares and Spiradon. She set off the bomb as she was hit from two directions.

Kintares never shifted from his frozen, crouched position over Spiradon's body. He did not make a single move for his weapon. He just watched her come. One moment he was crouched, the next moment he, Spiradon, and the girl were blown to pieces. Coda, Dram, and Thymi, the three closest guardsmen to the left flank, were also hit in the explosion, but only the girl, Kintares, and Spiradon were killed. It was the last attack of a suicidal cultist, and it was the most painful by far.

AFTERMATH

Guard Captain Waithe sat at his desk in his office in the Guard Headquarters building on the prime planet. The office was clean enough to pass inspection and decorated in a manner as to be unmistakably "career military." Plaques and commendations lined the wall in orderly rows. The desk surface gleamed. A neat pile of paperwork demanding his attention sat at his left hand and the only adornment that showed that the office was inhabited was the picture of a pretty, dark-haired woman that could have been a wife, girlfriend, or sister.

He stared at his computer screen for a long time without moving. This was the part of his job—his duty to the empire—that he hated most. There were three names on his screen, with their locations of the next of kin. Two had parents. One had a wife. The parents, he knew from experience, would be the easier visits to make. Parents had a way of accepting that their child was going into danger when they joined the Guard. Wives did not. Not usually.

This was not a task he would shove off on one of his many assistant junior guardsmen. Although they were all military men and women themselves, Waithe did not believe they would give the dead their due. They would not understand the gravity of the situation until *they* had led men and women into battle themselves and watched some of them die at their command. No, *Announcements of the Honored Dead* should have the attention of someone who truly understood. Thus, it was his job and his duty… a heavy one, but one that these fallen men deserved.

He touched the first name on the screen in his list. Guardsman Ermath. The official form of *Death in Battle* opened up and he began to type. It was all standard stuff until it came to the last part, where he was to put his official personal condolences that would be placed under the official *Announcement* document. Both of these documents would be delivered to the next of kin with the guardsman's personal effects. He hesitated, thinking of the right words to say, because unlike other Guard Captains, he would be delivering the news personally.

Finally, he wrote:

My deepest sympathies for your loss. Guardsman Ermath was an excellent guardsman, and one who always thought of his peers first. I cannot think of a day that he did not look to his friends and family within the Guard to see what hurts he could soothe. Always one with a kind word, Guardsman Ermath will be sorely missed. He died doing his duty and it was a good death. Our objective was achieved. He did not die in vain. Be proud of Guardsman Ermath. I am and I honor his memory. ~ Guard Captain Waithe

He worked on Guardsman Spiradon's *Announcement* next and wrote a similar heartfelt message of condolence tailored to the guardsman's taciturn ways but willingness to teach those who wished to learn. Waithe felt that sense of loss again as he finished up the official documentation and his computer screen focused on the last guardsman *Announcement* document to be completed.

Guardsman Kintares.

Waithe opened the document with a touch of his finger and all but rushed through the form, because he had written this part twice before. Then he got to the personal condolences section. When he reached this point, he sat back and considered what to say. *Kintares had been a good guardsman. Not the best and not the worst,* he thought. *He was... had been... in the middle of the pack and destined never to command his own squad. That didn't make him a bad man.*

However, Waithe could not get the image of a frozen Kintares—crouched over Spiradon's body, watching the suicidal girl's charge—out of his mind. He could not stop himself from wincing again and again as he was too late to stop her and the bomb went off. The Guard Captain could not stop seeing the blood and guts on the ground behind the stop line or his men's severed limbs twitching in the dirt. He had seen bodies before. But these were his people. His guardsmen. *His.* When the bodies were those of his people, it was never easy to dismiss them.

Do I blame him for his lack? Waithe wondered. He turned to the computer, pulled up the footage from the battle and replayed this particular incident again. It was a deliberate thing, as seen through the unfeeling eye of the camera instead of through the filter of painful flashes of memory. The camera had been mounted high on the hospital wall to cover all of the grounds right outside of the hospital entrance where the guardsmen had set their line. Waithe watched the fighting as the video timer counted the seconds and minutes.

He paused the footage the instant before the shots hit the girl and the bomb exploded. He studied the scene and tried to see it as Kintares must have seen it. Then, a small detail came into focus. Waithe restarted the footage and let it play through. He replayed the scene two more times before shifting his focus from the moments of Guardsman Kitares's death to earlier in the battle. Specifically, to the point at which Guardsman Spiradon fell.

Low-tech though the Believers were, that did not make their weapons any less deadly than the high-tech firepower of the guardsmen. Men have been killing each other with swords for thousands of years. While it seems crazy that a sword could kill an elite guardsman in this day and age, just because a civilization advances does not mean a sword is any less deadly. It was a sword that had taken down Spiradon: a lucky strike through the chest by a young man with only one arm. The other arm had been shot off just above the elbow.

Waithe watched as Spiradon fell, Kintares killed the sword wielder, checked the area for enemies, and then turned to Spiradon's supine body. Kintares's next action made up Waithe's mind for him. He returned to his document and began to write his final thoughts on Guardsman Kintares.

OFFER

Waithe sat in his office, ruminating over the choice to make Guardsman Kintares a hero instead of a failure when, in fact, the man had been both. He had worked to save his squadmate from a lethal wound, but had frozen when he should have acted. What Waithe could not decide now was whether Kintares froze because the attacker was a teenage girl or because he knew if he removed his hands from Spiradon's chest, Spiradon would die.

It's all speculation and hindsight at this point. Both men are dead and the proper forms and courtesies have been fulfilled. Let it go.

The suddenly tossed coin did not startle Waithe. Instead, it was a welcome distraction. He caught it with the automatic reflexes of a trained guardsman and looked up. "Hedari Araquez. What's this for?"

"Your thoughts." The handsome young man smiled briefly as he walked into the room and closed the door behind him.

"You don't want them." Waithe eyed his visitor. Full Explorer uniform, a serious attitude, and the closed office door. "And you aren't here for a social visit. Otherwise, we would have had this talk in my quarters."

"Sometimes, I think you live here." Araquez took a seat across from Waithe with the ease of longtime familiarity.

"Be that as it may, what can I do for you?"

"First, you may congratulate me on my new position. Mission Commander Hedari Araquez at your service." Araquez gave a little bow from his seat.

Araquez had meant the gesture to be light and casual. Instead, it had revealed just how uncertain he was. *Why would you be uncertain around me of all people?* Waithe wondered as he said, "Congratulations. What's the mission?"

"That's what I'm here to speak about. A star system has been found with at least one habitable planet. The new Explorer class ship will be going. Complement of five thousand. I need a Guard Commander for the mission."

Waithe sat back and considered his friend's words. A new, viable system was a rare and precious thing. "I'm a Guard *Captain*." He gestured to his rank pin.

"That will change."

"Why me?"

"Because you're the best, in my opinion." Araquez paused at the look that Waithe gave him. "Because we need to go to this planet. The Empress's oracles say that a great danger lies there, but the Empire's best chance for salvation is there as well. It's dangerous, and I need to know that the person who's going to be leading the Guard is someone I can trust."

"What's the catch?"

That startled a laugh out of Araquez. "I tell you that we are going into certain danger and you want to know what the catch is?"

Waithe was not smiling. "Yes. Tell me what you are not saying. The thing that makes you believe I'll tell you 'No' despite your offer of a promotion, exploration, and certain danger."

Araquez looked away and then back again, staring Waithe straight in the eyes. "Based on the nature of the danger, the crew complement will be about ten percent Hedari." When Waithe gave no immediate response, he continued. "I know you don't like our kind. I know I'm one of the few you tolerate. But we need you. I know you'll protect the Hedari—most of them scientists—despite your personal feelings."

Waithe reached out toward the picture of the dark-haired woman, but did not pick it up. "I lost my sister to you people. She died because she became Hedari. Now, you're asking me to protect five hundred of you?" His tone was soft and deliberate.

"Yes," Araquez nodded. "Because, I know you. I know you're a good Captain and will be a great Commander. I trust you with your people, the Explorers Guild's people... and with my people. There are few that I can say that about. We need you. The Empress will approve your promotion and your new assignment if I can assure her that you'll accept it."

Waithe frowned. "The Empress is involved personally?"

Araquez nodded again.

"I'll think about it. I'll give you my decision as soon as I can."

It was a dismissive statement and Araquez understood it to be so. He stood, bowed, and left without another word. Waithe watched him go, knowing already what his answer would be. But he needed time to think about the ramifications of that answer.

Also, he had another, more important, job to do first.

ANNOUNCEMENT

He arrived at Guardsman Kintares's home last... partly because he wanted to save the hardest for last, and partly because the guardsman's home planet was the farthest one out from the Headquarters planet. Ixon was in the Hayes system and was one of the two main water supply planets for this end of the system. A lot of men were stationed here out of deference to their families and were called away for a tour of duty several times a year to the more dangerous sectors.

While he was home, Guardsman Kintares had been an Acquisitions man for Base Aramanthe, making sure that all the equipment needed by the base was there. Not an exciting job, but an important one nonetheless. By all accounts, he had done his job well, and he would be missed.

One of the junior guardsmen gave Waithe a ride to Guardsman Kintares's home. While on the way, Waithe reviewed Guardsman Kintares's culture and how to appropriately address his widow. In this case, it was a first-name situation. *Gennabelle, his wife, and Natara, his daughter,* he thought, mentally repeating the names with the correct pronunciation. He knew these coming few moments would impact Gennabelle and Natara for the rest of their lives, and he wanted to make sure these memories would be as good as they could be under the circumstances.

"Please stay here. I won't be long," Waithe told his impromptu chauffeur.

"Yes, Guard Captain." The guardsman sat back and prepared to wait.

Guard Captain Waithe stood and pulled his Class A uniform in line. Even though he was a small, stocky man, he knew he was an impressive figure in this uniform designed more for the grips and grins of social events with aristocrats and leaders than for the somber occasion he was about to undertake. Still, the widow Kintares deserved to have the news delivered by someone who cared and looked like it.

When Gennabelle opened the door, he watched her very carefully. She had a smile on her face initially. Her eyes flicked over him, first to his face, then to his rank, then his medals, and finally his name. He saw her eyes widen as she recognized his name. Her smile faltered as the realization of what a visit from her husband's Tour of Duty commanding officer might mean. Then, he watched her face go neutral, all emotions hidden.

"Hello Guard Captain. What may I do for you?"

"Gennabelle. I have news. May I come in?" His voice was soft and courteous.

She stepped aside, closing the door after him. She said nothing as she passed him in the hall and led him to the main room of the living quarters. As he stepped in, she asked, "May I get you something to drink?"

"No. I thank you."

"It is nothing."

"It is to me." He said, completing the standard gratitude ritual. He paused for a beat before he asked, "Is Natara home? She may wish to be here for this."

"I'm here." The voice came from behind them. Natara stepped forward. Her face was also a mask of neutrality.

The moment that Waithe saw Natara, he was glad of what he had decided to do for his dead guardsman.

Both mother and daughter sat on the couch across from the chair Waithe chose. He placed the box of personal effects next to him, opened his case, and chose not to notice the collective wince at the sight of the *Announcement for the Honored Dead* certificate. He picked it up and handed it over to Gennabelle. "My deepest condolences," he said as she took the document from him.

"What happened?" Natara asked, looking up from the paper. "How did my father die?"

Guard Captain Waithe did not say, *Well, Natara, he froze in the middle of battle because a girl who could have been your twin ran at him with a homemade bomb. He saw you in her and died because of it.*

"He died on the line while trying to save the life of one of his squadmates. He had his hands full, covering a sucking chest wound when a suicide bomber came in and killed all three of them. Your father died a hero, and he is to be honored as such. He will receive a medal for his bravery under fire."

"I... we appreciate this." Gennabelle said. Her voice was soft and controlled. "More than you know."

"I have Guardsman Kintares's things with me." He indicated the box at his side. He understood the reaction to the news of death affected each differently. In this family, the chain of command and the decorum that went with it held tight.

Gennabelle stood. "If you don't mind, Guard Captain, I will open that in private."

He stood and handed the box to Gennabelle. He watched her walk out, leaving him alone with Natara. While her face was still neutral, her eyes had a wet and shiny look. "Tears are nothing to be ashamed of, Natara," he said, wanting to soothe her in some small way.

"A guardsman's daughter doesn't cry. My father taught me this." Her voice was tight with control and brittle with pain.

Waithe did not push. This family would mourn in private. Tears would not be shared with a commanding officer. In this family, that would be inappropriate.

"Did he really die a good death?" She looked him in the face, judging him, watching him for signs of falsehood.

He could see this was a very important question to her and nodded his affirmation. "He did. He died a hero."

"I'm going to be just as good and as brave as he was. I'm going to be a guardsman as soon as I'm of age."

There was a desperation in the declaration that Waithe understood far too well. Part of him wanted to encourage her path. Part of him wanted to dissuade her. *You're too young to be thinking of military service. You should be out there dating boys and wondering what to wear,* he thought. But, as he knew, children of a guardsman grew up living a very different life than other children. In the end, he simply asked, "Do you say so?"

She nodded at him.

"Then may it be so."

Those were the last words he spoke to her. As soon as Gennabelle returned, he took his leave. She paused at the front door. "Thank you for your words of condolence. They mean a lot. Natara will appreciate them, too."

At that point, he could not say, *It is nothing.* To him, it was something. He elected instead to say, "I meant those words." He returned to the waiting guardsman and his transport without looking back. After all, Guard Captain Waithe—who would soon be Guard Commander Waithe—had a new assignment.

The question of whether to serve on the new Hedari explorer ship had never really been a question at all. His duty was to the Empire and to her needs, no matter how hard the job would be. He had just lost three good men in the defense of a single Hedari explorer. It was always a possibility.

He would not hesitate now either.

This time, though, with a complement of five thousand, fifteen hundred would be guardsmen to protect, manage, and serve the three thousand explorers, and five hundred Hedari. Tours of duty on an explorer ship were never easy. Too much could go wrong. This tour of duty would not have an end date, because a new system was involved.

But "easy" was not what he'd expected when he'd signed up to serve. He pulled out his hand-held and looked at his waiting communications. Araquez had sent over the details of what the tour of duty would entail the same day they'd met. Waithe finally opened the communiqué and began to read. The Empire needed him, and it was his duty to serve.

I WROTE THIS FOR THE *What Fates Impose* anthology. *Set in-between books three and four of the Karen Wilson Chronicles (*Keystones *and* Chimera Incarnate, *respectively), I wanted to show more about John Corso and the Todari tarot cards. In essence, what he is willing to do to get one and what would make him give one up. This is after he fell hard for Karen in the books. Someday, I'm going to write about when he was younger, dumber, greedier, and what happened the one time he stole a Todari card then suffered the consequences of the forbidden action.*

A CARD GIVEN
(A Kendrick Story)

John Corso sat at the poker table. It wasn't where he wanted to be, but it was where he needed to be to get what he wanted. The traditional hexagonal poker table with green felt top was out of sorts with the flow of Japanese decorations of Sushi-Ya. But, there was no safer place to have a high-stakes game of this particular caliber.

Of the other three men and one woman at the table, only the man across the felt from John mattered. Sandeep Gowda was an older Indian with graying temples. He wore trousers of loose beige cloth, a silky mandarin-style white shirt, and a gold waist sash complete with a ceremonial dagger. John, on the other hand, wore his usual khakis, rumpled button-up no-color shirt, and tweed jacket. John appreciated what an odd contrast they were.

Akira Yamamoto, the dealer and one of the owners of Sushi-Ya, nodded to them. "Are you prepared?"

John glanced at his second, Mason, an older man in a business suit. "I am."

Sandeep patted the leg of his second, Puja, a gorgeous Indian woman in a loose cotton dress. "I am."

"Gentlemen and lady." Akira clapped his hands once. The tattooed men around the room left, sliding the rice paper doors closed behind them. "Sushi-Ya agreed to host this game. All in this room are bound by the rules of hospitality. All in this room agreed to them. The game results are final." He bowed to the room. "Remember, you came to us."

John tipped his chin to Akira. "I understand. I'm sure this will be a friendly game."

"I don't know about friendly." Sandeep shook his head. "Fair, though."

"A fair game, then." John fiddled with an unlit cigarette.

"Ante up, gentlemen." Akira's eyes crinkled into a mass of laugh lines.

Mason leaned to John. "Are you certain you want to do this? Really? Something this important… left to a game of chance?" He held a box out to John. It was about six by nine inches, and an inch tall.

"Poker is a game of skill, Mr. Steward." Sandeep's silky voice was filled with mirth. "I find it interesting, John, that your second is the mayor of Kendrick himself." Sandeep gave Mason a respectful nod. Mason returned it, his mouth a firm line of disapproval.

"Not so much skill as luck, considering the rules we've agreed upon." John tucked the cigarette into an inner pocket before accepting the box. "And I find it interesting that your second is a slave." He gestured to the tattoo on the woman's collarbone.

Puja flushed as she handed a similar box to Sandeep. Then she pulled the collar of her dress closed, hiding the small star-shaped tattoo.

Sandeep's smile cut like a knife. "My property knows to keep my property safe… or pay the price."

The two looked at each other, both reluctant to be the first to reveal their bounty. John shook his head and opened his box, revealing the exquisite Todari tarot card within. It was the eighteenth Major Arcana, the Moon. As always, the vivid colors made John catch his breath. This image was of a crescent moon. Sitting on the inner curve of the crescent was a beautiful woman with long flowing dark hair and a diaphanous white gown. Below her, on the edge of a lake, were two dogs howling and barking up at her as she looked off to the side, unconcerned. Crawling out of the lake from the other side was something that appeared to be a lobster.

Imagination, intuition, and dreams for you. But for one you love, bad luck may ensue. Unseen perils, possible woes. Deceptions abound with secret foes. John stroked the edge of the card with an affectionate finger. *Storms are weathered, peace at a cost. Practicality wins, imagination is lost.*

He held it out to Akira, speaking in a careful, formal tone of voice. "I give this card to you. It is my willing ante into this game."

Sandeep gestured, appreciative. Puja smiled at the dark haired woman on the card. Opening his box, Sandeep revealed that he had the Two of Pentacles from the Todari tarot deck. Not a Major Arcana card, but no less stunning.

John clenched his hands under the table to keep himself from grabbing at the card. He had never seen it before. Leaning forward, his eyes drank in the vivid colors of its image.

The Two of Pentacles card showed a young woman wearing a peasant's dress as she planted flowers. Ignoring the fallen autumn leaves, she planted these flowers in a box protected by an overhang. Two of the blossoms were in the shape of pentacles. One pentacle flower was already planted. The second was being planted. The young woman's face shone with hope, even in the lateness of the year.

John smiled. "That's the one." *Harmony and agility in changing times. New projects are running too far behind.* Although... *Juggled events fall apart. Forced laughter, not of the heart. Messages in writing, letters to start.*

"I give this card to you." Sandeep handed the Two of Pentacles to Akira. "It's my willing ante into this game."

Akira accepted both cards with the gravitas of a priest. He took a moment to look at them. "They are beautiful. I've never seen one in the flesh, much less two. Is it true? That they give you powers?"

"Yes," Sandeep said.

"They loan you their strength. Only the owners may share in it," John corrected.

"I would joke about now being their owner, but I know how many people have died trying to collect these artifacts." Akira's smile disappeared to be replaced with the no-expression he usually wore. "There will be three hands, no betting. I will gift the winner with these two exquisite Todari cards."

Akira placed the cards in front of him, face down. The effect was immediate. Everyone relaxed and focused on each other instead of the cards. Akira opened a new deck of mundane playing cards and began shuffling.

"I was surprised to get your call and the offer of the game." Sandeep tapped the edge of the table twice with his ring. "How many Todari cards do you have now?"

John took off his glasses and started cleaning them. "Would you tell me how many you had if I asked?"

"Seven. Soon to be eight." Sandeep's pride at this number showed in his bright eyes.

John nodded, still cleaning his glasses. "A respectable number."

"And you?"

"Thirty-eight. Soon to be thirty-nine."

The Assamese man didn't try to hide his shock as he took a breath and stared at John. "So many. I knew you were the foremost collector… but I had no idea."

John put his glasses back on. "Most don't."

Akira dealt each man five cards. John looked at his hand. A busted straight. Low numbers. Nothing to do but ask for four cards. Sandeep asked for two. John glanced at his cards. Nothing again. Not even a pair.

Mason murmured under his breath. "This is going well."

"Trust me." John nodded to Akira.

Akira returned the nod. "Please reveal your cards."

Sandeep revealed a pair of aces against John's garbage hand. "Ha! This *is* off to a good start."

John sat back with a sigh and watched Akira gather up the cards. "This round to you."

"Tell me, what power will my new card give me? It reveals enemies, yes? That's what I've heard."

"It gives you visions of the future." John glanced between Puja and Sandeep and back again. "What about the card I'll win? What will it give me?"

Sandeep scowled. "Visions of the future? Did you have a vision of this game?"

"Perhaps." John's face mirrored Akira's neutral expression. "The Two of Pentacles's power?"

"It mends that which had been sundered. It brings into balance those that need it." Sandeep gave John a quizzical glance.

"Interesting." He nodded to himself as if something had clicked into place.

Mason leaned to John. "You didn't know?"

John kept his eyes on Sandeep even as Akira dealt the next hand of cards. "No."

"But—"

"Later." He picked up the cards Akira dealt. Aces over jacks. John signaled for one card, hoping to get a full house. He shook his head as it turned out be a four of spades. Looking at Sandeep's face, John could tell he wasn't happy.

Akira nodded to each man. "Reveal your cards."

Sandeep muttered curses under his breath as his pair of threes lost to John's hand. Akira swept the playing cards to him and began the process of shuffling.

"That's one for me and one for you, Sandeep."

The dusky man nodded. "It is. It comes down to one hand. Are you certain you wish to do this?"

"Good question." Mason shook his head. "I must've been mad to agree to this game, much less to be your second."

"I'm sure. More sure now than ever." John's smile was hard, hiding his teeth.

Sandeep looked at the cards Akira was dealing and leaned forward. "Listen, John. I've changed my mind. Don't pick up those cards. We can quit the game together. Take our cards back." He glanced at Puja, his forehead moist with sudden desperation. "And you can have her. Keep her, free her. It's your choice."

John shook his head. "I—"

"I'll kill her after this game if I lose that card. I told her so before we arrived." Sandeep shoved Puja out of her chair. "Beg for your life."

Puja tumbled to the floor. Instead of getting up, she crawled under the table to John's feet. Even as John pushed back from the table, Puja grasped his leg. "Please, please, Mister Corso. Please, he *will* kill me. He promised.

You can save me and get your card back, too. I'll be your slave, your lover, whatever you want. I swear it."

"She's very skilled. Her mother sold her to me as a child. I've had her well-trained."

John looked down at her, his eyes hardening. She must have seen his rejection because Puja started to wail. "Please, God! Please!"

"That's not now this works. If we forfeit now, Akira owns both cards. Sandeep knows that. I will *not* lose them." Turning from her, even as she clung to his leg, John picked up his cards.

"So be it." Sandeep nodded. "Puja!"

John stared at his cards without seeing them. He felt Mason glaring daggers and refused to meet his friend's gaze. Sandeep smiled at his cards as Puja returned to her seat, her makeup smeared under moist, bloodshot eyes.

"One." Sandeep slid a card to Akira and received one in return.

Again, John looked at two pair. Kings over tens. He glanced at Sandeep and knew the man had something. John slid one card to Akira and got one back. John didn't even look at it. He slid it in his hand and nodded to the dealer.

"Gentlemen, reveal your cards. Winner takes all."

Sandeep revealed a flush of hearts. John put his cards on the table without looking, his heart hammering in his chest, his stomach sour with anxiety. Sandeep slamming his fists on the table told John he had won. Looking down, John saw the full house, and collapsed back in his seat.

Sandeep stood. "You've won. And I'm a man of my word." He pulled the knife from his sash, grabbed Puja by the hair, and stabbed her twice in the heart as an alarm rang throughout the restaurant. John and Mason leaped from their seats. Akira tackled Sandeep, knocking him away from the bleeding woman.

John and Mason stood back as the tattooed wait staff dragged Sandeep out of the room. Akira prayed over Puja, pressing his hands to her wounds. John leaned forward as Akira's hands began to glow and the woman took a shuddering breath.

"Thank God." John pulled the cigarette from his pocket and played with it.

Mason looked between them. "Did you know?"

"Later."

"'Later' better be a damn good story."

Puja opened her eyes and stared up at Akira. "I'm alive?"

"You are reborn." He touched the slave tattoo and it disappeared. "You died and were reborn a free woman."

"I don't... I can't... I've never..." Puja sobbed.

Akira pulled her into a fatherly hug. "Shhhh. We will care for you here until you're strong enough to fly in body and mind. The rules of hospitality apply to you, too. He cannot harm you further." Akira glanced up at John with unforgiving eyes. "Neither of them can."

John looked away, fiddling with his cigarette all the more.

As Akira called for one of the older women who worked at the restaurant, Mason indicated Akira's healing hands. "That's new."

Akira watched Puja as she left the room. He took a towel from his apron and cleaned his hands until nothing of the girl's blood remained. "Not new. Old. No one may be harmed in this place. We take no sides, follow no leadership but our own. And we do not allow the Lost to be abandoned."

He returned to the poker table and picked up the two Todari cards. "Mister Corso, I gift these to you. You are their rightful owner."

John accepted them. "Thank you. I accept them in the spirit they are given."

"I am neutral, but I'm glad I did not need to gift those to that man." Akira's laugh lines reappeared, but there was no joy in his eyes. "And I now know what these cards are worth to you."

John put both cards into the small box.

◆

"What in Sam hell was that all about? Did you have visions of what would happen at the game?" Mason's driver opened the car door for the two of them.

"I did. But before that… I had a different vision." John took his battered cigarette from his pocket. "Please?"

Mason nodded and the two of them cracked the back windows. "At least you smoke those good-smelling European cigarettes."

"American cigarettes are shit."

"So, vision?"

John took a long drag and held it in before exhaling towards the open window. "A vision that we need that card. It's going to sustain one of our allies."

"And the Moon, did it tell you what would happen at the game?"

"Yes."

"Even what happened to Puja?"

John wouldn't look at Mason. "I knew a woman would be hurt, but then the lobster pulled the woman away from the dog. So, I hoped."

"But you didn't *know*." Mason shook his head. "She could've died."

"There's only one woman I willingly give away a Todari card for, much less two. You know that."

Mason nodded. "I know. Karen. You're a cold man."

"You have no idea." John watched the passing scenery without seeing it as he smoked. His hands were still trembling.

"I'm slowly getting an idea." Mason sat there for a moment. "How is she doing?" His voice was carefully neutral.

"Karen?"

Mason nodded.

"She's… all right. Not hurt physically. But her heart… She's feeling the pressure of being the Master of the City's Representative. These past two years fighting the Children of Anu have taken their toll. So many people have died."

"That's not her fault."

"I know that. You know that. But she's been at the center of every major fight in the past several years. I used to think she was impetuous, naïve, and foolhardy. But now I know she's just trying to do what's right. And 'right' comes with the weight of responsibility. None of the factions blame her.

Not the Bacchanalia Coven, the Makah, the Brotherhood, the Special Unit. None of them. But she still feels the pain of every loss."

"Maybe that's why she's a good leader." Mason glanced at him. "And why she needs you."

"Yeah. So I do what I have to. The hard times aren't over. I need to make sacrifices to protect her." John took a long drag, then let the smoke dribble out his nose and mouth. "She makes me willing to make sacrifices. I didn't expect that. All in all, Mason, I'm a selfish bastard."

Mason gave him a half smile. "I know. But I'm glad she brings out the good in you."

"I don't know if there's any good to bring out."

"I'm sure. I have my family's legacy back and Kendrick is safe for the moment, partly because of you." He thought for a moment. "And I've done a lot I'm not proud of to protect my family and this city. So, if you say that card is worth what happened to keep Kendrick safe… who am I to judge?"

The two sat in companionable silence for rest of the ride to the Steward estate. John smoked his cigarette and wondered if it really would be worth it. Part of him cringed at the memory of condemning Puja to death. He was sure that was something that would come back to haunt him in time.

As the car stopped at the estate, Mason turned to him. "Nightcap and conversation?"

John shook his head. "Things to do and miles to go before I sleep."

"You gonna tell me the whole story?"

"Maybe. I still don't know it. Can I get a lift elsewhere?"

"Yes. Where?"

"Dock 14."

Mason gave John a careful look. "Really?"

"Really."

"Should I come with you?"

John shook his head. "I'd rather not."

Mason got out of the car as the door opened for him. "It's a good thing I trust you." He turned to his driver. "Dock 14 for John."

Waiting until the door was closed, John kept his voice low. "You really shouldn't trust me."

The last time John was at Dock 14, they—he, Karen, and a rare alliance of various supernatural factions in Kendrick—had gathered a strike force bent on rescuing a kidnapped ally. They had arrived too late. The Abbot, a good man, had been ritually beaten to death by the Children of Anu. John didn't like to remember what they had found in that dark, dank cave. He walked down the beach to a driftwood log and sat on it, smoking, waiting, thinking.

Karen. The naïve young woman had come into the supernatural world blind because the city itself had chosen her as its representative. She had been brash, reckless, and fearless in her quest to stop the casual acceptance of the war that had raged hot and cold amongst the supernatural factions for decades. Now she was a recognized leader among the hidden denizens of Kendrick. Betrayed, attacked, almost ritualistically murdered, she still held out hope that all could live in peace. Despite her losses, Karen never wavered from that belief.

How could a selfish, cynical man like him not love her? And she loved him back. He smiled, thinking about holding her as they talked about everything and nothing while Sebastian, the baby gargoyle who had bonded himself to her, cavorted in the antique store. Yes, he would do much to protect her.

John dropped his cigarette when the Gray Lady appeared on the log next to him. She still wore the long gray high-necked gown she always wore, but she looked old, translucent. "I wish you wouldn't do that."

"I apologize. I have little time or energy for the niceties of corporeal living." Her voice tickled his ear in a whisper.

"I had a dream." John lit another cigarette.

"I know."

"I have a Todari card."

"You have many."

John watched the lapping waves with their small whitecaps. Conversations with the Gray Lady were always like a game of riddles. The problem, this time, was the heavy feeling of doom instead of the usual feeling of confusion. "The dream. It warned me of a coming danger."

"Yes."

"What danger?"

"Tell me your dream, John. I may be the Queen of the Fair Court, but I am not all-knowing."

John glanced at her, saw the weary, patient smile. "Something was chasing me through a hallway of doors. It broke through every door I slammed shut. Except for the last one. The last one held. On it was a Todari tarot card, the Two of Pentacles. I touched the card and light came from me to it. The card glowed and the door grew roots, sealing it. All the while, the monster pounded and scrabbled at the wood."

"Did you see the monster?"

"No. But I knew that door was the last door and if it got through… I would die."

She thought for a moment. "We are more than tied to the land. We're often called 'the Goodfolk' because we're its guardians. But we're failing. Our places of power have been destroyed. They will take time to rebuild… if they can be rebuilt."

There was sadness in her voice that broke his heart and told him that he was doing the right thing, that he had made the right choice—no matter the pain. Taking the Todari carrying box out of his pocket, he opened it and looked on the beauty of the Two of Pentacles. It hurt him to have to give it up so soon. "Who is this for?"

The Gray Lady put her hand on his arm. "Me. If you would keep Karen and the rest safe."

Karen. How she had changed him and opened his world. "How will it help?" He took the Todari card out of the box, refusing to look at the Moon card beneath. He didn't want to see any more futures. Not tonight. Not for a long time.

"It will anchor me to the land. My hold is tenuous, the bindings sundered by the destruction of my keeps. The fair folk have ever been tied to the land and their places of power. When the Children destroyed them in their greed, they broke our protections. We, too, have our duty to those in Kendrick, though most never realize it." She paused. "They know the Veil is faltering. This will strengthen it for a time."

"They?"

"The Nightmares. The monsters on the other side of the Veil. The ones who would raze this land and subject its denizens to unimaginable horrors. The portent of your dream."

"Until?" He held the Two of Pentacles up.

"Until I can find the one who will come after me."

John tore his gaze from the Todari tarot card to look at her. "You're dying?"

"Oh, John, dear *Collector*… how can you look at me and ask that question?" Her rebuke was gentle and amused. "Yes. I'm dying. I will be replaced by another with a love and link to the land. Just as I followed the one before me."

"You're being unusually forthcoming."

"Impending death and doom will do that."

"Can we stop… what's coming?"

"Yes. Perhaps. With help from good people like you."

Good. Was he good now? He'd always hidden his selfishness under a veneer of civility and the guise of a rumpled scholar. But now… He held the card out to her. "Lady Gray, would you do me the great honor of accepting this gift?"

"You may not get it back." Her voice was barely heard now, a whisper on the wind.

He grimaced at the thought, his heart pounding his ears, but kept his hand out, offering her the precious card. "I know. I risked another card for it earlier. I even… I did something horrible… to get it. I give this card to you with my whole heart. I just hope it helps you and your people. I hope you survive. And… I hope what's coming won't be as bad as I think."

"That's a lot of hope in one gift."

John's stomach turned over, the selfish beast within roaring with want. He forced his hand to remain extended to her. "Please, please just accept it before my baser nature takes over."

The Gray Lady took the card from him. "I accept it with all that I am. I, too, hope for all of those same things. Thank you."

As soon as her hand took the card from his, her translucency filled in and she looked solid. Her presence became a weight he could sense, and his selfish beast was quieted, replaced with the satisfaction that the sacrifice was worth it. "Is there anything else I can do?"

She nodded. "Guard your dreams. Do whatever you can to guard your dreams and the dreams of those you love. The Nightmares are coming and we don't have the strength to hold them back."

THIS IS THE STORY WHERE I WANTED *to show the Mowry fans how the seemingly invincible Joseph Lamb could be hurt, potentially killed. No hero is interesting if he cannot be hurt. I also wanted to show the transition of Eric Hamblin going from being a passive host for Joseph to becoming a hero in his own right. Up until this point, Eric has done nothing but sit back and let Joseph do the dirty work. Also, the thing with the horse still gets comments years after it was published.*

IRON ACHILLES HEEL
(A Mowry Story)

"You ready?" Eric asked as he glanced from the sounds of gunshots and screams to the spirit on his right and back again.

"I'm always ready to do God's will," Joseph said. He looked through the bank office window.

Eric did not have to look again to know that Joseph had disappeared. He could already feel the avenging spirit taking control of his body, and let it happen. He knew all he had to do now was watch, listen, and learn. And, if necessary, warn Joseph of something the spirit had not already seen.

Like an experienced thief, Joseph slid the boot knife blade up between the window panes and flipped the latch. He swung the windows open and pulled himself into the bank's back office. There, he crouched behind the desk, waiting to see if any of the bank robbers had noticed him. Considering they were in the front with the terrified bank patrons and there was no backdoor, Eric wasn't surprised none of them expected an attack from behind.

Joseph and Eric had tracked this band of robbers for the past hundred miles or so through towns too small to be remembered on any map. Once they had gotten the gist of where the robbers were headed—Palmer, Arizona and the site of the most profitable of the small towns in the area—they had hurried on ahead with the intention of stopping the robbers before they made their mark there, too. However, only a day off the trail and just long enough to get the lay of the land, the gang had ridden into town and struck again.

But this time, there would be an accounting for their crimes.

"Please, mister, you have the money. Please, just go!"

"Never tell me what to do."

The crash of the gunshot was followed by a surprised gasp of pain that faded into a weak whimper.

Dammit all, they're shooting people.

"Not for long," Joseph murmured as he moved to the office doorway, no longer hiding. In front of him was the teller's countertop. Beyond that were a score of frightened folk and the four bank robbers he was set to stop and bring back—alive or dead. Joseph's first shot took the bank robber at the end of the counter between the eyes. His second shot swung wide as one of the robbers, the one closest to the front door reacted, shooting Eric's body in the chest.

"Move it, Daniel!" that robber ordered.

Daniel, the original target of Joseph's second bullet and the robber who had just murdered the bank manager, cursed, shot wildly in Joseph's direction, and ran to the door. Joseph leveled his gun, but stopped as Daniel grabbed the nearest woman and used her as a shield. Both men backed out the door, Daniel still holding the crying woman hostage.

The fourth bank robber, to the left of the door, stared as Joseph used his left hand to pluck the bullet from his chest and his right to aim and fire. The fourth robber gurgled as he dropped his gun, and clutched at his throat to stanch the blood that spurted forth. He went to his knees, still staring at Joseph, before toppling over.

Eric knew the bullet to the chest had to have hurt, but Joseph was a master at ignoring pain. When you could heal all wounds within a matter of moments, all you had to do was wait it out. And all Eric had to do was mend yet another bullet hole in his shirt. Fortunately, his body rarely bled while Joseph spirit-rode him.

Joseph headed toward the front door, but stopped as one of the women, a girl from the General Store, frantically shook her head. "No!"

"What is it?"

She drew back from him as if understanding that Eric wasn't exactly himself. "Those two are the Marlin boys. They wait and shoot anyone who comes after them."

Joseph nodded, curt and polite. "Thank you, ma'am." He turned from her, walking to the back of the bank, stepped over the first robber he shot, and returned to the bank manager's office. He slid himself out the window and crouched down, listening. There was a cry of a woman—not a mortal cry, but one of distress and outrage, followed by the sound of men's rude laughter and the pounding of two horses pushed into a gallop.

"Looks like a chase then."

Better for the townsfolk. Less likely to get any of them killed.

Suddenly in charge of his body again, Eric knew what was expected. He whistled for his horse. In all the time he and Joseph had been together, the spirit still had not learned to whistle.

Eric had never thought he would get used to being a passenger in his own body, watching the gunfight with a sleepy eye, like a man who has seen the same vaudeville act one too many times. But here he was; nothing more than a human vessel for the Lion of God, Sheriff Joseph Lamb, doing his sworn duty to smite sinners and bring justice back to this wild land. It was the pain that broke him out of his complacency; pain in his hand and pain in his neck. Something he had never felt before while being spirit-ridden by Lamb.

Then he was falling.

As he hit the dirt, the pain in his hand and neck was replaced with the jarring sensation of his teeth clacking together and the scrape of rocks against his cheek. The sound of his horse galloping toward parts unknown covered the other man's groans until Eric rolled over and saw Joseph lying in the dirt, blood streaming between fingers clamped to the man's throat.

"Joseph! Holy God! What happened?"

"My gun," Joseph croaked. "What happened to the gun?"

The gun in question was a Colt 1851 Navy revolver with a series of intricate flame engravings on the barrel, and a well-worn handle. It was the Sheriff's weapon. Decades ago, it had been used to murder him. Eric saw it lying in the scrub a few feet from where he'd landed. He limped over to it, picked it up and saw the deep notch in the barrel of the pistol where the bank robber's bullet must have hit it. One in a million shot.

Eric turned back to Joseph as he held up the pistol. "It's here. A bullet hit it." He rubbed a finger in the bullet groove and Joseph gasped in pain. Eric frowned and touched the bullet groove again and saw Joseph wince at the same time. "You didn't tell me you could get hurt," he said as he walked over to where Joseph was.

"Didn't know it until now." Joseph struggled into a seated position.

"Huh. The almighty Lion of God is not invulnerable after all."

The spirit looked up at his companion with a wry expression. "Appears not."

Eric hunkered down next to Joseph and stuck an experimental hand through Joseph's incorporeal arm. "That hurt?"

"No."

He touched the bullet groove on the pistol and did not have to repeat his question. Joseph winced in pain. "Well, hell and damnation, Lamb. How am I supposed to get you fixed? Your body isn't of this earth and any touch to the gun makes you weep like a child."

Lamb shrugged a little. "I don't know. Never been hurt like this before. But the bleeding's stopped. I think I'll live. It'll just take time to heal. A lot of time. More time than we have. We've got a job to finish."

Eric holstered the revolver and stood. "Not like this we don't." He turned in the direction the bank robbers had gone. West, toward the setting sun and the Mexico border, or maybe a slight turn north, and they'd be in California in the same amount of time. Either way, the Marlin boys were home free. "You're too hurt."

"You're right. *We* can't do anything. *You* need to finish the job."

"Like hell." Eric turned on Joseph, only to find him gone. The next words Joseph spoke were from inside his head.

If you let these men go because of your yellow streak, it'll be one more step on your road to damnation. We made a promise. The words you spoke were your own. I did not force you.

"Damn you, Lamb."

Not likely. We don't have much time. I'll be with you the whole way. You aren't helpless. You're not some mewling child. Now call your horse back. There's work to be done.

Eric resisted the urge to pull leather and bash that Colt revolver with a rock until it, and the spirit of Sheriff Joseph Lamb, were no more. Instead, he took a breath and whistled for his horse, Dusty; he used the whistle that promised the gelding a treat even though it was a lie.

As the fire-red coal of the sun touched the horizon, Dusty picked his way through the darkening desert landscape. Eric kept an eye out for leg-breaking holes. He also scanned the line where the fading light met the blackness of earth, looking for sign or silhouette of his quarry. All the while, he tried not to think of just how frightened he was of facing the Marlin boys alone.

No, not really alone. He had not been alone since that day in the church just over a year ago. There, in that haunted place, he had sought refuge from outlaws, found the gun, and with it, the spirit of the murdered Sheriff. He had agreed, fearful and shaking, to do the Lord's work at the threat of his immortal soul, rather than die at that moment with his place in heaven assured. He wondered, and not for the first or last time, if he had made the right choice.

You'll need to dismount soon and go on foot.

No. Never alone. "You want me to keep going in the dark?"

I'll help you to see as best I can. With all the ground we lost, this is our best chance to catch them before they cross the border.

"How you feeling?"

Joseph came forward just enough for Eric to feel the aching throb in his right hand and the searing pain in his throat; it was a pain so great he had to muffle a groan, and tears limned his eyes.

I've felt worse.

"Really?"

Honestly, no. This is bad but I don't think I'm gonna die… again. I think the Lord still has work for me to do.

Eric dismounted and tied his horse up in a loose hitch. If he died, he wanted Dusty to have a chance without him. He took a breath and continued following the trail on foot. There was nothing left to do now but go forward.

It wasn't long before he and Lamb spotted the faint glow of a campfire in the distance. It was low and unobtrusive in the gloom. Just enough coals to warm some food and keep the night from getting too cold. It was also the last mistake the Marlin boys would make, Eric thought. After the shooting they had done this afternoon, he was going to shoot first and demand surrender second.

Ill thoughts from a man doing good works.

Eric wanted to curse Lamb for his eavesdropping. "You said it first, 'sometimes a man has to do bad in the name of good.' These men are stone cold killers and think I'm already dead. I'm not going to give them another chance to actually put me in the ground."

Watch that hole.

He looked down and saw he was moments from plunging his foot into a leg-breaker that would have stopped this foolish quest as well as his life. Eric stepped over it, balancing with one hand against a stone still warm from the heat of the day. He kept close to the rocks and the scrub to keep his own silhouette from announcing his presence.

"In any case," Eric said, "there's two of them and one of me."

You get the drop on them and they might surrender.

"Or they might blow my fool head off."

You never know, but we're about to find out.

Eric halted his careful steps through the darkness and unfamiliar land to look up. Before him was a small hill—a mound, really—with the silhouette of a man propped up against a rock at its apex. The glow from the dying campfire gave scant details: Stetson pulled low, a bushy beard and both hands limp upon his chest.

Remembering to pull his ordinary revolver from his left holster, Eric moved with swift, silent motions. Revolver now in his right hand, Eric acted on instinct. He took cover behind a rocky outcrop, cocked his gun, and aimed at his target. However, instead of shooting first, he yelled, "Hands up! I've got you covered! Hands up or I shoot."

The Marlin boy—the older one, Jebadiah, Eric thought—did not move. For a moment, he wondered if the man was asleep and where the other one, Daniel, was. Then Jeb twitched. Instead of reaching for the stars, the man's right hand came down toward his thigh.

Eric fired twice. Both chest shots hit and Jeb fell over.

His heart pounding, Eric waited to hear what he would hear as the echoes of his shots died away—the scrabbling of Daniel fleeing, the crunch of rock underfoot, the yell of an angry, grieving brother or the clack of a pistol being cocked.

Nothing.

The seconds ticked by.

"I think you need to come up here and see this."

The voice was Joseph's, and Eric saw him now standing above the still form of Jebadiah. Eric hesitated, looking around, flash-burned eyes still seeking the other Marlin boy.

Joseph nodded with approval. "You're learning. It's clear. I wouldn't lead you into danger."

"What do you think you've been doing for the past year?" Eric scoffed as he put his normal revolver back in its holster and clambered up the mound to the makeshift camp. Immediately, he saw what Joseph wanted him to see: Jeb's throat had been cut, and deep. The wound had been hidden by his beard. Now, the almost dried blood glistened black in the light of the coals.

"Congratulations. You just shot a dead man and let his murderer know we're on his trail."

"Daniel did this?" Eric's eyes traced the outline of the gash in dead man's neck before looking at Joseph. He saw that Joseph had tied a kerchief around his throat and, while the blood was staunched, he saw the blood on the cloth and that Lamb's neck was also black in the light of the firelight. Once again, he wondered at how a spirit could bleed. "Why?"

"'For the love of money is the root of all kinds of evil. And some people, craving money, have wandered from the true faith and pierced themselves with many sorrows,'" Joseph quoted. "In short, he got greedy. Money does funny things to a man. Guess he decided he wanted the bankroll for himself. From the looks of it, he planned it that way. Snuck up on Jeb here and cut his throat while the man slept. Then he ran." Joseph pointed toward the place where the last shades of red met black.

"And now he knows someone's coming for him."

"Yep."

Eric gave the camp a brief look over, saw that everything worth taking was gone, and nodded. "Then we'd best go get him."

They did not immediately chase down Daniel, as Eric wanted. Joseph pointed out that it would be best to wait until moonrise, as it was a clear night and the moon would give them better light to follow the trail. Instead, they argued about Jebadiah's ring.

With time to kill, Eric inspected what was left of the Marlin camp. Daniel had done a good job of ransacking it. There was nothing useful left. Then he saw a glimmer of light from Jeb's left hand. Upon removal and some squinting in the scant starlight, Eric discovered that it was a wedding ring.

"Huh. I didn't know he was married." He turned the ring over and around until the starlight reflected the engraved words. "With Love, Anne."

"Even outlaws find love," Joseph said. "You know you can use that as proof of your kill."

"My kill?"

"There's still a bounty on Jebadiah's head—dead or alive. That ring you just pocketed proves you deserve it."

Eric scowled. "No, it doesn't. I didn't have anything to do with Jeb's death. I'm not a murderer."

"Ah, but you are."

"No." He shook his head. "You spirit-ride me. You do the killing."

"While you get the reward and accolades?"

Eric swung his head from side to side. He wasn't hearing Joseph's voice in his head. That meant the Sheriff was around, but for some reason the spirit stayed hidden. He wanted to face his accuser, but suppressed his growing anger at the man's accusations. "That's not why I do this."

"Then why'd you take the ring?"

Eric's voice was quiet. "Even an outlaw's wife deserves to know her husband's dead and who really killed him."

Joseph did not respond. He remained quiet until they were well on their way to finding Daniel Marlin.

Once the moon rose and turned the desert landscape into a myriad of dark and light silver-tinted shadows, it was easy enough to follow the double horse track trail to the darkened camp recently fled by Daniel. Finding nothing but an abandoned pot of water over smothered coals, Eric and Joseph continued on. But this time, the double horse track was rushed and spoke of panic. Eric did not like it. A panicked man did risky things... like push a horse through a desert full of leg-breakers after dark.

There is something up ahead.

Joseph was back within Eric and he felt the Sheriff's lingering pain on the edges of his senses. He pushed it away and concentrated on the moving thing in his path. His heart sank as he got closer. It was a downed horse. A live one, in pain.

With his pistol drawn, he approached, looking all around. The horse groaned loud when it saw Eric. Its eyes begged him to stop the pain. To help it, somehow. There was a touch of a squeal in its next, more urgent groan and Eric saw the front foreleg was broken. "That bastard left you to suffer."

No. I think he left her here as a way to tell how close you were getting.

Joseph was right; Eric knew it and did not need to question his mentor's comment. The choice was to either immediately end the horse's suffering with a bullet in the brain or to cause more pain and a slower death with a cut throat.

What will you do?

"I don't know. What would you do?"

This is your hunt. Your choice. Joseph paused and added, *Choose with your heart.*

"Are you testing me again? Because if you are, it's starting to irritate me."

What will you do? Joseph asked again.

"The right thing." With that, he put his pistol to the suffering horse's head and told the outlaw exactly where he was… also told him the kind of man who was tracking him.

◆

They both knew it was a trap when they saw the next horse left in the dirt. This one whinnied and tried to toss its head at their approach, but the bridle and bit held the horse's head close to the ground. Eric pulled leather as soon as he saw it and searched the shadows for the outlaw.

Sounds came from all around Eric. Pebbles thrown to distract him. Adrenaline pushed into him, honing his abilities. He listened for the scrabble of boot heel on rock and the cock of the gun. His eyes searched as he moved in closer to the horse. He was distantly aware of the horse's struggles to get up, and the pain from Joseph's wounds. None of that was important. What *was* important was—

There. The scrape of spur on rock. That was all the warning he had before Daniel opened fire on him from the base of a nearby cholla cactus. Eric dove to the ground, firing two shots at the muzzle flash off to his left as he fell and heard Daniel grunt in pain. The sound of metal hitting the earth told Eric that Daniel had dropped his gun. He listened to the man's moans of pain for a few moments before walking over to where Daniel lay.

Daniel Marlin was a slight man. Young, in his early twenties, but he had the weather-beaten face of a man ten years older. He was curled up on the ground with his hands to his chest. It reminded Eric of Jebadiah's death pose. He saw the fresh blood, black in the moonlight, staining the front of

Daniel's shirt.

"Help me. You've got to help me," Daniel wheezed at him. There was a high-pitched sound of escaping air coming from the man's chest.

"Help you like you helped those people back in town? Helped the banker even after he gave you the money? Helped your own brother?" The righteous anger built up as Eric spoke, softening his words into the threat they were.

"You got to, lawman. Your... duty."

"Don't got to do anything, Daniel. Not a lawman, just a bounty hunter." It was the blood on Daniel's spurs that made him do it. Blood from the horse he had run until it had faltered. Then left to die, leg-broke and keening in pain. Only Eric wasn't going to take that kind of chance with this kin-killing outlaw. He fired twice more: another shot to the chest and one to the head. "I do God's work."

He looked down at Daniel's limp body and watched the last breath escape already dead lips. Watched as the man's chest fell and did not rise again. "That's what you've been trying to tell me, isn't it, Joseph? I really am a killer. Like you. Like him. Have been for the past year... no matter how much I've told myself I wasn't."

No, Eric. Not like Daniel. He killed for the joy of it. You kill because it is God's will. You too are a Lion of God, or you never would've been chosen to wield me.

"Wield? All I do is sit back and watch you work."

You do more than that, and it's time you understood. We're cut from the same cloth.

"How do you know?"

Look at your hand, my friend, and see that it is God's will.

Eric looked down at his hand and saw that he had not pulled his normal gun from the left hand holster. He was holding the God-blessed revolver. Its engraved flames danced along the now-unmarred barrel of the pistol in the moonlight. To be certain, he raised the revolver up and swung the cylinder out to confirm what he already knew: it was not loaded. The last two shots he had made, the ones that had killed the outlaw in cold blood, had been his choice, but they had also been God's will. It was something to think about.

"Are you well?"

By the grace of God, I am now.

But not tonight. Tonight was reserved for freeing the trapped horse, recovering the bankroll and backtracking his trail to his own horse. Later, after property was returned and a widow was informed, Eric would think about this revelation. Until then, he would soothe himself with the mundane tasks of being a famous bounty hunter.

THIS IS ONE OF MY MYTHOS STORIES, *a stretch goal for Lillian Cohen-Moore's* Village by the Sea *Kickstarter. She and I always joke about how her hometown has the makings of a Lovecraftian setting with its twisting roads, local legends, and general coastal city weirdness. I jumped at the chance to write within the setting. This is a favorite of mine because it is based on a vacation my husband and I took soon after I agreed to write the story. The plot came to me as I watched him build a sandcastle on a deserted beach.*

SANDCASTLE SACRIFICES

Lynn shoulder-bumped David as they sat around her childhood home's kitchen table. He bumped her back and then leaned in for a kiss. The two snuggled for a moment before returning to their coffee and toast.

David pointed to the French on the mug he was drinking. "What's this mean?"

"It's our family motto. '*La famille avant tout*' or 'The family before all.' We mostly just say '*La famille*' these days. Everyone in the family knows what we mean when we say that."

"Interesting. This is your family crest?" He looked closer at the shield with the fishing boat on it.

"Yep." Lynn grinned. "The Bozeman family is very close to the sea. A lot of us have jobs that involve the ocean in some way." She shrugged. "The family shield goes back to a legend of one of my ancestors doing something to save the Village."

"An ancestor doing something, eh? So specific. I vote you for family historian." He winked a baby blue at her.

"That's me. Keeper of the Details. It just means that duty and loyalty to the family are of utmost importance."

"Look at you two." Lynn's mother entered the kitchen. "Being all cute and stuff. It's like you're on your honeymoon or something."

"Good morning, Mrs. Bozeman. I mean Elizabeth." David straightened up, hiding his smile behind his coffee mug.

"Just call me 'Mom.' You're family now."

"Yes ma'am. I mean 'Mom.'"

Lynn rubbed her new husband's thigh under the table. "Relax. All is well."

"Yes, it is," Elizabeth agreed. "Can I make you eggs or pancakes?"

"No thanks." Lynn and David said at the same time and then burst out laughing.

"You two are in a good mood." Elizabeth gave them a fond smile. "Especially for being up so early. The sun's barely up."

"In the Pacific Northwest at this time of year, that just means 7 a.m. And we're still on East Coast time." David sipped his coffee.

Elizabeth looked out the window. "True. Storm's coming tonight." She turned back to them with a sparkle in her eyes. "Oh, are you going to build the sandcastle this morning?"

"Mom, no!" Lynn's voice was sharper than she meant it to be. She shook her head, but the damage was already done.

"Sandcastle?" David looked between mother and daughter.

Elizabeth looked abashed, turned away, and rummaged in the cupboard for a coffee mug. "It's nothing. Just a little family tradition. I thought you knew."

"I hadn't told him about it yet." Lynn wouldn't look a David.

David poked her. "Sandcastle?"

When Lynn didn't respond, Elizabeth answered, her voice light. "Oh, it's silly, but we all do it. When the married couple comes to the Village, the husband builds his new wife a sandcastle below the high tide mark at Deception Beach. Then the two of them watch it get eaten away by the tide. It's symbolic of the husband making a home for his wife… and a warning that, without care, it could all be washed away. The Bozeman girls have done this for generations." She shrugged. "It's just one of the reasons I was so glad you two decided to honeymoon here and take in the sights."

"Wow. That's really cool. I like it. Meditative and stuff. It's great that you have family traditions like this." David turned to Lynn. "Let's do it. When's high tide today?"

"Ten. Just about." She gave him a tentative smile. "I just thought you'd like to see more things before you built the sandcastle for me. Sometimes, it can seem kinda heavy, you know?"

"No way, hon. We've got two and a half hours to get there and for me to build you the best sandcastle I can. I know you've got beach stuff around here. Let's go!" He hugged her and slid out from behind the kitchen table.

She grinned at him, his enthusiasm infectious. "Okay. We'll do it."

David kissed her on the forehead and disappeared to change clothes.

Lynn and her mother exchanged a glance and Elizabeth mouthed the words "I'm sorry" to Lynn as she followed her husband.

Lynn was quiet as she drove the long, winding, cliffside road to Deception Beach. David noticed. "What's up, love?"

She shook her head. "Nothing. I'm glad you don't think our family tradition is stupid. I was worried about it."

"Don't be. I like it here. If you're worried about where we'll live, I say we can look around here and Seattle for jobs." David watched her face as she pulled into a nondescript patch of graveled dirt that could barely be called a parking lot.

"That's good. We don't have to be right next door to my parents, but I'd like to be within driving distance. And near the shore. I've always lived near water."

"Me, too."

Lynn paused. "It's going to be a bit of a hike."

David looked around at the lack of civilization and the cliff top mansions in the distance. "Yeah? Private beach?"

She opened the car door. "More like a private cove. Mostly locals use it. Or clients at the Zimmerman B&B, when Minerva tells them about it. Deception Beach is a popular fishing place in the summer and great for bonfires in the evenings. Cops check on it from time to time, but they don't like the hill much."

They gathered the beach supplies—a towel for Lynn to sit on, a thermos of coffee, a plastic shovel, a pail, and a beach umbrella. Lynn didn't think they would need the umbrella. The sun hadn't burned off the morning haze and probably wouldn't by the time the sandcastle was done, but she let him bring it all anyway.

At the bottom of the hill, where you couldn't see the road anymore, David panted and waited to catch his breath. As he set up the towel and umbrella—*Maybe it'll rain instead*—Lynn watched with a smile.

"Don't forget to take in the sights. There's the Storch Island with the lighthouse." She pointed to the south. "It's been there for ages. I'll have to show it to you after this. We'll charter a boat."

"You got it, babe." David gave her a kiss before heading to below the high tide line, where the sand was wet and workable.

Lynn settled in on the towel to watch, turning on her iPod to listen to a selection of instrumental music David put together for her. She figured they had about an hour before the tide would reach the sandcastle.

Almost immediately, the small plastic shovel broke. They both laughed and David put the handle to the side and used the shovel head to dig a moat around the castle he was building. It was easy to love David as she watched him work with the rising tide behind him. There was just something beautiful about the image of it. Something she wanted to keep in her heart forever.

The arrival of a brown, medium-sized, enthusiastic dog brought her out of her thoughts. Pulling her earbuds out, Lynn got up to greet the puppy before she got licked to death. "Loa! Hey girl." Lynn then turned to the puppy's owner, Chuck, a grumpy old man in a young man's body. "Hello Chuck."

"Mornin'. You're out early." Chuck snapped his fingers at Loa, who had gone to investigate David and his sandcastle. He adjusted his glasses and smoothed over his beard in a nervous habit. "Loa, heel!"

Lynn smiled as Loa loped back over to Chuck's side and then ran around the two of them as they talked. "Just introducing my husband to the Village."

Chuck gave David a once-over as he walked up, squinting one eye at him. "Husband, eh?"

"Yes, sir. I'm an honest man." David offered his hand.

Chuck ignored it. "Honesty doesn't protect you here."

David and Lynn glanced at each other.

"Pardon?" David dropped his offered hand and wasn't certain how to respond.

"You watch yourself, young man. Never turn your back on that ocean. She's one treacherous bitch. Our charming motto, *'Where the sea calls you home,'* isn't just a pithy phrase. It's a warning. You understand?"

David nodded to Chuck. "Yes, sir, I'll do that."

"Good. See that you do. And you take good care of our Lynn, too."

Lynn gave David a tight squeeze. "He already does, Chuck."

Chuck looked them both over. "Good. Fair winds to you both."

"You as well." Lynn waved as Chuck clucked his tongue at Loa and the two of them continued up the beach toward a beaten path through the scrub that went over a hill and out of sight. Loa ran around her owner in happy circles. At the top of the hill, the pup paused, facing the ocean and giving it a low woof that Lynn almost didn't hear.

David watched Chuck go and waited until he was out of sight and earshot. "'She's one treacherous bitch'? Really? Did that just happen?" He laughed.

Lynn smiled. "It did. The Village has all types. Chuck's just one of the colorful characters that live here. Don't worry about him. He's harmless. An old salt born young, my mom used to say."

David shook his head. "Okay. But I'll watch my back. You know, the sea, she's *treacherous*." He chuckled all the way back to his sandcastle.

Lynn's smile disappeared as she glanced the way Chuck had gone. She wondered how much he really knew. Putting her earbuds back in, she pushed the thoughts of the warning away and settled in to watch David and the sandcastle building. He was doing a great job.

Leaning back on her elbows, she watched him finish the moat, build a couple of small side towers, and then a large central one. That feeling of love and contentment came over her again.

Until she saw the shapes in the water, and knew that it was time.

She stood as David called to her. "I just need to get a big rock to act as a drawbridge." Lynn held her breath as he spotted one close to the waterline. She wanted to scream a warning.

Instead, Lynn turned her back to the ocean and turned up her music—an orchestral soundtrack to something. Probably *Lord of the Rings*. She did not want her last memory of David to be one of terror. *Possible* last memory, she amended, and silently prayed as she let her eyes follow the tracks that Chuck and Loa had left behind, counting each paw print and footstep.

After a count of three hundred, she risked a look. David was gone. There were signs of a struggle, and the dragging of someone into the water. "Not someone," Lynn forced herself to say aloud. "Signs of a struggle and David being dragged into the ocean to be judged by the rest of the Bozeman family."

Blinking back tears, Lynn sat back on the towel to watch the rising tide wash away the signs of the sandcastle David had built for her. This was her part of the ritual, and she had to see it through. Although Lynn did not know the reason for the judging, for the sandcastle, for any of it, she knew that it was one of the many things the Bozeman family did to protect the Village.

Elizabeth was waiting for Lynn in the kitchen. She had coffee and scones ready, but all Lynn wanted when she came in was a long hug. The sobs she had held back out of a need for public decorum bubbled forth, and she howled her fear into her mother's shoulder. Elizabeth, understanding completely, held Lynn tight, murmuring reassurances until Lynn was coherent again.

"I didn't think it would hurt so bad," Lynn hiccupped as her mother led her to a kitchen chair.

"I know, honey. I know."

"What if they don't approve of him?"

Elizabeth handed her daughter a clean dishtowel and sat across from her. "Well… there's a storm tonight. If they don't approve… he'll be found in the morning. But, you chose well. I'm sure it'll be all right."

Lynn tried to keep control of herself as her mother pushed a mug of coffee toward her. She took a deep breath and let it out, calming herself. The dishtowel was rough against her hot face as she wiped at her tears and nose.

There were a million questions in her head and all of them were jammed together in a Gordian knot of words, feelings, and barely controlled hysteria. Gritting her teeth, Lynn went through the motions.

Focusing on the coffee helped. Burning her mouth on the coffee helped more. When Lynn looked up, she saw her mother watching patiently, and knew that all the questions she had would be answered in one way or another.

After a few minutes of forcing herself to focus on the coffee and scones, Lynn was able to ask the questions. "What happens if they do approve?"

Elizabeth smiled. "Then David will return to you tonight. The judging of worth never takes that long."

"Will he be okay?" Lynn didn't like the way her mother hesitated. "Mom? Will David be okay?"

"The judging changes a man." Elizabeth frowned, clearly remembering something. "He'll know so much more about the Village and world *we* live in." Her mother paused again. "It changes a man. But he'll still be David under it all. Just remember that."

We. Lynn knew she meant the Bozeman family. It was this judging that always made the man take the Bozeman last name. "Wait... what if I had a brother? How would the ritual work then?" Watching her mother's face, she saw she'd hit a sore point.

"They're judged. It's a different ritual passed from father to son. But, if the son fails, he's allowed to live. It's just... it's not a good life." Elizabeth looked away from Lynn. "My brother failed. He told me he wished they'd just killed him. But, there was a chance he'd find a strong enough Village girl. Instead, he abandoned the Village a couple months after his judging... and disappeared."

"I'm sorry, Mom."

"Don't be. Kevin was weak. If he's not dead it's because he fled inland instead of doing his duty to the Village and our family."

The flint of hate in her mother's eyes surprised Lynn. "What do the unmarried girls in the family do? Is there a ritual?"

Elizabeth returned to the here and now. "Sometimes. But don't worry, honey. I'm sure David's coming home. Your father liked him. That's saying something."

"But if he doesn't. What happens to me?"

"You're young and beautiful. You'll find another husband." Elizabeth sipped her coffee. "If you don't, well, we'll see. The family line must go on."

Lynn drank the rest of her coffee in silence.

The storm raged outside, just as the weatherman and Lynn's mother had predicted. The sun had said its goodnights hours ago. It was impossible to see out of the rain-lashed windows, and yet Lynn still strained her eyes. Despite her pacing, Lynn was having a hard time staying awake. She didn't know if… *when, not if…* when David would return. But she wanted to be awake when he arrived. As she leaned against the balcony door, she knew she wasn't going to make it.

Maybe it's better if I just go to sleep and let him wake me up, Lynn mused. It would be like Christmas morning. She made sure the balcony door was unlocked, as per her mother's instructions, and went to bed with a book. Part of her still wanted to stay awake to greet him. Part of her lied, saying the book was to make sure she did go to sleep.

Hours later, sleep won.

It was the sound of the storm, suddenly loud, that woke Lynn. The balcony door stood open. The wind and the rain danced in the opening, chilling her as her heart pounded loud in her ears. Lynn was standing, robe in hand, before she was aware of what she was doing. Wrapping the terrycloth robe around her tight, she called, "David? David, are you there?"

There was no answer but the wind and the rare, faint peal of thunder.

Hurrying to the door, wondering if the storm forced it open, Lynn stopped when she saw a man standing on the balcony in the rain. It was David. He was naked and facing the roiling ocean.

"David…" Lynn could barely breathe.

He turned to her and smiled, baring too many teeth. "Hello, Lynn."

She ran to him and hugged him tight, ignoring the rain that pelted her and the wind that pulled at her hair. "I was so afraid." When he didn't answer her, she pulled back from him. Even though he was holding her, he was still looking at the ocean. "David?"

"It's beautiful. I never realized how beautiful the ocean was."

His voice was strange to her ears. Something was wrong. She tugged him inside and turned on the light. He looked around the room with dark, almost black, eyes.

"Are you okay? Did everything go well?" Lynn stepped back from him even as she spoke.

This time, when he looked at her, a stranger stared from behind her husband's eyes. "We were judged worthy. We will have many strong children." He bent down and gave her a brief, cold kiss on the lips before he closed the balcony door.

As Lynn watched the stranger in her husband's body move about their room, touching various things, her mother's words came back to her.

It changes a man. But he'll still be David under it all.

Lynn wondered how many generations of Bozeman mothers had lied to their daughters on their honeymoons. She also wondered if this man... if he was still a man... would be as kind to her as David had been.

Family loyalty had never looked so bleak.

THIS IS ONE OF MY TIE-IN STORIES.

It was written for Elementary, *the second anthology based in Mercedes Lackey's Elemental Masters universe. I had written for Misty before, but I was particularly pleased to write for this anthology because it allowed me to play in my favorite weird west genre. This was a joy to write, but difficult to end. I had two endings, both just as hard on the story as the other. I finally decided on the ending here because it was where the story wanted to go most. I still feel bad for the fire elementals though.*

THE PRICE OF FAMILY
(An Elemental Masters Story)

The smell of the cooling pasty in the cold morning air was too much to resist. It'd been two days since Josie had last eaten. Stowing away on a train to Carson City hadn't come with any benefits except for getting away from Salt Lake City. From what little she had seen of the place, it was worthy of its title as the capital of the Utah Territory. Not surprising—not with all of the gold miners looking for a claim at the Comstock Lode.

Josie had spent last night in a burned out husk of a farmhouse. It had been better than nothing, but not by much. Not even wild grain to scrounge. It had been a bad fire. Her walk in search of something—*anything*—to eat took her from the dead farmhouse into Carson City proper. The town was alive with a bustling main street, already awake in the dawn light. It was why she had moved away from the crowd to this side street. And why she now had eyes on the best-looking thing she'd smelled in days. If she was lucky, the pasty would have both savory and sweet in it. It didn't matter either way. What she needed was something to stop the cramps in her tummy.

So intent was she on her prize in the open window that Josie didn't even know the man was there until after she had snatched the pasty and felt bony fingers dig into her shoulder.

"Gotcha, you little mudsill!"

"Lemme go!" Josie twisted and turned, but the man held her tight as he pushed her around the corner of the building. She fought to get free while still trying to keep her prize, but she was small for her age, and he was a grown man. Even as scared as she was, her tummy cried out for the hot food. With a final hard shove from her captor, she tumbled to the ground, the pasty flying out of her hands to land in the dirt.

"Whatcha got there, Bosh?"

"Little thief. He stole one of the pasties I made. Didn't want you to think I shorted you."

The second voice was much deeper than the first, but Josie wasn't listening. She scrabbled forward, grabbing the pasty and hugging it to her chest. She was caught—might as well get as much of it in her as possible before the beatings came. Only when her mouth was full of flaky crust and peas mixed with potatoes and dirt did Josie look up and back at the man who had caught her.

He was a lean man with an almost skeletal face. Clean-shaven, his face was all angles—as was the rest of his body. Clad in brown homespun trousers and shirt, he wore the half apron of a baker. He had enough flour covering him to prove her assumption. Josie turned back to the man with the deeper voice.

Standing above her was a tall, old man with a full white beard, sucking on a pipe and holding a mallet in one hand. His shirt was the no-color of dirty white from countless washings, and his patched gray trousers were frayed at the bottoms. Only his thick leather apron looked to be in good shape. Behind him was a forge. He was a blacksmith. His lined face was ruddy from the heat of the fire, and he looked tired. Though his eyes smiled at her.

"Looks like your 'he' is a 'she,' and a hungry one at that."

That stopped Josie in mid-bite. She touched her hair with a grimy hand and winced. Her braid had come untucked from her shirt in her fall. She knew she should've cut her hair off. Now it was too late. Things were always worse for girls on the road.

The baker shook his head. "A thief's a thief."

"Bosh, it's a hungry child. Go on, man. I got her."

"I didn't short you."

"I know. Just bring a couple more pasties at lunch and add it to my tab."

Bosh gave Josie a withering look as she stuffed another bite of pasty in her mouth. Then, he turned away and disappeared around the corner of the house.

"Hungry, eh?" The blacksmith nodded to her and then to his left. "The dog's hungry, too. Give him the rest. You can have one that doesn't have dirt on it."

Josie looked around and saw a mutt of a dog watching her with keen attention, his tail thumping puffs of dirt. She didn't want to give up her meal, but the blacksmith was watching. She stood and offered it to the dog.

"Sit, Dog." The blacksmith's quiet voice was so full of command that Josie almost obeyed him. "He won't bite."

The dog sat, its eyes never leaving the half-eaten pasty in her hand. She walked to him and held it out.

"Go on." The blacksmith's voice was kind. "Gentle."

Dog reached out and mildly took the pasty from her. As soon as she stepped back, he wolfed the food down in a couple of hasty bites. Josie nodded, understanding that kind of hunger.

"C'mon, little one. You can wash up here. We'll have a meal inside and find out your story."

Freshly scrubbed, Josie sat on the edge of a rough, wooden chair at the only table in the room, looking around the blacksmith's small house while he got breakfast together. It was two rooms as far as she could see: a main room with a kitchen area, rocking chair and hearth, and a back bedroom. Based on the fact that his plates looked like the special ones they brought out for important visitors at the orphanage, Josie saw he was doing well in this rough and tumble town. She'd expected plain tin plates. These were stone and had a glaze on them.

"Name's Huff. Edward Huffington. But Huff'll do. That's what everyone calls me." He pulled a cast iron pan from the fire and checked the cooking eggs and bacon before scraping the food onto two warmed plates.

"Josie, sir."

"Not 'sir.' Huff." He put both plates on the table, giving her a good, long look as he sat across from her. "What's your story?"

The smell of breakfast made her tummy rumble again, but she made no move to eat. Instead, she watched Huff as she figured out what to tell him. The silence grew. Finally, she shrugged. "Ran away from an orphanage."

"Why?" He picked up his fork and shoveled food into his mouth. There was no recitation of prayer, no pretense of the etiquette and manners that she'd been forced to learn.

"Girls disappeared from it all the time. They'd show up in bad places, and I wasn't going to be a painted lady." Josie watched the food disappear into his mouth, bits of egg falling into his beard.

He nodded, then waved his fork at her plate. "Eat, child. I ain't gonna bite."

Josie didn't hesitate, and she didn't bother trying to be ladylike, either. She'd learned that food needed to be eaten as quickly as possible—never mind the taste or the heat.

"What now?" he asked.

She looked up at him, still chewing, and shrugged. She'd gotten this far, but it was as far as she'd planned.

"How old are you?"

Again she debated, and then opted for the truth. "Nine."

Huff nodded. "Looking for work?"

"Yeah." She paused long enough to point her fork at him. "But not as anyone's jilly."

He nodded again. "I got that. I'm an old man. No salt left in me anymore. But..." He looked around. "I could use some help around here. Cleaning, cooking, mending, fetching. That sort of thing."

"Where would I stay?" She couldn't keep the suspicion out of her voice.

Huff threw back his head and laughed. It was halfway between a coughing fit and a crow's cawing. "Trig. The bedroom's mine. I can make you a bed by the fire. For now. We'll see how we cotton to each other." He shrugged. "After that, we'll figure something out. Get another room built or something."

Josie looked around again. The place was a mess, but no worse than Saint Beatrice's Home for Lost Children. Less people to clean up after, too.

"What's my pay?"

"Room and board." Huff gave her a shrewd look. "A penny a day. More if you help in the forge. But that's hard work, girl."

She nodded. Her plate cleared, her tummy full of warm food, the prospect of a roof, regular meals, and actual money was appealing. She stuck out her hand. "It's a deal, Huff."

"Good." He smiled at her with yellowing teeth, and a twinkle in his eyes. "You can start now. I got to get back to work. The new city hall building's keeping me busy."

Josie had slept in worse places. The nest of blankets and Dog made for a comfortable bed. Huff had given her one of his old shirts to sleep in. It came down to her knees and smelled pleasantly of the old man's pipe. Still, something kept her awake. It sounded like someone crying. She put her ear to Dog's side and listened. It wasn't him whining in his sleep.

Sitting up, she listened hard. It wasn't Huff. He was snoring away in his bedroom. The noise sounded like it was coming from the hearth. She leaned toward the fire, the coals giving off a pleasant heat. The crying was louder there. Josie shook her head. That wasn't possible.

She decided she'd ask Huff about it in the morning.

Of course, she didn't. By morning, Josie wasn't certain she hadn't dreamed up the crying. And she didn't want Huff rethinking the deal so soon. It was nice to know where she was staying for a while. Even if Bosh glared at her when he arrived with the day's pasties for both she and Huff. Josie just smiled, politely greeted him, and continued sweeping out a house that had not been swept in months, maybe years.

By lunchtime, the place had a clean look that it hadn't seen in ages, and the small window in Huff's bedroom had been pried open to let the stale air out. The biggest mysteries were the weird-looking symbols Josie had found scratched into the walls all around the house. Symbols she'd never seen before. She decided she'd ask about them later. After she'd gotten a good gauge of the man.

Huff came in and nodded at the state of the house. He grabbed two of the three pasties, eating half of one in a single bite. He washed it down with water. "Going into town with an order. I'll be back by dinner. Figure something out, eh?"

Josie nodded, knowing the cold box was scant on supplies but the larder had enough staples to get by. She'd talk about that with him tonight, too.

"And don't forget to play with Dog. He needs his exercise."

She grinned as he winked at her and was gone. Josie took the other pasty and went out to the forge yard. She felt good. Food, sleep, a place to stay, and a dog to play with. There wasn't much more she could ask for.

There was singing. It had been going on for hours. A wordless song in the back of her mind.

At first, Josie didn't realize she was humming along to the tune. It was a sad song, full of loss and longing. It made her think of the parents she'd never had. Josie finished her pasty, giving the last of the flaky crust to Dog, when she realized that the music she was hearing wasn't just in her head. Like the crying from last night, it was faint, but it was definitely there. Almost like music from the next room, but she heard it in her head and her ears.

Walking around the yard, she traced it to the back of the covered forge area. Josie swore the singing came from the forge itself. Creeping forward, she peeked in at the glowing coals and realized two things at once: the coals and wood were actually stones, and there was something—a creature—dancing within the flames.

She gasped and jumped back. When nothing followed her, and that wordless singing continued, Josie took two hesitant steps forward and looked into the forge again. This time, when the creature appeared, Josie stood her ground, her heart pounding hard, and watched it.

It was about a foot long, a cross between a lizard and a fish. Its body was red and orange, with flashes of white along its tummy. It was long and sinewy, with a series of small, fluttery fins running down its back. It cavorted through the flames on four stubby legs, its claws finding purchase on the impossibly burning rocks. Turning its snouted face to her, its eyes looked like white-hot, glowing coals.

"So pretty…" she murmured.

The singing stopped and the creature came to the edge of the stone forge. "You can see me?"

Josie nodded, her eyes wide with surprised pleasure. It was something she'd never seen before. Not even heard about. And yet, there it was, fins fluttering in the flames. She looked around to make sure no one was watching her talk into the forge. "You can talk and sing!" She looked at Dog to see if he could see what she could see. From his low tail and head, she thought he could, and was afraid. Turning back to the undulating creature, she wondered if she should be afraid.

"Yes. I sing." The creature's voice was like the crackling of fire.

Curiosity won over caution as Josie leaned into the heat as far as she dared. "But why is the song sad?"

"I sing for my lost child."

"Lost?"

The creature tilted her head. "My lost child, who feels no flame."

"I'm sorry." Josie stared at the creature. "What's your name? I'm Josie."

"Seneca."

They looked at each other for a long moment. Finally, Josie asked, "Where did you lose your child? I could help you look for him."

"Ask the master what happened to my Scintil. Ask him."

Josie shook her head. "I don't understand. The master?"

But Seneca said no more. She disappeared back into the forge and blended in with the flames until she disappeared. Try as she might, Josie couldn't coax the fire creature back out into the open.

Two days passed before Josie could bring herself to ask the questions she knew might change the good thing she had going. A warm bed, a roof, regular meals, and a guardian who didn't yell at her were powerful incentives to do nothing about what she knew. It was almost like having a real home. But every night she heard the crying by the fire, and it killed her to know that it might be from Seneca's lost child.

"I met Seneca." The words were out of Josie's mouth before she realized they'd bubbled to the top of her mind. She continued wiping the last of the dishes, half-hoping Huff hadn't heard.

Huff kept rocking in his chair near the fire, puffing on his pipe. "Seneca?"

"She lives in the forge." Josie watched his bushy white eyebrows bounce in surprise.

"You can see her?"

She nodded.

"Seneca's her name?" He rocked slowly back and forth, the creaking wood making its own rhythm to fill the room. "Never occurred to me that she'd have a name we could understand."

Josie wanted to know why not. Instead she asked, "What is she?"

"Fire spirit." He gave her a keen look. "You haven't had your menarche yet, have you?" At her blank look, he waved his pipe at her. "Woman's blood."

Flushing, Josie shook her head. "No."

"And yet, you can see her. Talk to her." He nodded before she answered, still contemplating her.

"What are fire spirits?"

"Elemental spirits. Earth, air, water, fire. I'm surprised you can see her, talk to her. You've got the talent, Josie. It's rare."

"You've got the talent, too?" She didn't want to ask more. But she knew she needed to figure out if he was the "master" Seneca talked about.

He puffed his pipe and nodded. "Been a master for decades. It's rare to find them out here in the west. I don't know why. I think the Chinese brought these with 'em. They look like Chinese art."

"You're a master? What does that mean?"

Huff shrugged. "I can control them. Get them to do things for me. They need that. Fire spirits are wild. Dangerous if not controlled. Burn the whole city down. The one in the forge... she *is* the forge. She's the main reason I can make my living without the backbreaking work of getting wood. I'm too old for that now. Just change out the rocks now and then." He looked at Josie again, a keen interest in his eyes. "I never thought I'd meet another with talent. I could teach you..."

Josie put the last dish away and wiped her hands, thinking about that. "Teach me. Is it magic?"

The old man chuckled. "Yes, Josie. It's magic and it's real."

Josie lay by the hearth, snuggled deep into her makeshift bed of blankets and Dog. She couldn't sleep. There was too much going on in her head. Huff had talked for hours about magic, talent, training, and about the different types of elemental spirits. He knew about all of them, but his specialty was the fierce and wild fire spirit. The untamed ones. The ones who kill you where you stand if you don't have protection.

And yet... there was the crying. *In the hearth, up the chimney,* Josie thought, *a baby fire spirit cries while outside, in the forge, a mother fire spirit sings for her lost child.* It didn't match with what Huff said about the wild, dangerous, free fire spirits. He'd never even thought to ask Seneca her name.

After one particularly mournful wail, Josie couldn't stand it anymore. She threw off the blankets and crawled across the barely-warmed brick of the hearth. Braving the still-glowing coals, she looked up into the chimney and thought she saw metal glinting there.

"Scintil?" Her voice was a whisper, but still sounded loud to her. "Scintil? Is that you?"

The crying stopped.

"Scintil?"

There was a tapping on metal.

"Is it you, Scintil? One for no, two for yes."

There were two taps on the metal.

"Are you stuck?"

One tap.

"Trapped?"

Two taps.

"Do you miss your mama?"

Two taps. Then two more taps. Then a third double tap.

Josie sat back on her haunches. She had a choice to make, and she knew it. On one hand, Huff was offering her a home, a safe haven, *and* magic training. On the other hand, if she accepted, it would cost Seneca and Scintil their family for who knows how long. And now that she knew, she'd be a part of keeping mother and son apart. She could forget this now. Or she could go tell Seneca where Scintil was.

She bowed her head, aching at the choice, and then got up, pulled on her trousers, and padded to the door with Dog following.

It was cold in the darkness of early morning, and the forge glowed a dull orange of banked coals. Picking her way through the yard to the forge, Josie looked into the heat, looking for Seneca. After a moment, the fire spirit came into view. She looked up at the little girl, her eyes dull.

"I found him. I found Scintil."

Seneca flared in a sudden light of flame. "Where? Where is my son?" She flowed out of the forge in a sinewy slither of rasping curves onto the worktable, moving amongst the tools.

Dog took off, running from the house and spirit. Josie stepped back, too, surprised. "I'll take you to him, but you have to tell me something. If you could leave the forge, why stay? Why not look for Scintil on your own?"

"The master hid him from me. I had no eyes to see."

Josie tilted her head, looking at the fire spirit that looked more and more like the dragons the Chinese who worked the trains talked about and drew.

Seneca tilted her own head. "And it's a pleasure to burn..." Her voice almost sounded guilty. "I didn't want to leave him. I had things to burn."

"So, you agreed to work the forge?"

"He had my son. I couldn't leave."

"Why did he trap your son?"

The creature shook her head. "Take me to him. Please. It's been so long."

Josie couldn't resist the longing in that voice. She understood it all too well. The want—the need—for family. She nodded and led Seneca to the blacksmith's house.

Once there, both Josie and Seneca were surprised that the fire spirit was unable to enter. The barrier flared as Josie passed through it, but the fire spirit was stopped at the lintel. "My baby. The master is keeping me from my baby." Seneca flared brighter in her agitation.

Josie held out a calming hand. "I'll try to get him. If not, I'll get Huff to free him." She turned and hurried to the hearth on quiet feet. Almost climbing into the still-warm fireplace, careful to avoid the barely glowing coals, Josie reached up into the chimney and felt around. Her hand encountered a small, warm metal thing on a chain. It moved as she touched it.

"Shhh. I got you. You'll see your momma again." Josie pressed herself against the sooty stone as she reached up to find where the chain was hung. It was a hook. A little fiddling and she freed the chain.

"Hurry! Hurry! Before the master comes!"

As Josie pulled herself out of the hearth along with what looked to be a small incense burner—like they used in church—Huff's bedroom door opened. "Josie?"

She froze, hugging the small metal pot to her, while Seneca gave a wordless cry of rage and began to beat herself against the ward.

Huff took this all in, his eyes widening. He reached for her. "Don't! You don't understand!"

"You've kept them apart. That's not right." Josie's heart broke as she betrayed the man who had been so kind to her.

"He was wild! Burned down two farms. She wouldn't rein him in." Huff nodded at the enraged fire spirit trying to force its way through the wards. "He killed two families! You have to understand."

Josie remembered the burned-out farm as a feeling of horror grew in her stomach. The metal in her hand suddenly flared so hot that it burned her even before she could drop the small, enclosed pot. Josie gasped, looking at her swelling, reddening hand. The burner's heated metal was already making her blankets smolder. Hurrying from the hearth, Josie grabbed the nearest thing she could find to protect her hand—the dish towel. She wrapped her good hand in it, then returned to grab the burner's chain, pulling the burner from the blankets before they could catch flame.

When she looked up, Huff was returning from his room, wearing a thick gold ring with a ruby on one hand and holding an ornamental knife in the other. He was focused on Seneca at the door. Josie could see that fire spirit had cracked the ward and was breaking through. Huff was repairing it.

He stepped into the living room, still looking at the ward as he spoke to her. "If you free the fire spirit, we die. Who knows how many more will die?"

"But it's her baby. Her family."

Huff didn't say anything. Josie knew he'd turned his attention back to Seneca and the ward. She could actually *see* the magic flowing from him, feel it like you could feel the air after a thunderstorm. Seneca was nothing more than the embodiment of flame and rage now. Huff pushed her back, capturing her in his magic, forcing her into the yard. Scintil cried out in his prison, a wordless wail of longing and despair.

Josie took one last look at Huff then closed her eyes and made her choice. It was the hardest decision of her life.

"I'm sorry," she whispered to Scintil's prison. "I'm sorry. If you've killed… If you can't be tamed…" The wailing grew louder as Josie returned to the hearth and hung the burner in its place in the chimney again. Tears spilled down her face as she knew exactly what she was doing: sacrificing one family for the new family and home she had gained.

"I'll find a better way to free you. I promise." Josie spoke to the hearth, but wasn't sure Scintil could understand. She turned away and silently repeated the promise. Then she ran to find out what had happened with Seneca and Huff.

In the yard, Josie watched as Huff forced Seneca back into the forge.

The fire spirit lashed out at him and everything around him, scorching the ground as she went. Once Seneca was secured, Josie watched Huff scratch those strange symbols into the forge's stone and metal sides. Seneca raged inside, glowing white hot in her anger.

Huff stepped back and bowed his head. "That was closer than I ever want to admit." He looked over his shoulder at her. "You did the right thing. That fire spirit… it would've rampaged. Could have lost the whole town."

Josie was still looking at the white-glowing forge. "Is she a prisoner now?"

Huff nodded. "She has to be. She knows where he is. She won't stop trying to reach him."

Josie stared at the ground, not seeing it as more tears welled up and spilled down her dirty face. She knew what she had done. Feeling a warm, kind hand on her shoulder, she looked up.

"I'm proud of you, Josie. You did good."

Sobbing, she threw herself into his arms. The feeling that welled up at his praise battled with the guilt of her betrayal of the fire spirits. She had her family now. She had Huff. Someday, she would free Scintil and Seneca. But not today. Today, Josie had a new father, and that was what mattered. It was a price she was willing to pay.

I WAS ONCE AN AFROTC CADET

and I got to experience the joy known as "base visits." This is where you and two dozen other cadets descend on a military base in organized chaos to see what military life is like. The one I remember most is Bangor, Washington, to visit the Trident submarines. I wanted to bring this experience to an SF story, even though the only real similarities between what I did and what my protagonists experienced was the act of visiting a military establishment outside of school. In reality, we never stayed for more than three days and we weren't put to work.

M.O.V.E.
(A Kember Empire Story)

Senior Cadet Natara Kintares looked out the Space Station Command and Control window and saw her future. The view was filled with military vessels of all types coming and going from Space Station Killingsworth. Her future probably did not involve this particular space station, but it was a possibility. As a graduating military cadet, these Military Observation Visit Experiences—or M.O.V.E.s—were designed to give the student a taste of what was to come. Natara could not be happier. Ever since she was a little girl, she had wanted to join the Guard and to work in space.

"Cadet, look at this screen and tell me what you see."

"Yes, sir," she said, paused and then restated her response. "I mean, yes, Guardsman Harber."

The middle-aged man gave her a severe look softened by the twinkle in his eyes. "What's wrong with this situation?"

Natara studied the monitor. "You're gonna have a jam in Port Alpha-3. The two Explorer class ships are too big to be rubbing hulls in there."

"Good. How would you fix it?"

"Shift the *IIS Lifeline* to Port Charlie-2 and shift the two smaller scout vessels to Alpha-3."

"Good. Anything else?"

Natara thought about it and shook her head. "I don't think so."

"That plan will work fine, but there's one more thing to do—give everyone an extra five minutes lag to allow the switch and trajectory calculations. It'll take a bit more time and some will grouse, but the extra fifteen minutes isn't going kill anyone. Just because you shift things on the computer doesn't mean they shift automatically. The pilots of these ships are human, with human foibles."

"Yes, Guardsman."

Harber was about to say something else, but the sudden influx of ship signals detected on the edge of one of his screens made him pause. A moment later, he said, "You're dismissed, Cadet. Go to your quarters." He turned from her and hit a series of buttons on his console. As she left, knowing that a large fleet of ships was suddenly descending upon the space station, the first battle alarms sounded in the corridors.

Instead of returning to her quarters, Natara stood in one of the viewing rooms on the observation ring, watching the orderly dance of large military supply ships being shunted to one side while the space station all but vomited its short-range fighters to set up a protection grid between the advancing armada and the strategically-placed military base. She sighed as the observation ring rotated away from the ports she had been watching and showed the next quarter of the station. She turned to hurry to the next observation room and almost ran right into Soolee.

"I knew you'd be here. Are we gonna be all right?" her bunkmate, and the only other female cadet on this M.O.V.E., asked.

Natara shrugged, ignoring the implied disregard of orders—admittedly, something she was known for. "I don't know. I think it's the Epiets. I got kicked out of CnC before I could get a good look at the ships' silhouettes. But I'm pretty sure it was them."

"Why are they attacking?"

Natara shook her head, "Don't know. Maybe because this is a strategic station on the border between their space and ours? Not sure. I do know if they take the station, there'll be trouble. It breaks the treaty the Council of Primes ratified." She paused, "You've got dirt on your face."

Soolee rubbed at her nose, smearing the dirt rather than cleaning it up. "That's what you get when you crawl around the hydroponics gardens: dirty. My M.O.V.E. has been all about 'move this' and 'move that.'"

"Lucky you. Mine's been all observation. Look, but don't touch. I should be up there right now. I should see what really goes on in CnC when there's an emergency." Natara looked out the observation window and frowned at what she saw. In the distance, a lone scout-like ship was headed toward the space station. It was coming in from the opposite direction of the fighting. She stared at it, trying to identify its type. Her frown became a scowl when nothing came to mind.

"What? What's wrong?"

"That ship. Do you know it?" She pointed at the rapidly growing speck.

Soolee looked out the viewport and shook her head. "Not my area of expertise."

"I don't know it either."

"So?"

"You don't understand. I don't recognize that silhouette. There are four hundred and two space-faring races in the Kember Empire. From those, there are three thousand six hundred and eighty nine different types of military space-worthy ships, averaging nine different types of ships per race. I just passed my identification class. I'm the third cadet in the past ten graduating classes to get the silhouette test perfect. I identified all three thousand six hundred and eighty nine ship types based on the silhouette alone... and I don't know that ship."

Soolee whistled. "Impressive... but also bad. Maybe it's a civvy ship?"

"No. Can't be. Shouldn't be. Civilian traffic is restricted in this part of the sector, due to the... ah... contested nature of the border. Besides, it's too small to have come in on its own. There's got to be a mother ship somewhere within range." She looked out the viewport again, but the rotating deck had moved them out of view of the unknown vessel. "C'mon."

Natara and Soolee hurried down the empty corridor. Everyone was either at their battle stations or in their quarters staying out of the way. They ducked into the next observation room that was rotating into line-of-sight of the unknown ship. It was much closer now. Natara pressed against the viewport, trying to get a better view as the ship came in towards the station.

"It's got to be all right, right?" Soolee asked. "They wouldn't let the ship this near if it wasn't."

"Probably. But I want to know what it is."

The two cadets watched as the small ship—the size of a one- or two-man scout vessel—dived down away from the docking port ring and flew parallel to the station's body. "Oh, that's not right. Ships aren't supposed to…"

"What's it doing?" Soolee pressed herself against the viewport. "Why's it doing that?"

"I don't know," Natara admitted.

"Why isn't anyone doing anything about it?"

"I don't know," Natara said again. "There should be tug drones out now, trying to move the ship back to the space lanes. It's an automatic thing but… nothing's happening. It's like they can't see it."

"We can see it."

"We're using our eyes and not machines. It's got to be a new stealth technology." Natara watched the small ship land itself on the space station like an insect landing on an animal too big to notice it. "This is bad."

"Real bad," Soolee agreed. "That's the hydroponics ring."

Natara turned to her classmate. "Are you sure?"

"Yeah. I'm sure."

"We need to report this.

⚡

"Please, I really need to talk to Guardsman Harber," Natara tried to keep her voice level and professional as she faced the guardsman in the doorway to CnC. Behind him, hunched over their consoles and talking in quiet, tense voices, were the Command and Control personnel and Guardsman Harber.

"Cadets, you're supposed to be in your quarters," Guardsman Oberman said with little patience. He eyed them up and down with irritation. "You need to be elsewhere. We don't have time for inconsequentials."

"But this is important," Soolee insisted, disregarding Oberman's fearsome glare, as she remained at attention before him.

Inside, Natara cringed. She knew this old Guardsman could only see a couple of young girls, much less mere cadets, and not the trained Guardsmen they were becoming. She wished Soolee had not said anything at all. Oberman wanted and needed details.

His eyes narrowed. "What is so important that two cadets need to interrupt someone in the middle of an attack?"

"There's an unknown ship. It landed on the station but not—"

Oberman interrupted Natara, "There are thousands of ship types out there. I'm not surprised you don't know one. The Guardsmen in CnC have a handle on things. They know what's coming and going."

"But—"

"But nothing, Cadet. I've read your M.O.V.E. file, Kintares. I admire your enthusiasm, but this is neither the time nor the place for it. I've also read about your tendency to bend the rules. That doesn't fly on a real space station, and we *will* discuss this on our shift tomorrow. Count on it." He raised a finger to forestall another protest. "One more word from either of you and I'll have you both thrown into the brig for disobeying a superior officer. Return to your quarters. That's a direct order." He turned his back on them and shut the door to the control center in their faces.

"Damn. What'd you do to him? Piss in his morning drink?" Soolee asked.

"You idiot," Natara muttered to the closed door and blew out a gusty sigh. "I've only had one shift with him, but I get the impression he really doesn't think females should be in the military, much less in CnC."

"What are we gonna do?"

"Not talk to the Cadre, that's for sure." Natara wondered what else was in her M.O.V.E. file. Then her scowl turned into a smile devoid of joy. "We're going to deal with this ourselves. Are there any back ways into the hydroponics ring? The section that the ship landed on?"

"Oh, yeah. Lots. I've been spending most of my time doing maintenance in them. You wouldn't believe how dirty hydroponics can get."

Natara looked at Soolee's smudged face and half-smiled. "Yeah, I would. Let's go."

Within minutes, the two made their way to the hydroponics ring, avoiding as many of the station personnel as possible. The one time they did run into someone, they bluffed the Guardsman into ignoring them by pretending to be on an errand.

"Guardsman Rillion will have our heads if we don't get this to hydroponics maintenance yesterday. Come on!" Soolee said and pulled Natara's arm. The Guardsman barely looked at the cadets as they quickened their pace, passing him in the hallway.

Natara let Soolee pull her along until they reached a door marked: Maintenance 26-D. Soolee waved her ID bracelet next to the security pad and they were rewarded with the opening of the door. Once inside, they breathed a sigh of relief. "We're good now," Soolee said. "All we have to do is slip into the maintenance tunnel that leads into the garden."

"What do you maintain in the tunnels?"

"The water lines, nutrition to the plants. That sort of thing. Why?"

"Just wondering how dirty it'll be."

Soolee rolled her eyes. "Some. They run a tight station here. At least, Rillion does on the hydroponics ring. 'An ill-maintained garden makes for an ill space station.' I'll go first. I know where to pop out so it won't be right next to where the ship landed."

"Good. Then, I'll take the lead."

True to her word, the maintenance tunnel was small but relatively clean. There were no leaky pipes and no puddles of dank water. Still, it was not comfortable. Too short to stand up in, they had to crouch or crawl to move. It was slow going. The lighting was sparse and motion-sensitive, so it felt like they were crawling in circles within a bubble of light.

Still, Natara was impressed. Coming from an acquisitions base with water as the main export, she knew just how tough it was to keep containers and pipes completely watertight. Even so, crawling on hands and knees wasn't the cleanest thing around, but it was required. Natara vowed not to tease Soolee about the dirt smudges again.

Natara could have shouted for joy when they paused and Soolee took a small tool from her belt to unlock the maintenance panel. She did not like the cramped space, and mentally urged Soolee to move faster. But her companion worked in slow, silent motions to free them from the maintenance tunnel. Once unlocked, Soolee pushed the panel out and slid it to the side, taking care to be as quiet as she could. Then she and Natara crawled out of the maintenance tunnel. They hunkered down and listened before Soolee replaced the panel. They could hear movement; soft, under the hum of the machinery around them.

Soolee brought them to the far side of the hydroponics garden where the hanging plants, filled with ripening fruits and vegetables, hid them from view. The walls and ceiling sprouted both plants and water spigots, while the grated floor, littered with specialized hydroponics tools, revealed the softy humming fans that kept the air moist and the room clear of plant detritus.

Natara crawled forward, parting the plants in front of her, and then stopped. She motioned Soolee to her. When the other girl came forward, she saw what had stopped Natara. It was an Epiet. She could tell by his basic humanoid appearance, grayish skin, and the iridescent scales on his head and neck. He had two vials of liquid, and was pouring the smaller one into the larger one, changing the liquid's color from clear to murky green.

"What's he doing?" Natara asked, keeping her voice low. "What's that thing he's standing over?"

"It's one of the water sample valves. It feeds into the water supply for this garden."

The answer made Natara feel cold and then angry. "We need weapons."

Soolee pointed at two gardening tools on the floor nearby. One was a metal-handled net and the other was a pair of long-handled clippers.

"Those do?"

Natara nodded as Soolee crawled behind the hanging plants to get to the tools. She handed the cutters to Natara, who dropped into Guardsman hand language and signed, *You go high. I go low.*

Soolee nodded and stood. Natara maintained her crouch and scuttled forward, through the plants into the open, staying low. The Epiet was fully involved in whatever he was doing to the water supply and did not see the cadets creep up behind him. With a signaling yell, Natara dove low at the Epiet's knees, swinging the clippers so that the metal head of the tool hit behind the Epiet's right knee. At the same time, Soolee brought the net down over top of the intruder's head and yanked back, putting him off-balance.

As the Epiet went down with a hiss of surprise and pain, he dropped both of the vials he was holding into the open water valve. On the ground, tangled in the net that Soolee held down on his head and neck, his hand went to his sidearm. But Natara used the clippers to break his wrist with a single sharp blow. Soolee gave the Epiet two hard kicks to the head, and the alien lay still. Natara took the sidearm from the Epiet's unmoving body and stepped back.

Both girls panted with excitement and suppressed terror at what they had just done. Natara nodded. "Good. Good." She looked at the weapon and then pointed it at the Epiet's leg. The energy pulse struck the Epiet, but the alien did not move. Both cadets jumped at the sound the weapon made.

"Seeder's Balls, Nat! Why'd you do that?"

"I needed to know if the weapon was bio-locked to the species. Besides that, the weapon fire should bring security."

Soolee crouched over the Epiet. She placed her palm on the alien's chest. "No heartbeat. But that doesn't mean he's dead. He may have dropped into stasis."

She nodded. "You should restrain him."

"Yeah," Soolee agreed and rummaged around for tie-down cords. "Why didn't an alarm go off when that thing cut its way in?" she asked, cords in hand, working to restrain the unresisting Epiet.

Natara looked at the opening in the space station wall, "There's no pressure change. The ship must be sealed to the station. With no pressure change, there's no hull breach to detect." She walked to the opening and looked inside the Epiet's ship.

It was compact and highly sophisticated. There were three chambers that she could see, and probably a fourth one she could not. Natara recognized many of the Epiet language symbols, but did not know enough of the language to understand the symbols on the doors.

Soolee came up behind her. "He dropped the vials. I have to know what they were. Get an untainted sample. We need to know what he did to the water supply."

Natara nodded. "I've got to see what stealth programs are running. Security should've been here by now. Whatever technology it's running, it has a larger radius than the ship." She looked over her shoulder at the unmoving body of the Epiet. "He secure?"

"Yeah. Five minutes. Five minutes to do what we can do and if we haven't figured something out, we hand it over to security. Any longer is too dangerous for the station."

"Agreed." Natara stepped into the Epiet vessel and put her hand on the pad next to the door nearest her. It opened with a soft hiss. "Control. Excellent. Check the other rooms."

She stepped into the control room of the small scout ship and marveled at its engineering. Every inch of space was used for controls, screens, and devices she had no hope of understanding in the five minutes they had given themselves. But she knew military intelligence would be all over a ship like this. There were blinking symbols, lights, and buttons everywhere. It was a lot to take in. As she stared at the pilot's center, she heard a noise and turned around, whipping the Epiet gun up into a firing stance.

"Natara?" Soolee's voice sounded strange. "I found something. Could you come here?"

Natara frowned. The five minutes was not up. She stepped to the doorway of the control room, keeping the Epiet weapon at her hip. "What is it?"

"I… I found the samples. You need to see them."

"All right." She stepped forward, cautiously looking into the doorway that Soolee stepped through. The tall redhead stood at an angle to the door, not looking at it. She was looking at something else in the room.

For one instant, Natara was sure someone else was in the room with Soolee. In the next, she was positive she was being paranoid. Her next step told her that her gut instinct had been correct.

Another smaller Epiet was in the corner of the room with a weapon pointed at Soolee while looking at the door. The Epiet opened its mouth to speak, but Natara did not hesitate. She opened fire on the alien. The first shot missed, hitting the cabinet next to the Epiet's shoulder. The second shot hit the target square in the chest. The Epiet got off one shot, grazing Natara's left arm. Natara yelped in pain and fired again. She struck the Epiet in the chest again. This time, the Epiet dropped its weapon and slumped to the floor. As its last living act, the Epiet reached over and twisted something on its belt. The light in the small ship blinked from the standard white to an ominous yellow.

Natara dropped the pistol and reached for her wounded arm, only to be stopped by Soolee grabbing her wrist. "Don't. It'll hurt worse if you touch it."

"It hurts now."

"Yeah. Well, it'll stop hurting permanently if we don't figure out what she just set off."

"She?"

"Yeah. She. Small, more purple in the scales. My area of expertise."

Natara turned for the control room. Inside it, the main console displayed what clearly was a countdown. Everything was bathed in yellow light. "It's a self-destruct."

"Ya think?"

"Yeah." She put her hands on the glowing hand prints next to the countdown display that had not been there before. Nothing happened. Her heart sped up. "Ideas?"

"Hit the big yellow button there?"

"You do it. My hands are full."

Soolee reached over and hit the yellow button in-between Natara's hands. Again, nothing happened, except the countdown continued to get smaller.

Natara raced over ideas in her head. "I've got one last idea and then we run for it." She turned from the glowing console and ran into the other room. Grabbing the dead Epiet by the arm, she yanked the body toward her and dragged it through the ship, back into the control room. As soon as Soolee saw what Natara was doing, she hurried to help. Between the two of them, they each managed to get the Epiet's hands pressed to the glowing handprints. Natara slapped the large yellow button in the middle and prayed that it was the right thing to do.

It was. The countdown disappeared and the light in the Epiet vessel returned to normal.

Natara collapsed into the nearest seat, and then jerked herself back into a standing position with her hands in the air as space station security personnel shouted for them to freeze and to identify themselves.

Soolee responded first. "Soolee Moore, Cadet, Senior Class, 992-236-510-288."

"Natara Kintares, Cadet, Senior Class, 611-444-972-313," Natara added on the heels of Soolee's answer.

The faceless security personnel in their combat helmets did not relax their guard as they pulled the cadets from the Epiet vessel. The girls saw that security was covering the male Epiet who was still down or unconscious while the female Epiet was dragged from the vessel and dropped to the floor next to her companion. They all stood there, cadets with their hands raised, covered by two security men, while a third reported the situation.

"Your sponsors, Guardsmen Haber and Rillion are on their way, Cadets. I hope you have a good explanation for what happened here," the security officer said as he got off the com-unit.

"We do, sir. It's one for the books," Natara said.

"I'll bet. At ease."

Soolee and Natara dropped into a semi-formal parade rest stance. They glanced at each other and smiled. Disobeyed orders or not, they had saved Space Station Killingsworth from a sabotage attack, and that was something that could never been taken away. If the two of them could just get through the next day with their skins intact, they would be all right and they would both have one hell of story about their M.O.V.E.s to tell their peers back home.

THIS IS THE SECOND MOWRY STORY
I sold. Inspired by Seanan McGuire's Sparrow Hill Road *and her stories of the hitchhiking ghost, Rose Marshall, I wanted to see what a hitchhiking ghost story set in the weird west would look like. I think it came out nicely. It has all the hallmarks of the hitchhiking ghost story—the mysterious hitchhiker, the disappearance, the need to set the wrong right, and, most importantly, to show how the mythology of Eric Hamblin and Joseph Lamb changed in the telling of it.*

A PROMISE MADE
(A Mowry Story)

Joseph saw the man before Eric did, even though they used the same set of eyes. Hard-bitten or hard-beaten, the man was only a few hundred yards off the dirt-packed road that their horse-drawn wagon plodded down. He wasn't crawling, not yet, but the disheveled man was just a few stumbles short of it. Joseph pulled himself out of Eric's body and sat shotgun with him on the wooden seat.

"Something?" Eric asked, feeling the spirit of Sheriff Joseph Lamb leave him.

"Something," he answered and said no more.

Eric scowled in irritation as he stopped the wagon and set the brake. He was sure this was yet another one of Joseph's lessons. He looked around to see what had put his mentor on alert. Seeing nothing at first blush, he halted his horse and stood.

"Now, if it was Apache, you'd be dead."

"If it was Apache, you'd still be in me with that damn gun of yours drawn, waiting for me to determine if we could talk or just shoot."

Joseph leaned against the backboard. "You can be taught. And that's 'blessed gun,' if you will."

But Eric was no longer listening. He had spotted the stumbling man. Watching the stranger made Eric hurt. It was clear he was wounded. There were large splotches of dried blood on his shoulder and stomach. So much blood stained the man's rough clothing that Eric wondered how he could still be moving.

"I'm surprised you didn't see him sooner," Joseph said. "He's the only thing moving out here in the desert at this time of day."

"He's not going to be moving for long."

The stranger stumbled to a halt and saw them. He had enough strength in him to raise a hand in supplication before he keeled over in the dust.

Eric jumped down from the wagon and ran toward the downed man, dust flying from his boots. He was panting by the time he got there and sweating in the heat of the afternoon sun. When he dropped to his knees, he was certain that the man had died. With one shaking hand, he turned the stranger over and was rewarded with a soft groan of pain.

"Soft, cowboy. I gotcha. You're gonna be fine."

The man's eyes opened, and their brightness showed what kind of fever he was in. "Water," he whispered, his voice cracked and dry like a husk. "Please."

Eric shifted his waterskin off his shoulder and dribbled a few drops into the man's mouth. Swallowing hard, the man opened his mouth again, wordlessly begging for more. Eric obliged again with a few dribbles. Not too much. Not enough to choke the fellow.

"Thank you," he whispered and closed his eyes.

Need to get him out of the sun, Joseph said from within.

Eric did not answer. Instead, he replaced his waterskin and then scooped the man up. As small as the man was, Eric was still surprised at how light he was.

※

Under the wagon was the only shady place. Eric wiped down the man's face and neck with a damp handkerchief. It took some time, but the stranger regained his senses.

"Peter's my name. Peter Foster from Tucson. My wife's waiting for me."

"Where'd you come from?"

"About two miles west of the road. We had a claim. We were working it."

"We who?"

"Brother-in-law. Scott. From back east. Told me… my sister was murdered by savages. Murdered and eaten." He panted with the effort to speak. "Told me... he needed to get away. I went and got him."

"We'll get you home," Eric lied as he looked at the bullet wounds in the man's shoulder and stomach.

No, we won't, Joseph said. *Those wounds were meant to maim and not immediately kill.*

Maybe the other guy was a bad shot. Eric scowled and then spoke aloud, "How'd you get these, Peter?" His fingers grazed the shoulder wound and as he leaned forward to look closer at it, he smelled the sick scent of infection.

Although Eric's touch was slight, Peter groaned low before answering. "Scott. He, he shot me. Don't... know why."

Eric tried to be gentle as he cleaned the blood away from Peter's shoulder wound. Every touch made the man hiss in pain. He stopped, looking at the wounds, his heart sinking.

He's not going to make it, Joseph said.

I know, Eric thought back, bile rising in his throat. As he watched the man's eyes flutter open and closed, Eric saw how Peter struggled to hold onto life.

"What's your wife's name, Peter?"

"Margaret. My... lovely... Mags. My... wife."

"Tell me about her," Eric whispered.

"Pretty... as... sunrise," Peter said, taking great gulps of air. His eyes went wide, and he clutched at Eric's shirt. "Afraid." There was no need to say what he was afraid of. Death was too close to deny.

Eric pulled the man's grasping hand into his own and held on tight. "It's okay, you're not alone. Just think about Margaret. Just think about your pretty wife."

"Take me home... to Mags."

"We'll get you home. We will."

"Promise."

The word was nothing more than the exhaling of breath; his last one.

"I promise," Eric said, knowing that he was already talking to a dead man.

He bowed his head for a long moment, praying for the man's soul before he opened his eyes and reached out to close the unseeing ones.

After Joseph gave Peter's body a blessing for the departed, all that was left was to wrap the body in one of Eric's blankets and put it in the back of the wagon. Once everything was resettled, Eric climbed up onto the seat and flicked the reins to get the horse moving again.

"Didn't figure I'd be delivering a body on this trip," Eric said.

Joseph, sitting shotgun next to him again, nodded. "Good thing we were headed to Tucson anyway."

"I don't get it. Why'd Peter's brother-in-law shoot him?"

"His wife was murdered. Sometimes, that makes a man crazy. Then again, he said they were working a mine. Maybe it was simple greed."

Eric shook his head. "He walked two miles gut-shot. He was lucky to get away."

"He didn't get away, Eric," Joseph said. "He just prolonged his pain."

There was no answer to that.

They rode in silence for hours until Joseph's voice cracked through the air, startling Eric out of his desert daze.

"Whoa!"

Eric's head jerked up as his hand slapped leather. He had already pulled the wagon to a stop and was crouching down behind the backboard, looking for danger.

"The body's gone."

Eric looked at Joseph as if he were mad. "What?"

Joseph was scowling. "Peter Foster. His body is gone."

Relaxing his combat-ready crouch, Eric looked into the back of the wagon. Sure enough, the blanket they had wrapped around Peter's body was flat. He set the wagon brake, jumped down from the seat and walked around to the side of the wagon as he holstered his gun. He stared at the blanket for a long moment and then grasped the wool in one hand. Lifting and shaking the blanket confirmed what he already knew: the blanket was folded together as it if had been wrapped around something.

"No bloodstains," Joseph said.

"I see that. What in God's name is happening?"

Joseph shook his head, "I'm not sure. I've not had anything like this happen before."

"There was a man, Peter Foster."

"Yes."

Eric's voice softened."He died in my arms."

"Yes."

"I wrapped him up in this blanket."

"Yes."

"I'm not insane or sun-struck."

"No."

"Then where is the body?"

Joseph shook his head. "I don't know."

Eric threw the blanket back into the wagon. He stood there, looking around into the desert and back the way they had come.

"What are you thinking?"

"I'm going back."

◆

Joseph did not argue with Eric as they returned the way they came. Each was lost to his own thoughts about what had happened. A man's cooling corpse does not disappear from a moving wagon. Not usually. Eric looked for facts while Joseph considered the spiritual side of the matter. While they rode, Joseph watched Eric's jaw clench and his hands squeeze the reins until his knuckles were white.

"What has you so riled?" Joseph asked as they approached the place where they'd tended to Peter. "I understand this is unusual and upsetting, but there's something more."

"What do you mean?"

"I mean, this isn't just a mystery to you. What are you thinking?"

Eric halted the wagon. He shaded his eyes from the sun, low in the west, as he looked in that direction. He sought and found one set of tracks to a disturbance in the dust where Peter had fallen and where Eric had picked him up. He headed in that direction, leaving the wagon and horse behind.

"Eric." Joseph's voice was calm and curious as he kept pace with his host. "What are you thinking?" he repeated.

Eric halted at the disturbance and looked over his shoulder at Joseph. "I made a promise to get him home to his wife. Maybe I made that promise to his ghost. I don't know. But, a promise is a promise. I'm going to get his body home." Now that he'd said what he was thinking, he felt better. It sounded crazy... and right.

Joseph nodded. "I see. Two miles west. That's what he said."

"He left us a trail to follow." Eric pointed at the tracks of a single man taking slow, unsteady steps. The trail was as clear as if it had been outlined in gold. His eyes followed the line of footsteps as far as he could see them, and then let his gaze drift towards the horizon. It was broken by a butte. He saw spatters of green brush and a tree at the base of it. "There."

Joseph said nothing as he continued to walk alongside of Eric.

As the sun set, the scent of cooking meat—pork or some sort of sausage—wafted on the air. The rocky hill cut the blinding light of the sun at the horizon line, allowing them to see the glow of a small cooking fire in the distant shadow of the butte.

"It'll be full dark by the time we get there," Eric said.

"I know."

"This will be ugly."

Joseph glanced at Eric. "How so?"

"A man who can eat after murdering his brother-in-law is not one who'll go down without a fight."

"You're looking forward to that, aren't you?"

Eric's silence was answer enough.

I was wrong. That isn't a man, Eric thought from his hidden vantage behind a cactus.

No, it's not a man. I've heard tell of such monsters, but I've never seen one in the flesh, Joseph answered from within.

The creature they watched might have been human once or worn a human disguise to fool its prey. But now, it was in its full bestial glory, secure in its privacy. It was an emaciated, skeletal monster wearing the torn and dirty trousers of a businessman. Its skin was the color of ash, and its overlarge teeth gleamed yellow under blackened lips. Its eyes were sunken into its skull and shone black into the firelight.

Worse than what the monster looked like was what it was eating. In one clawed hand was the partially consumed arm of a man. That man, Peter Foster, was hanging naked by his feet near the fire. Two bullet wounds showed in his dead flesh—one in the shoulder and one in the stomach. His throat had been cut, and his blood had been drained into a bucket that still sat beneath his dead form.

Wendigo. Eaters of man. The Algonquin Indians from back east speak of them. They're spirits of gluttony, sometimes transforming humans into cannibals.

We're not back east. This is Arizona, Eric thought.

His brother-in-law was from there. Perhaps he was possessed by the spirit that killed his wife.

Perhaps he's the one who killed his wife.

Eric felt Joseph's agreement. *It's possible.*

Is there a man in that thing that can be saved?

I don't think so.

Eric stood, pulling the Colt 1851 Navy revolver with the intricate flame engravings on the barrel from its holster. "Then it dies."

At the sight of Eric rising from his hiding place, the wendigo roared its rage and hunger. Almost too fast to see, the monster leaped for Eric, its claws flashing in the firelight as they slashed at his chest. Eric fired two shots before the beast was on him. Using the wendigo's momentum, Eric pushed the monster past him even as its claws raked his side.

Joseph dulled the pain but did not take over Eric's body as he usually did in combat.

Clutching the wound in his side, Eric turned with the wendigo, firing another shot that struck the creature in the throat, but still it kept coming. Charging again, the wendigo leaped for Eric again, knocking him to the ground, but not knocking the revolver from his hand. Eric raised the gun and shot the monster between the eyes. It finally keeled over onto Eric, pinning him, its last breath wafting the fetid stench of carrion.

Eric laid there under the body of the wendigo until Joseph took over, killing the pain of his wound and shoving the monster off him with his otherworldly strength.

Why didn't you take over sooner? Eric asked.

"I thought this was something you wanted to do for yourself," Joseph said in Eric's voice.

Maybe.

While Eric's body healed with Joseph's supernatural ability, Joseph cut Peter's body down and laid it out next to the fire. He took the bedroll from a nearby pack and, once again, wrapped Peter's body in it.

We can't return that body to his wife with two bullet wounds and shy an arm, Eric said.

"I know. But he deserves a decent burial."

Get his wedding ring. We can return that to her.

"Small comfort."

It'll allow me to keep my promise, and it's better than nothing at all.

"I know."

Eric pushed himself forward and back into his body, with Joseph's consent. Over the next hour, he dug a grave for both Peter and for Scott, whose body had regained its human shape in death. After covering the double grave with stones to keep the coyotes and other such animals from savaging the bodies, Eric sat in the camp of the dead men and stared into the dying fire, wiping grime from his brow.

"How come we didn't know?" Eric asked.

"Know what?" Joseph sat across from him on the other side of the fire.

"Know that Peter was a ghost? I mean, I carried him. I held him. I felt him die in my arms. How could I have done all that if he wasn't really there?"

"Because he was there."

Eric scowled at Joseph, "You know what I mean."

Joseph sat back and stared into the fire. "Perhaps because of me and the gun. You are God-touched and spirit blessed for as long as you carry that weapon. Maybe that's why you could actually touch him even though he was spirit."

"Then... how will we ever know when we're speaking to spirits and not normal humans?"

Joseph's smile was slight and troubled. "We won't. We just have to trust that if they need us like Peter did, they'll let us know."

I HAD BEEN THINKING ABOUT THIS *Kendrick story long before the stretch goal for* Time-Traveled Tales 2 *anthology had been met. Set long before the* Karen Wilson Chronicles, *this tells Kendrick fans who and what the Gray Lady is, what her relationship to the Makah people is, and, in truth, how the city of Kendrick came about in its current form. The trouble with backstory is that it usually stays in the back. I was really glad I got a chance to tell some of Kendrick's most important bits of hidden history.*

LEY OF THE LAND
(A KENDRICK STORY)

The boy looked up at the old man standing in the shadow of the stone totem pole. Sees-the-Wind gestured to his apprentice, Eric Iron Eyes. "Sit. Today is an important day."

Taking his favorite spot in the circle of sitting stones across from the pole, the ten-year-old looked up at the Pillar of Memory and wondered at it once more. Eric kept his tongue as his great grandfather, shaman of the tribe, sat next to the object of his fascination. As always, he could see the power radiating from the pillar into the ground and the air. He knew that he was one of the few who could see this. It was one of the reasons he had been chosen as apprentice.

"What do you see before you?"

Eric eyed Sees-the-Wind, looking for the trick in the question. Such deceptively simple questions always had complex answers. "I see you, Grandfather. Sitting next to the Pillar of Memory."

"Tell me about the Pillar of Memory."

He screwed up his face, trying to remember what he had been told about the sacred artifact. "It represents the oldest pact the Makah have with the outsiders. It's as wide as a man and twice as tall. It is made of stone not from here. I see its connection to the land. Um..."

Sees-the-Wind tilted his head. "But what does that mean?"

"Which thing?"

"The pact. The stone not from here. What do these mean?"

Eric shook his head. "I don't know. No one really talks about it. Even when I ask. They just say to ask you."

The shaman nodded. "As it should be. Some knowledge is too dangerous to be known... and too precious to be forgotten."

"You're going to tell me?" Eric leaned forward.

He gave his apprentice a brief smile—a white crescent moon within a mass of dusky wrinkles. "Yes. And you will need to remember everything I tell you." The smile disappeared. "This is a true thing, and you *must* remember it."

Sees-the-Wind tapped the drum he used for storytelling, beating out the slow cadence for the tale to come.

Long before the white man arrived to take our land as their own, the People were invaded by another. The Pillar of Memory was once a huge stone boulder that appeared one night during a storm of immense power. A great bolt of lightning struck the ground, opening it up and allowing the boulder to rise from another world into ours. This was witnessed by the shaman and his apprentice.

The boulder was more than mere rock. It was a gateway to another world. And out of that gateway came creatures of beauty and light, both terrible and marvelous. What we, the Makah people, did not know was that these creatures were fleeing a lost land. All we saw was the invasion of creatures we did not understand.

For many years, a war was fought. For many years, the creatures of light and the Makah people were lost to a fight to hold the land as ours. Until one day, the shaman's apprentice fell into a hidden ravine and almost died. He was found by the greatest of the creatures of light—what looked to be a gray lady with a white flame crown. Knowing he was done for, he said, "Before you kill me, let me know your name so I may take it with me."

Seeing a man-child before her, the Gray Lady took pity upon the shaman's apprentice and, instead of killing him, she healed him and helped him from the ravine. When she touched him, shared herself with him in the healing, it changed both of them and both people knew more. He knew that she was their queen and that they wanted nothing more than peace. And she knew the fear and misunderstanding the Makah had of her people.

It was because of this meeting, the gray lady's kindness, and the shaman's apprentice new understanding of what the creatures were that a healing between the two people could begin. From that day, the shaman's apprentice was the one to meet and speak with the creatures who called themselves the Goodfolk. It was because of this one act of kindness that the Pact was born.

For many years the Makah and the Goodfolk lived in peace and harmony with the land. The more the Goodfolk worked with the Makah, the more they looked human. Still made of light. Still not of this world. But kindred spirits. The Makah protected the Goodfolk, and the Goodfolk protected the Makah.

"Who was the shaman apprentice?" Eric couldn't keep the question to himself any longer.

The old man stopped beating his drum and looked at his apprentice. "The name he took upon becoming the tribe's shaman was Sees-the-Wind."

Eric blinked at his elder for a moment. "You're named after him?"

Sees-the-Wind shook his head. "No, young one. I am him."

Laughter bubbled up before Eric could stop it. He shook his head. "You can't be. That would've been… hundreds of years ago. You're old but—"

Eric's voice cut out as Sees-the-Wind seemed to grow tall and fierce, power rolling from him in waves that dwarfed even the power radiating out from the Pillar. "Do not mock me or our history! I do not lie. This is a true thing. One that must be remembered."

The boy found himself cowering on the ground even after Sees-the-Wind regained his old man's stature and demeanor. "I'm sorry," Eric whispered.

Sees-the-Wind nodded once. "Are you ready to hear more?"

He shifted back into a sitting position. "I am, Grandfather."

As I grew into a man, I became the shaman of the tribe. I continued to be the ambassador to the Goodfolk, and every year we renewed the Pact of Protection. Then one year, we—the Gray Lady and I—met on the anniversary of the Pact… we both had had warnings, prophecies, of the coming white man. It was then that we spoke of our love of the land and the worship of the bounty we had enjoyed. It was at this meeting that we knew we needed to do something more to protect that which we loved. We could not stop the coming tide but we could make a safe harbor.

It was the Gray Lady that proposed the Binding of our peoples and the sacrifice needed. One of each of us would give of ourselves to the other… and they would become one. It would bind us, both our people, to each other, and to the land. But, this Binding needed more than our approval. It needed the whole of each tribe to agree.

This great decision was not easy. I offered myself to the Binding, but the Makah would not hear of it. A great debate raged for days until Falling Petals, the chief's youngest daughter, spoke up and offered herself. I wanted to deny this, for I had long loved Falling Petals. I wanted her as my wife. But the good of the people came before my selfish heart. In the end, her father and I both let her go.

The Goodfolk had also had a long debate, for it was the Gray Lady who offered herself to the Binding. Some of the Goodfolk feared how it would change them. What happened to her, happened to them all. But it was as the Gray Lady had foreseen. Her long sight was stronger than mine.

The Binding was when the Goodfolk gained substance… and it was when the Makah gained the Guardians who protect Changer's Claw. Changer's Claw was used in the Binding, but I know not how. Only those in the Binding know.

───── ❖ ─────

Sees-the-Wind's voice grew silent in the face of Eric's growing questions. The boy tried very hard to keep his tongue, but his impatience overwhelmed him. The shaman's brief scar of a smile appeared and disappeared. "Ask your questions, boy."

"But how are you alive still? How did the Binding give us Guardians? How did it give the Goodfolk flesh? I don't understand." Eric fidgeted in his seat as he looked between his elder and the stone pillar. "And how did the Gateway boulder become a pillar?"

The old man nodded at each question. "These will be answered. Patience a little longer. And remember my words."

The Binding was beyond anything I had ever seen. It was as if Falling Petals and the Gray Lady walked into the distance without leaving our sight. It was a ritual that all witnessed. They spoke together, they mingled blood and light, then walked towards the Gateway boulder... that is now the Pillar of Memory... and continued walking until they were almost too small to be seen. Then, where two walked forward, only one returned. The change was immediate. The Goodfolk were more than light. There was a substance to them.

For the Makah, the change was... not immediate. The one who returned looked much like Falling Petals, though her hair was white and her clothing gray. She returned to us as Queen of the Goodfolk, but also of the Makah people. She returned and offered herself to me as wife. The Gray Lady was Falling Petals... and the Falling Petals was the Gray Lady. Both, it seemed, loved me despite my flaws.

I accepted this, and for ten years she lived with the Makah as one of us. She bore us three healthy sons and one beautiful girl. Each of them was changed. Our children were the first Guardians. While the blood doesn't always run true, every Guardian is of my blood. And every apprentice to me has been of our blood... the Gray Lady who was Falling Petals and mine.

After ten years, the Gray Lady needed to return to her people. She offered me a gift of life and a choice. First, she gifted me with the ability to live as long as she did. Then... when it was time for a new Binding, she promised me the choice of whether to continue on with her. I have witnessed three Bindings.

"But why?" Eric's question burst out of him before he could stop it.

"Why what?"

"Why go on? Isn't she someone different now? The Gray Lady isn't Falling Petals anymore. Right? She doesn't even look Makah."

Sees-the-Wind bowed his head. "She is and she is not. There are memories there. And, in the ley of the land as well as the people, I wanted to see the legacy I created. I wanted… to make sure that the sacrifice was worth it."

"Was it?"

For a long moment, Sees-the-Wind did not answer. Then he continued the true story that needed to be remembered, his drum beating out the slow cadence once more.

My grandchildren were just born, proving the Guardian blood true, when the white man came. Colonel Reginald Kendrick and his true aide, Sergeant George Stewart. They came to the land and found it good. Unlike most who simply took what they wanted, Colonel Kendrick and Sergeant Stewart traded and bartered for what they wanted. The Colonel wanted to found a new town that would be a safe haven for those who had fought in too many wars. Sergeant Stewart had pledged himself to the Colonel.

It was from this that Kendrick was born of the People, the Land, the Goodfolk, and the white man. I don't believe the Colonel ever really understood this, but I know that the Sergeant did. He made himself an ambassador to the Makah. He respected our ways as much as he could understand. He even took one of the Makah as his wife. It was for this reason that the Gray Lady blessed him and his with the ability to sense the land and all within its borders.

There were trials and tribulations, yes. There always are. But the Binding of the Makah and the Goodfolk did protect the land we loved. It was Sergeant Stewart's firstborn son, Marcus, who suggested that part of the Gateway stone be used to carve a statue of the Colonel to honor him. Marcus was touched by the land and by the Goodfolk. He understood that using the Gateway stone, placed at the town's center, would permanently bind the city of Kendrick to the land itself.

When the stone was carved, leaving the Pillar, one of the Goodfolk known as the Maker came to me and asked if he could carve what was left into a monument to the Pact and the sacrifices made. I and the council agreed. With one of my apprentices, the Maker crafted the Pillar of Memory you see now.

"And a lovely monument it is." The Gray Lady's voice, light and amused, broke the spell of the telling.

Eric jerked, startled by the woman's sudden appearance at his side. Sees-the-Wind did nothing more than still his drum and nod to the fey queen.

"You always did have a lovely storytelling voice… and I wished to meet this one again." She gestured to one of the sitting stones that circled out from the Pillar. "May I?"

"You are always welcome to join me and mine, Lady Gray."

Eric watched as the Gray Lady sat upon the stone as if it were a throne and arranged her long gown about her legs. He looked between the two eldest in the land and saw a hint of the love the two of them had once shared in the mingling of glances. This was not the first time he had seen Lady Gray. The twins—Thomas and Thomasina—had once taken him to her secret home for tea. But that had been years ago, when he was just a baby.

"The twins will miss him when he's grown. Already, his iron eyes fail to see them from time to time."

Sees-the-Wind nodded. "Ever it is so with the young ones. They don't stay young for long."

Eric frowned as they talked over him. "How many?" he demanded. "How many apprentices have you had?"

The old man shook his head. "Many and many." He raised his chin and finished his telling.

Binding the city of Kendrick to the land did more than protect the land. It gave safe harbor to many who can see beyond this plain of existence. Powers grew as the city grew. As the city's borders grew, so did the borders that we were all connected to. And where there is power, dark forces amass, drawn to it as a moth is to the flame.

It became our duty to protect the land from more than those who came to claim it. Now, every year upon the anniversary of the Pact, it is renewed. The spirits are consulted. The dangers assessed. Plans for protection made. Responsibility assigned. There are many evil creatures that would dearly love to rip out the heart of Kendrick and consume it whole. Some of these creatures are already denizens of the city itself.

The Makah and the Goodfolk are the oldest guardians of the land, and it is a responsibility we will not shirk. We will protect the land we worship until we are no more.

Sees-the-Wind stopped for a moment and gazed at Eric. "That is the true story that must be remembered."

Eric looked between Sees-the-Wind and the Gray Lady. "Is it the anniversary of the Pact?"

"No. That comes in the fall, on the Autumn Equinox."

"When light becomes dark," the Gray Lady added with a secretive smile.

"Then, why are you here? It's not for me… is it?" Eric's voice held both a note of fear and pleasure.

She shook her head. "Not just for you, Iron Eyes." The Gray Lady turned her attention to Sees-the-Wind. "I have foreseen… things."

The shaman glanced at Eric with a question in his eyes. "Let me stay. I'm his apprentice now." Eric knew the plea would be ignored, but he had to ask it anyway.

"Terrible things." Her voice was neutral, neither permissive nor dismissive.

Sees-the-Wind nodded to her and shook his head at Eric. "Not this time. Soon. But not now." The old man gestured with his chin. "Go, and tell no one. We'll speak again soon."

Knowing better than to argue, and still remembering the brief terrible visage of the old man's anger, Eric slouched off with his hands in his pockets and his shoulders slumped.

The two eldest watched him go until he was out of sight. Then they sat together in companionable silence for a time. Sees-the-Wind murmured, "Terrible things."

"Yes."

He nodded. "I've had troubling dreams lately."

"As have I."

"What have you seen, great Lady?"

"I have foreseen the end of me."

Sees-the-Wind gave her a sharp look and saw no fear and no lie in her eyes. "A new Binding?"

"Perhaps. Perhaps not. The path is not clear, but the end of things… of me… as I am now is coming. Dormant powers rise. All of Kendrick is in danger."

"How soon?"

The Gray Lady looked into the distance again. "A few years. The blink of an eye. Iron Eyes is there and almost a man. It's why I wanted see him as he is now."

"There is time, then, to stop this?"

She shook her head with a sad smile. "No, dear one. What will be, will be."

He nodded. "When you end, so will I."

"Not necessarily." She stood in a smooth motion and crossed the circle to sit next to him. "I may not die. Just change."

Sees-the-Wind looked into her stone gray eyes. "Binding or death. My end comes. I have seen too much. I do not appreciate a young man's youth anymore. The world has changed too much to be what the tribe and the land needs."

She put an arm around his shoulders and pulled him to rest against her. "I have sensed this for a time. It's why I came now. A warning, and the promise of respite. I did not understand why you chose to stay at the last Binding. You were tired then."

He rested against the warmth of her and pretended, just for a moment, she was Falling Petals once more. "It was not time." A pause. "He has her eyes."

"Yes."

Sees-the-Wind pulled away and looked at her, searching her face, and seeing the same gray eyes his grandson—so many times removed—had.

Lady Gray smiled at him. "I, we, can see ourselves in him. It's why the twins love him so and will mourn the loss of their childhood friend to maturity."

"He has her eyes, her temperament… and her talent."

"A worthy successor."

"Finally." The weight of the ages lay in that single word. Then the shaman shook himself out of his melancholy. "But the foretelling. The rising power. What do we do?"

It was the Gray Lady's turn to be silent for a time. Sees-the-Wind did not interrupt her or press her with words. The two had each had centuries to understand how the other thought and worked. The words would come in time.

When she spoke, the Gray Lady's voice was distant. "A girl will come who speaks for the city, for Kendrick. It will be a terrible day of theft and betrayal. Much hinges on what this girl does. Support her. Have the tribe support her. I believe through her—rather than my death—will my change come."

"She will Bind with you?"

She shook her head, not a white hair falling out of place, "That will be for another. I cannot really see her yet, but she is a child of the city, with a bond to the land. The path is unclear, but it is not the one who speaks for the city."

Sees-the-Wind took a long, slow breath. "And I will know her when I see her?"

"Yes."

"Then I will trust my instincts."

"It is all we can do."

He reached out and took her hand in his, squeezing it gently. "Thank you for the warning… and for the promise. We will save you, but I admit I look forward to my rest."

"As do we all, dear one."

They sat together for a very long time in the shadow of the Pillar of Memory. Both heard Iron Eyes sneak away with his companions.

"I have her eyes," Eric said with awe as he touched his face. He looked at Thomas and Thomasina for confirmation.

As Thomas nodded, Thomasina spoke for them both. "Yes. You are their child through and through. The strongest we've felt in a long time. We believe the land senses the growing danger and has gifted you with its bounty." She bit her lip. "It's one of the reasons we love you and why we helped you listen."

Eric nodded. "The Lady is in danger."

"Danger and more. The city, thus the land, is in danger." Thomasina sighed. "The Binding always changes us in some way."

"The Goodfolk?"

"Yes. We are of the Lady and she is us. She was one of the first… and the first to drive back the monsters."

Eric frowned as he looked at the twins. "Are the monsters coming here?"

Thomas nodded as Thomasina shrugged. "We think they might. They've ever searched for a way in. And, there's little else that concerns the Lady."

"What happens if she dies?"

The twins paused, silently consulting each other. "We sleep," Thomasina finally answered. "We don't actually die… but we would sleep within the land for an age, unable to fulfill our part of the Pact with the Makah and with the land."

"I don't want you to go. You're my only friends."

Again, the wordless exchange. This time, Thomas spoke. "We can make you a promise. If the Lady survives the coming danger, when the Binding happens, we'll *change* for you. Just me and Thomasina. Not Theodore and Theodora."

"Change how?"

"Grow up with you."

"Be there for you." Thomasina added.

"Because I'll be the shaman of the tribe?" Eric looked between them.

Thomas shook his head. "Because you're our friend."

"And we need you as much as you need us." Thomasina grabbed his hand for a moment then pulled back into herself again.

"Promise me." Eric put out his hand, palm down. "Promise me you won't leave me."

Thomas and Thomasina placed their hands on top of his and spoke in unison. "We swear that we won't leave you for as long as is possible. In this, we'll serve the Lady as best we can."

Eric felt the power of the promise binding the three of them together and relaxed. "Thank you. I'll be strong, and brave the danger when it comes, with you at my side."

The twins nodded. "We'll be brave together."

◊

The Gray Lady looked up from her quiet reverie with Sees-the-Wind. "Those scamps."

"What is it?" He tilted his head at her amused smile.

"It appears that yours and mine have *bound* themselves together. This… might change things."

"For good or ill?"

She gave a small shrug. "That remains to be seen. The wit of youth often amazes me."

"The Binding of the Goodfolk and the Makah can never be bad. You and I have proven that." Sees-the-Wind nodded to her. "But it can make for unexpected happenings."

"Then we must wait and see." The Gray Lady smiled at him. "He really is our child... and maybe the best hope for us all in the coming trials."

"Then may I train him to the best of my ability."

"It is all any of us can ask for and do."

The two settled comfortably together as they briefly became the young couple they had once been. Husband and wife, hand in hand, in duty and love of the land.

THIS STORY CAME ABOUT BECAUSE *editor Bryan Thomas Schmidt challenged me to write about "the dangers of privatized space travel and colonization." I think because he knows I really believe it will be private companies that really pave the way for humanity to colonize the stars. This is also my first political satirical piece, taking the idea of "corporations are people" and extrapolating it to an outrageous (but distressingly plausible) end. I also wanted to play around with the concept of having to sign a EULA before moving onto a space station. Really, no one ever reads the fine print in a EULA.*

AN INFESTATION OF ADVERTS

"There! There it is!" Mrs. Sutter danced in place as she pointed out the brightly-colored advert.

"Yes, ma'am. I can see it." It was hard not to see the advert with its flashing LED back against the garish background of her cerulean blue dining room wall. "Just step back and let me do my job." To my relief, she did as she was told. At least her husband—Todd, I think his name was—had the sense to be elsewhere while I worked.

Modeled after insect hive creatures, adverts were fast and semi-intelligent. I knew I needed to be careful and quick to catch it without hurting it. The advert sensed my movement and ran around within view, doing its job of telling me all about the new formula for Hi-Tang. I happen to like Hi-Tang, so it made me smile. Then I struck.

"Gotcha." My quarry was snared in my Class-A trap: a bell-shaped jar. Sometimes, going old school was the best with these new AIs. They don't see non-electronic things as a danger.

I pulled the advert out of my trap and looked at it. "Interesting."

Mrs. Sutter looked over my shoulder. "Huh?"

My job as Sweeper is both to catch the adverts and to inform the public about them. "This is one of the older Morgan-Lee models." I flipped the advert over, exposing its rectangular tummy and corporate stamp. "You see, these guys are second-generation models, invented by Michu Lee, and were originally used by the JP Morgan company. They were so successful that a bunch of other corporations started using them. Interesting, though, that it's advertising Hi-Tang."

Mrs. Sutter peered at it, wincing at every wave of the advert's many legs.

It was trying to flip itself right-side-up. "So… what will you do now? How will you kill it?"

"Mrs. Sutter!" I pulled the advert away from the bloodthirsty woman, disgusted, and ignored her wounded look. "I am a *Sweeper*. Not an exterminator. My job is not to 'kill' adverts, as you say, but to sweep them from your home and set up ultrasonic stations that will make adverts turn away. I am not a murderer."

The insensitivity of people astounds me. No one understands the job of a Sweeper. All they want is for me to "get rid of" the adverts for doing their job. Oh, sure, the colonists all say they read the EULA when they arrive on the station, but no one ever does. Otherwise, they'd know that adverts come with the territory. But no one wants to hear my rants. That's not what they are paying me for.

I put on my most professional smile. "I'm sorry, Mrs. Sutter. I must be careful with my charges. I don't kill adverts. I don't have any special privileges in my job. I can only relocate them to a more acceptable area—like the shopping level, where they can pick up coupons for you to use. But first, since you've said that you've seen a bunch of these little guys…"

I petted the advert I held captive, soothing it. "Once this little guy is calm, I need to let it go so it can run back home. Usually, when one feels like it's in danger, it hides instead of going back to the nest. I need to figure out where the nest is and if it has a Queen."

"Oh. Okay."

And there's the look—the blank sheep-like look that most colonists give me. I swear, those who lived on the planet below are bred with less compassion and less smarts than station- born. I continued my practiced smile, the one they taught me in Sweeper school. The training keeps us sane and in control. "If you could just stand very still and not move or speak at all…"

As I spoke, I continued to stroke the advert until it stopped waving its little robotic legs in panic and curled up to rest on my hand. I went down on one knee and put my hand to the floor. For a moment, the advert did not move.

I'm not surprised. One client was terribly upset at the fact that her son had made a pet out of one particularly smart advert and could call it to follow him throughout the station. At that point, there was nothing I could do except to suggest she either get used to the adverts or get Advert-B-Gone glasses. Personally, the glasses make them look too much like real bugs.

The Morgan-Lee scampered out of my hand in a sudden rush of flashing LEDs and flailing legs. Mrs. Sutter gave an almost inaudible squeak of terror. I gave her the hand in a sharp gesture that froze the woman in her place. I was good at the "stop" gesture. Good enough that I knew I didn't even have to look at her. I couldn't look at her. I had to follow the advert.

That lovely little bit of technology that so many people hate scampered under the table, up the wall, and into the hallway. I followed it in Sweeper-trained silence, making sure I didn't reactivate its "show me" programming. As soon as I saw it squeeze its way into one of the closets with old-fashioned opening doors, I knew where the hive was.

You see, as much as adverts seem like insects, they aren't bugs. They're small machines, and they can't actually squeeze their bodies into anything. That would distort their advertising message, and no one wants that. So, they need to find gaps in the floor, wall, or ceiling plating and under non-sliding doors to get in. Again, if the colonists would just read the damn EULA, they'd know all this. But no… they want swinging doors that use the space inefficiently, because that's what they're used to.

Bah. That's another rant for another day. I had my target. Opening the closet door, I saw the gap in the floor panel where—by design; the station is corporate-owned after all—an advert could travel through the maintenance spaces in-between levels to get from place to place. I pulled the shoes out of the closet, shaking my head at all of them. Station-born natives only need three pairs of shoes: daily, formal, and spacewalking.

As I pulled the floor panel from its place, I became aware of several things at once: I had found the advert nest; Mrs. Sutter had crept up behind me with a Sweeper's quiet step, which impressed me; this nest was one of the largest I had ever seen; Mrs. Sutter wasn't ready to see that many adverts in one place; neither was I.

Mrs. Sutter actually screamed.

Well, partly screamed. I moved before I realized it and had a hand over her mouth, but the damage was done. All I could do was try and keep her calm under the onslaught of moving adverts. "It's all right, Mrs. Sutter. It's all right. They're reacting to noise and movement." I kept my voice pitched to calm and soothe—thank Corporate for the training—as hundreds of adverts streamed out of the closet and up the walls around us. I needed her to see adverts like I did: beautiful machines that did no harm.

"It's part of their programming, Mrs. Sutter. They won't hurt you. I promise. You aren't dirtside where there are bugs that bite. These are adverts. Harmless, little adverts. All they want to do is show you their message." I saw the panic dying in her too-wide eyes. It looked like I was getting through to her, and that pleased me. "I'm going to let go of you now. Okay? Please don't move or make a sound. Please."

When I felt her try to nod, I let go of her head. She looked around in wonder at the myriad of adverts all around us, winking, flashing, and scrolling their messages. It was a wondrous sight to these jaded eyes. Even I had never seen so many types in one place. Thank Corporate that their programming kept them on the walls and ceiling. I didn't have to worry about stepping on one.

I unslung my backpack and pulled out the big gun: the Sweeper 2000. It could safely hold two thousand adverts and ten Queens—adverts designed to both do the job of a normal advert and to receive updates from headquarters to disseminate through the rest of the adverts attached to it. I turned it on and, as always, all of the adverts in the area lined up in perfect rows for loading. First to load was the Queen.

Except there were two Queens.

"Well, look at that. I guess we had a merger recently. It's very rare that you see multiple Queens in a nest." I picked them both up and flipped them over, curious and amazed. With the Sweeper 2000 working, the Queens were calm. "Morgan-Lee and Google-Zunger. Huh. That's interesting."

"What is?" Mrs. Sutter's voice was soft and filled with wonder.

I looked up and saw the panic was gone. There was nothing but curiosity in her face now. I wanted to hug her. A colonist who could learn was a beautiful thing. Because she could pass on the message to her other colonist friends. They tended to clump together. It was really very much like the adverts. I decided I would see if I could make her a colonist Queen.

"I don't know for sure, but it looks like at least one branch of the J.P. Morgan Corp. has merged with a branch of AmazonGoogle. Which means, the Morgan-Lee and the Google-Zunger adverts can now carry both Corporate messages to everyone. It's rather like a marriage when it comes to adverts. These two types of adverts are now siblings."

Mrs. Sutter smiled at the family terminology. "I see. Some of them are really kind of pretty. Now that I can see them."

"Did you know, you can request specific adverts? Just e-mail the address on this card and ask for a survey. You never know when you'll see exactly the right advert for what you need. I'd mark down all of the brands you use." I handed her one of the cards I always kept in my pocket. It was usually part of my goodbye spiel, but this seemed as good a time as any.

She nodded, accepted it, and looked at it. "Can I ask to never see a specific brand?"

"Yes." I put the Queens in their private boxes, their messages glowing dull in sleep mode. "Though, with mergers, things can slip. I recommend doing the survey at least every three months." I pressed the button to call the rest of the adverts into the Sweeper 2000. They entered and stacked themselves on top of each other by size and style.

"That's amazing. But, what about the ultrasonic stations?"

She sounded like she didn't want them anymore, and that was a step in the right direction—welcome words to my ears. "I don't have to put them up if you don't want. It would cost you less in maintenance and rent." I started to say more, but Mr. Sutter burst into the hallway from the other side of the apartment.

"I got the bastard!" He held something small and metal in his hand and my stomach sank. There were other adverts still coming in from the rest of the apartment.

Mrs. Sutter and I looked at each other. I stood and was careful not to step on the stragglers as they trundled toward the Sweeper 2000. "What's that, Mr. Sutter?"

"This bloody advert. It's been startling me for weeks. I finally got him."

I didn't want to ask for more details, but it was my duty as a Sweeper to do so. "What happened?" I held out my hand for the unmoving machine.

"It was running around on the wall and then the ceiling. I was trying to get it. Then it suddenly dropped, hit me in the shoulder, and then fell to the floor. It ran for the door but couldn't get out. I had it trapped."

I was barely listening to the man as he gloated. The half-crushed advert in my hand was one of the brand new Amazon-Sutherland models. It had once been a beauty of technology to behold. Only twenty centimeters long and ten centimeters wide, it was a miniature TV screen. Noise laws kept it from sounding out jingles, but its picture was clean and clear. Nine of them could get together and show a large picture of their message.

"Trapped?"

"Yep. I saw it and decided this time the damned thing wasn't going to get away. I closed the bathroom door."

And when I started up the Sweeper 2000, it tried to come home. My heart lurched. It was my fault the beautiful advert was dead.

"…and stomped on it."

I looked up. My goodwill toward the Sutters turned to ice water in my veins. "What? You trapped it and stomped on it? Clearly, it was an accident, right?"

Mrs. Sutter must have seen the sick look on my face. "Yes, I'm sure it was an accident…"

"Hell, no. That thing's been bothering me for weeks. Always in the bathroom! A man needs his privacy."

"Todd… I'm *sure* it was an *accident*."

I heard her stress the words. I saw the panic growing in her face. Suddenly, I realized she had read the EULA, but just hadn't remembered until now. Or didn't want to remember. Again, I realized that Mrs. Sutter wasn't like the rest of them. Not like Mr. Sutter… and everything hinged on what he'd say next.

I tried to help her, despite my sick fury. "Yes, Mr. Sutter. An accident. You didn't mean to—"

"Accident my ass. I finally got the damn thing."

"Oh, Todd."

I heard the distress in her voice even as I gave a deep sigh and stepped back. Three times confessed. The man was unrepentant and, while I didn't like him, I didn't like what I had to do next either. "Mr. Todd Sutter, I have no choice but to put you under arrest for the willful adverticide of an Amazon-Sutherland model. I am required to report you at once. Do not run. You're on a space station. There's nowhere to go."

His face turned bright red in shock and surprise. "You've got to be kidding me."

"No sir, I'm not. In Section 23 of the EULA, Subsection 14, the willful adverticide of any advert is a class one felony on the S-Brin Colony Cylinder." I turned my back to him and called it in. "This is Sweeper Arlington. Class One Adverticide to report. One Todd Sutter in Delta-227. Three times confessed."

As I heard the confirmation beep, Mr. Sutter grabbed my arm and spun me around. I turned the spin into a Sweeper attack and brought him to his knees with an arm behind his back and my forearm slammed against his neck, crushing his face against the wall. "Section 23, Subsection 14, part C: Sweepers may make arrests of S-Brin inhabitants who confess to adverticide. Sweepers may also defend themselves as needed if arrestees become hostile."

My voice was calm, despite my anger at the whole situation. I noticed my hold wasn't perfect. I saw that it was because I was still holding the poor dead advert. It was now evidence, and I didn't want to damage it any more than this willful idiot already had. I didn't think it could be revived, but I didn't know for sure. I'm a Sweeper, not a mechanic.

"If you struggle or attack me again, I will be forced to hurt you. Now, if I let you go, will you stand peacefully until the Units arrive?"

I let him up as he nodded with a whimper. I was still on alert, this part of Sweeper training deeply ingrained in me. Many of the station's inhabitants disliked Sweepers as much as they disliked adverts. I understood. So few colonists really know what it means to live on a Corporate-owned space station—even when they live here.

Mrs. Sutter stood back from her husband as if his crimes could contaminate her. Her face was pale and resigned. I felt for her, but we all had a job to do on this station, and sometimes, my job sucked.

After five awkward, stiff minutes, the Units arrived and Mr. Sutter was taken away. His shoes—those clumsy, dirtside shoes—were bagged as evidence. So was the Amazon-Sutherland. Even the Units were dismayed at its destruction. They dragged him off, reading him his colonist station rights.

As the apartment door slid shut, Mrs. Sutter touched my arm. "What will happen to him?"

"Trial and punishment. He three-times confessed to both of us. Don't be surprised if you are called to the stand." I saw the reluctance on her face. "As adverts are the progeny of Corporations as stated in the Corporations Are People Act, spouses may be called to testify as hostile witnesses." I softened my voice, hoping she would understand. "It's better if you testify willingly."

Mrs. Sutter nodded, her face hardening into something neutral. "And the punishment?"

"If you get a good lawyer, the best is a year's maintenance duty in the trash department. The worst… revocation of Colonist status and deportation." I shuddered at the thought of being condemned back to dirtside.

Her brows knit together in thought. "If I don't want go, too?"

"It's not you who would be deported, but you'd be required to get a roommate or to move to a smaller apartment. Most likely, you'd want to divorce; especially if you wanted to make a life on the station. Deportations are permanent, and visitation rights only go dirtside." I tried to give her the options as neutrally as I could.

"I see." Her face was a mask of pain as she tried to figure out what to do next.

"What's your job?" I don't know why I was asking, but I felt like I needed to help her. I guess I still wanted to make her a colonist Queen.

"Forum moderator of the Macy's Homeworks line and the makeup line."

In other words, not paid enough to afford even a single bedroom apartment on her own. I tried to think of her in a Coffin apartment and couldn't do it. "You ever professionally blog?"

She nodded. "Yes. For Macy's, Amazon, and Royal Dutch. I freelance sometimes."

"I know the Sweeper blog is always looking for a good blogger. It's a hard job but pays well. Not many sympathize with us. But if you do well with that, maybe moderating one of the advert or Sweeper forums could be next. It's possible to do that in addition to your current freelance jobs."

I paused, letting her think about her options. "You know, to be able to afford things like lawyers. I'll give you the contact info for my boss and my recommendation. I can see you've... come to understand adverts in a new light."

Mrs. Sutter smiled at me, understanding my desire to help. "Thank you, Sweeper Arlington. I appreciate it."

I nodded, gathered up my equipment and left. I didn't know what she'll do—hire the lawyer or get a divorce. Only time, and the courts, would tell.

Thank Corporate this sort of thing doesn't happen all that often. I hate to see my adverts destroyed. I do think, however, I got through to Mrs. Sutter. I hope she becomes a Sweeper blogger no matter what happens. I think she could do good work spreading the word of how the world of adverts and Sweepers really works.

THIS IS THE FIRST TIE-IN STORY

I did for Mercedes Lackey. It's one of those that make me pinch my arm and grin like an idiot. This is my life. I've written for the Valdemar universe. I remember how much Valdemar kept me going through college. How much I needed the strength of the Heralds and mercenaries throughout those years. I remember talking to John Helfers at a convention (he worked at Tekno Books at the time) about the universe and saying something like, "I'd love to write a story about the bards of Valdemar." And he nodded, saying, "We need more bard stories. I'll talk to Misty about getting you invited to the next anthology." I smiled, thinking it was just convention talk. But no, a couple of months later, I had an invite to pitch a story. This is that story. I've written more for Misty and Valdemar, but this one will always be a favorite because it was my first.

DISCORDANCE
(A Valdemar Story)

Rax wept into what was left of his ale as the bard finished the ballad of love lost and betrayal. It wasn't like Rax to lose his composure outside the house, but things had been so difficult this season, and he didn't see them getting any easier with the baby on the way. As the bard struck up the next tune--a war chant with a heavy drumbeat—Rax called out to the bar wench.

"Sarry, get me another, and another after that." He felt the chant beat in time with his heart and felt his blood rise to combat the sorrow.

Come, come, come to the beat of the drum, drum, drum.
And kill, kill, kill with your shar-pened sword!
To take, take, take every last crumb, crumb, crumb.
And do as you will!

Sarry, distracted by a handsome man with coin, ignored him, fussing over her target for a tip and possibly a tumble later, if the stars aligned.

"Sarry!"

She glanced over her shoulder at Rax and offered a tightlipped smirk that told him all he needed to know before turning back to the man before her. "Is there anything else I can get you, Seder?"

Before Seder could answer, a clay mug sailed past Sarry's ear and crashed against the wall in a shower of shards and dregs of ale. Sarry turned to see Rax standing tall and shaking with anger. The mood of the tavern turned ugly with the beat of the drum and song of violence. Rax took a step toward the bar wench, only to be stopped by another growling man—already angry at the sound of Rax's voice.

She didn't see the first punch or who threw it. Years of experience in rough places told her this was going to be trouble, and it wouldn't stop until blood was shed. As she fled to the back of the tavern, the room erupted in chaos—men yelling and swearing, the pummeling of fists on flesh, the crash of furniture thrown and the sharp sound of metal weapons being unsheathed.

Mathias grabbed her and pulled her behind the bar. She let him do it, thinking that he was trying to protect her. Instead, she found herself flattened face first on the dirt floor with him behind her—one hand holding her down, the other fumbling with her skirts. She had a brief moment of confusion. She had trusted Mathias. He'd always protected her. Now, this? Sarry let the rage of being attacked flow over her. The pounding of her furious heart beat in her head like the sound of the bard's continuing drum.

Sarry screamed her fury, bucking her body up as she reached for a weapon. Her hand found one: a large serving fork. As Mathias wrestled with her, trying to hold her down, she twisted her body around and stabbed the man who had been her friend, protector, and boss in the throat. Blood spurted from the wound as he reared up in pain and she yanked the fork back. They both screamed now, two more voices in the din of the total tavern melee. She plunged the fork deep into his stomach.

On the other side of the bar, Rax already lay dead, his head caved in by a chair. Seder was dying; a sword pierced through his chest, and his enemy was being beaten to death by two other men using clubs and their feet. Those who were not fighting were dead.

Except for one.

No one noticed when the music stopped. Nor did they notice when the bard picked up his pack and drum and walked with careful steps through the violence and out the door.

The only survivor of the night, Sarry, would not remember what the bard's name was or what he looked like.

Terek frowned at the letter in his hand. Usually, letters from home were a thing of joy. Not today. There had been a brawl at a tavern, and people had died. People he knew. Mathias had been a brother to him. His death was a shock. He closed his eyes and rubbed his brow. *There is more to this,* he thought. *People don't murder each other over ale. Maybe in the slums of Haven, but not in Woodberry. Not in a tiny settlement like that.* Something within his Gift told him he was right.

"Terek?"

He opened his eyes and smiled at the always fashionable Mari. She was a bard who knew those worth knowing in the court, and she looked the part. "Yes?" He frowned at the worry lines around her eyes. "What's wrong?"

"I'm not sure, but I was listening to a couple of Heralds talking and I think something's happening."

He gestured for her to come in and sit down. "Tell me."

"I'm not sure," she repeated. "I got a letter from home. A friend of mine died while carousing with his friends." She bit her lip, marshaling her thoughts. "Then, I heard the Heralds talking. They'd just come off circuit and there was a bit of bad business in the North. They had to judge a murderer. The thing is, at first, I thought they were talking about the death of my friend, because everything was the same—the victim had been killed in a huge tavern brawl. But, they were talking about someone else. So, I asked them more about it. Two different villages, next to each other, had the same thing happen about a sennight apart. Bar fight, unusual amount of death."

Terek nodded, his heart thumping hard in his chest. It sounded far too much like his letter from home to be coincidence. "It's been a hard season in northern Valdemar," he allowed.

She shook her head, her hair flying in its vehemence. "Not that hard. Look." She pulled a rolled up piece of paper from her bag. When she spread it out on his desk, he saw that it was a map, with small marks over four villages in the north.

As soon as Terek saw the map marks, his stomach dropped in horrified recognition and his mouth dried. He sucked air in through clenched teeth.

"These villages," Mari said, pointing to the places they both knew well, "have all had horrible events with people dying in taverns, or…" She stopped and took a breath before continuing. "Or have had a bunch of people kill themselves. Valdemar has had hard seasons before, but this is different. I looked into it. This is one village after another in a line."

"In a circuit," Terek corrected and tapped Woodberry. "Make that five villages. Maybe more." He drew his finger over the map from village to village in an oblong circle. "What aren't you telling me?"

Mari paused in her reluctance to speak, to brush invisible lint from her ruffled, crimson sleeve. "There's a bard involved. Only, no can remember him after the carnage. They just know he was there the night of the deaths, but no one can find his body, and he isn't in town the next day."

"One of ours is doing this on my old circuit." He looked up at his former protégé, his eyes bleak. "One of ours. And it must have something to do with me."

He listened to his lord's voice as it instructed him where to bury the shard. Eyes closed, he stepped forward or to the side as it commanded. He felt the power flowing through him as he dropped to his knees and dug a small hole. As he placed the shard, chanting the words that had become his mantra, his prayer, his obsession, he knew his revenge was nigh. Either the object of his hate would come to him, or everyone who had lauded the old bard would suffer for ages to come.

Poisoned stone planted on the edge of the village, he stood and brushed the dirt from his hands. He hefted his pack with its evil secret, put on a real smile in anticipation of the carnage that would happen that night, and sauntered down the road into the village, where kindly folk pointed him toward the nearest tavern.

It was a modest thing, with only one story and small windows, but it was one of the nicer buildings in the square, with uncracked walls and a freshly painted sign of a mug frothing over with ale. He nodded to himself and entered the tavern. Empty at this time of day, only the proprietor sat at one of the tables, eating from a bowl of steaming porridge. He didn't get up, only gestured the stranger forward with his wooden spoon.

"Good day, I'm Sorrel. I'm looking for a room, and a place to show my skill." Sorrel tapped his drum for emphasis.

"Daven, here." The proprietor gave Sorrel a critical once over. "Bard, eh?"

"No, good sir. Merely a wandering minstrel. I wear not the red of an esteemed bard." He watched Daven calculate in his head for a moment.

"Then I can't pay you bard wages, but I can make sure you have a warm bed and a full belly, and maybe a coin or two to rub together as you leave."

"Excellent. For that, I will give you an evening of entertainment you won't forget for a long time to come."

◆

"May I sit with you?"

The old man looked up at Sorrel's smiling face, glanced at the mostly full tables around him, and nodded with a grunt.

"I'm Sorrel," he said as he sat, arranging his pack and drum next to him on the floor.

"Aaron." He gave Sorrel another look and then returned his gaze to his ale.

"You local?"

"Nah. Traveling through."

"Where to?"

Aaron looked up again. "Why?"

Sorrel pulled back and raised a hand. "Just curious. I'm a traveler, too. Thought I'd make conversation. Sorry."

The old man gave a long, gusty sigh. "Nah, I'm sorry. Heading to Woodberry. Got grandkids to look in on. Their Da died."

"Woodberry. Bad bit of business there."

"You know?" Aaron paused, his mug in midair.

Sorrel nodded.

"What've you heard?"

"Big brawl. Lots of people died. It was a mess."

"You were there?"

"Nah. Just picked up the word on the road. Avoided it."

Aaron drank deep from the mug and clonked it on the table. "Yeah. That's what I've heard, too."

"It's why I travel." Sorrel saw Aaron's questioning look. "To spread joy, and leave a place a bit lighter than when I arrived." He tapped the drum on the ground.

"A bard?"

"Just a minstrel."

Aaron nodded. "Playing tonight?"

"Aye."

"Good. I could use some music. It lightens the soul."

Sorrel gave him a smile with too many teeth. "This will be a night to remember. Speaking of which, it's time for me to earn my supper."

Word of the minstrel had spread throughout the small village. Music was always welcome, and the villagers came out in force. The sounds of wooden mugs clopping to the table mixed with the smacking of satisfied lips and the laughter of good conversation. However, when Sorrel took his place in the corner where the singers and dancers performed, the place quieted with an anticipatory buzz of people whispering to each other what they knew of the stranger. Two beats of a drum later and the tavern was almost silent.

"Tonight, a dream of mine is about to come true, and all of you here will witness it unfolding." Sorrel reached down into his pack and pulled out something small and black. "Terek, this is for you." With that, he tossed the black thing toward Aaron.

It is the most natural thing in the world to catch something tossed to you in a casual manner. Terek's hands were already wrapping themselves around the cursed item as Sorrel's drum sounded out a slow beat and Terek realized that his real name had been used. By then, it was much too late.

He rocked back as the power of the thing; a statue with large, blank eyes and a larger mouth filled with sharp teeth caught him in a spell. Staring into the statue's eyes, Terek knew that Sorrel had captured the rest of the audience in a spell as well, and they would be no help to him. He felt his own power draining from him as he fell into the statue's trance.

"Before me stand three promising youngsters, but not every dream can come true." Terek recognized himself from years before while riding his last circuit. He had been asked to judge the children in the village for potential. And judge he had. *"You, young Sorrel, you have some skill, but lack both the Creativity and the Gift of a true bard. You will be welcome at campfires to come, but not in the halls of the Collegium."* With a shake of his head and a turn of his shoulder, he dismissed the boy. Terek saw the boy's anguish as he fled the square, but that was no longer his concern. These other two children were.

"Aric, you have proven yourself to be both skilled and creative. I have spoken to your parents and they have agreed to send you to the Collegium. You won't go alone. You will take with you my personal recommendation. You will be welcomed in courts and merchant houses around Valdemar after your skills have been honed." Terek gave Aric a scroll tied with a crimson ribbon whilst the villagers applauded. He patted the boy's shoulder and gave him a gentle push toward his beaming parents.

Terek allowed the power of his trained voice to carry his pleasure as he made his final announcement. *"Mari, my dear child, you have proven that you have the skill, the Creativity, and the Gift to become a master bard. I have spoken to your parents and you will travel with me, finish out my circuit, and then enter the Collegium as the most esteemed of students. You are what every bard strives to become and the kind of apprentice every master bard seeks. You end my quest."*

Locked in a vision of the past, Terek could feel his power, his Gift, being torn from him bit by bit. He struggled to bring his considerable will to bear, but this trap was too well laid and too long in coming. He had fallen for it, and this knowledge settled heavy on his heart. All around him, he was vaguely aware that even his hidden companions, Kolan and Pala, gifted bards both, were locked in Sorrel's spell. He wondered how the ungifted peasant boy could have become so powerful. As if in answer to his query, a new vision clouded his mind.

Fleeing through the trees, Sorrel sobbed as his heart broke. His one dream in life—to become a bard, to show the village he was good enough—was gone. There was nothing left for him now. It was the end. He tripped over a tree root and fell headlong into the dirt. He stayed there, trying to choke off the sobs that threatened to overwhelm him again. He wished he would die.

No, little master, no. Don't die. I can help you.

Sorrel lifted his head, looking through wet lashes into the forest around him, tears smudging his dirty face, but the sobs had halted in surprise at the voice in his head. He shuddered as he took in a breath and wondered if he had gone mad.

Not mad, little master. Far from it. You have found me, and I can make all of your dreams come true. Would you like that?

As he looked around, he felt something smooth and cold under his hand. Sticking up from under a tree root was a glossy black stone. He dug until he could pull it out of dirt. It was a squat thing, just longer than his hand and as thick as his fist. Carved on the front of it was a frowning creature with large eyes and a large mouth with thick lips. On the back, the same hideous creature was smiling, open-mouthed, showing off rows of sharp teeth. "Make my dreams come true?" *Sorrel marveled at the thing in his hand as it spoke in his head.*

All I need is a sacrifice of blood. Feed me and I will be your slave.

"Sorrel?"

It was Aric. Most likely come to tell him of his failure, too. "Here," *he called as he stood up, statue in hand. He waited for Aric to appear. He'd show him the statue and the two of them would figure out what to do—just like they always did.*

Aric burst into view. He was smiling. Before Sorrel could say anything, Aric grabbed him by the hand, "I did it! I'm going to the Collegium with Master Terek's recommendation! I did it."

Sorrel stared as his friend broke his heart all over again.

"I'm sorry you didn't make it, but I was thinking after my training, you could travel with me, anyway. You're really good on the drum. You could be part of my entourage. I'm going to have one of those, I'm sure, after I'm done. We'll still be together and making music!"

Hot roses bloomed on Sorrel's cheeks as Aric added insult to injury. Come be part of Aric's entourage? Become one of Aric's lackeys? An unfamiliar emotion rose out of the shards of Sorrel's dream. Hate. Hate for his friend and his good fortune.

Heedless of Sorrel's clenching fists and flushed face, Aric continued on, dancing around his friend, "Maybe they'll let you come to the Collegium with me anyway. Maybe I can say I won't do it without you. Or, maybe, I should just take you with me and we'll just see what happens. We're going to get out of here! Isn't that great?"

I need just one blood sacrifice, and all your dreams come true. Will you sacrifice him to me?

"Yes," Sorrel said and stepped close to the boy lost in his own dreams.

Aric grinned at Sorrel, not realizing that his friend had not answered him until the first blow came. By then, it was much too late.

Terek groaned aloud as his vision showed him Sorrel beating Aric to death with the statue. As each blow landed, he felt as if he were being beaten himself. His vision clearing, he saw blood on his hands. Where it was from, he did not know. All around him, he saw people fighting with each other. The heavy drumbeat dominated the sounds of chaos. Sorrel's voice was strong and overwhelming. Terek felt the power of it. It was as if Sorrel had a corrupted Gift.

As if sensing his thoughts, Sorrel looked through the melee of bodies when Terek raised his head and their eyes met. That one look told Terek everything. This *was* his fault. He was the reason so many people had died. He had been callous, careless, and mean to a boy who had not deserved it. As the thoughts slammed into his head, Terek realized that they weren't true thoughts, but the thoughts forced into him by foul magic. Be that as it may, he also knew he was going to die. Still, Terek fought will against will, praying that Kolan or Pala would be able to break the spell.

Then the tinkling of finger chimes cut through the drowning drumbeat, and a high soprano voice powered by the Gift brought forth a light. The sounds of love and laughter on the music gave Terek the strength he needed to push back against the draining force of the cursed thing in his hands. Sorrel's beat faltered and Terek saw why: Mari stood in the doorway of the tavern and Sorrel stared at her as she sang familiar words of their past.

You and I together,
Far from all that ails.
Young and loved forever,
And forever we will sail.

She strengthened her song, singing of childhood days and the innocent love the two of them had once had, long ago. Terek could breathe again and now he brought forth his own voice in harmony with Mari's. Sorrel's face hardened once more and he turned his focus back on Terek, willing the statue to finish its task, but Terek met him, voice to voice, will to will, while Mari sang her own attack.

The village folk who had stilled at the first sounds of Mari's song now stirred as if awaking from a bad dream. Those who could, fled the tavern, limping, bruised, beaten, and bleeding. Mari stepped into the tavern over to where Kolan and Pala had regained their senses. Mari's finger chimes urged the village folk on as the other two Gifted bards raised their voices to Mari's, allowing her to lead them in the fight against Sorrel and the evil artifact.

Terek stood, statue clenched in one fist. He stepped toward Sorrel, whose wide, hate-filled eyes refused to give in. The bard raised his shaking fist and forced it open to reveal the small statue: a twin to the original one that Sorrel had found in his grief. He showed it to Mari and the others, who turned their voices on it, and all at once the statue vibrated and then shattered.

As black stone shards flew in all directions, cutting unprotected flesh, Sorrel's head snapped back, and the music stopped: his, Mari's, Terek's. Sorrel staggered backward, hit the wall behind him, and slumped to the ground. It was only then that the bards saw that the largest of the black stone shards had taken one last bloody sacrifice by embedding itself into one of Sorrel's eyes.

Terek rushed forward and went to his knees, but it was too late. Sorrel was dead, leaving the old bard with questions and an apology unspoken on his lips.

Terek sat in his office, staring at the one shard of black stone he had kept.

"We found the rest of the shards and buried statues at the affected villages. They've all been taken care of—except for that one," Mari said from the doorway to his office as she gestured to the one in his hand.

"I feel like I should keep it to remind myself of what my hubris has wrought."

"You can't blame yourself. Not all dreams come true. Sorrel chose his path."

"But..."

"But nothing." Mari stepped forward and held out her hand.

Terek hesitated before handing it over. "Why did you follow us?"

She shrugged. "I always wondered why Aric didn't make it to the Collegium, and I always wondered what happened to Sorrel. Once you decided this was happening because of you and your past, I realized that I was part of that past and that, perhaps, I could help."

"You were right."

She smiled. "It happens sometimes." She turned, paused, and turned back. "We're about to have the Herald-mages do a seeking to find the statue you described from your vision. We know it's still out there. Want to help?"

Terek did not say anything for a long moment before he stood. "Yes. I started this, I should help end it. One last circuit to complete."

I WROTE THIS BECAUSE TOO MANY
friends came home from war changed and feeling guilty for surviving. Too many watched their military brothers and sisters killed in the line of duty. Too many have been hurt far beyond the physical. This story is one of the ways I process my complete inability to help them as they fight demons only they can see. I gave this story a good ending because I have hope for my friends and their struggles.

MEMORIES LIKE CRYSTAL SHARDS
(A Kember Empire Story)

Guardsman Atric left the spaceport with both love and dread in his heart. The familiar sight of the city trees and the loamy smell of dirt tinged with the sharper scent of metal told him he had made it home. Finally. After all the pain and sorrow and loss, he was home. He dropped his bag, closed his eyes, and let the sensations of his world sink into his battered skin.

"Guardsman!"

Atric saw a human guardsman waving to him with big arcs of his arm. He whistled an acknowledgment and added the customary human arm wave in return. He picked up his satchel and walked as fast as his wounded leg would let him over to his new superior officer.

"Senior Guardsman," he said as he stopped, dropped the bag again, and gave the man the traditional Erdant military salute.

"Just 'guardsman' here, or 'Joe' if you like." The senior guardsman returned the Erdant salute and then extended his hand. "Joseph Landen. Welcome home. Your family group is waiting for you on the main platform. I'm here to escort you in."

Atric took Joe's soft, pink hand in his red and yellow calloused hand and shook it twice, as per human custom. "The main platform?"

"That's where returning heroes are welcomed, isn't it?" Joe's smile was close-lipped, and his eyes were dancing with excitement. "I've never seen the hero's welcome before."

"Yes. It is," was all Atric could think to say. He covered his confusion by reacquiring his bag, and stowed it in the back of the forest rover. Human or not, Joe was the type of offworlder who could probably read Erdant body language. The human had followed all Erdant customs—the proper salute, not showing his teeth, not taking Atric's bag despite his obvious injury—of one of the anthropologist guardsmen who were often assigned to non-native planets to be both guardsman recruiter and scientist.

Atric glanced at the human next to him. He looked like most humans, with soft, smooth skin, dark hair on his head and peeking out of his uniform collar and cuffs, and the average height of an Erdant just reaching maturity. Atric wondered what Joe saw when he looked at his new guardsman. Did all Erdant look alike to him, with their hairless, toughened, multicolored skin, flat faces with fluted cheekbones, and three-fingered hands? Or did he recognize the subtle coloring in the mottled skin, the hints of blues, purples, oranges, and reds? Obviously, he would note the *dusamez* if it were not covered, it being in the middle of the chest. What did he think of that? Was he one of those who thought of it merely as a smooth, gemstone-like bone spur?

"You want to know why I'm here, don't you?"

The question startled Atric. "I... yes." It was the simpler answer.

"It's the singing you Erdants do. It's the most wonderful sound in the universe."

Singing. That's what offworlders call the non-verbal communication Erdant did when in the forest and wanted to be in harmony with their surroundings. "Thank you."

"I've been here for," he paused, counting, "three full cycles. I only have a cycle left. I'll miss this place, but I know you'll do well here."

"Why do you say that?"

"You're a hero, Atric. One of the first in a very long time."

I don't feel like a hero, he thought but remained quiet as they arrived at the center of the city trees. The sight of the giant trees of Erdant lessened Atric's confusion and sadness. It was hard to be sad with all of the comforts of home around him.

"Your honor guard," Joe spoke, his words just above a whisper, as the lift descended and five Erdant warriors in full traditional garb came into view. "Your Prime Elder said that I was allowed to take a place among them as you will be working with me."

Atric nodded, knowing that Joe's position would be that of the youngest or least of the guard. It was a place of honor, and yet it was not. He did not explain this, as he did not want his new boss to feel slighted.

Later, after the Welcoming Ceremony, Atric mused how much the beginning had seemed like the first day of the guardsmen training he had been put through. First, he was hustled into a small room where he was stripped of his clothing and cleansed. They were particularly careful of his wounded leg, re-bandaging it with Erdant medicine and wraps. Then he was dressed in appropriate clothing for what was to come. Only, instead of being yelled at in multiple languages by strangers, everyone treated him with respect. Instead of showering with dozens of beings in an open washroom and given a scratchy uniform, he was pampered with a scented bath and dressed in the richest cloth the planet provided. The only thing that had not changed was the complete lack of privacy. There was always someone there to hand him something, to take something, or to assist him with the unfamiliar, traditional clothing.

The rest of the Welcoming Ceremony was both a dream and a nightmare.

The city trees surrounding the main platform were more than ten thousand cycles old. They were the five centerpiece trees in the Prime port city. Old enough to be hollowed out for living quarters and meeting halls, and young enough to still flourish in the growing cycle. Most offworlders would take many days getting used to trees taller than the towers on their own worlds. The suspension bridges, once built from vines, were now crafted from strong, light fiber and metal that served as tethers and balances for the main platform. Many other ties and hidden technology ensured the main platform's safety.

Even so, Atric was surprised at the number of people crowded onto the platform for the Welcoming Ceremony. He could not help but glance at the primary support cables as he was escorted to the dais at the center of the platform, where all of the Elders of the Prime City stood. At that point, Atric had no choice but to forget his worry about the platform supports to be certain he did not mess up his part of the ceremony as the Hero, which, fortunately, was only to stand there and accept the gifts that were brought forth.

As the Elders spoke and whistled Atric's honors—a commendation from the Guardsmen, acknowledged by the sector's Prime, success in a decisive military mission that won a vital asset in the ongoing war and being the sole survivor of his unit to return—he stared out at the crowd before him. The sea of colorful Erdant natives—the bold reds and yellows for the males and the subtle greens, blues, and purples for the females—was a feast to his color-starved eyes after so long in space with uniformed humans. There were people he knew, and his own family group, of course. But there were so many more people he did not know that it was terrifying to see the adoration on their faces. It took all that he had not to shout at them that he was no hero. He was just one lucky guardsman who had not died.

But to say such at this time would not be proper. There had not been such a Welcoming Ceremony performed in his lifetime. Instead, Atric tried to look humble instead of horrified.

The gifts, offerings, and tithes began with the lowest family groups first. These were the offerings of gathered fruits, vegetables, and livestock. Then came the furnishings and household essentials. Next was the fine clothing made by the oldest children of each family group. Then, weapons presented by the lead warriors of the city. As the pile of gifts grew, Atric's heart felt heavier. He had no idea what he would do with so many things, but to turn away even one would be a grave insult.

After the gifts of finery—luxury spices, jewelry, clothing, and a weapon presented by the Second Elder—the Prime Elder came forward and announced that his tithe to the Conquering Hero was a home within one of the five trees supporting the platform. All the Hero need do was indicate which one he preferred. Panicked, Atric whistled a low query to the Prime, who tilted his head and returned the low whistle indicating what he was to do—pick the city tree to the left. Atric accepted the gift of a new home with a grateful nod, and gestured toward the appropriate tree. Then he gave a sigh of relief. Surely, this was over now.

However, while the Prime ordered the waiting workers to carry all of the gifts up to the Hero's new home, a final Erdant stepped forward with a heavily-veiled woman at her side. Suddenly, Atric thought he was going to be sick despite all of his military training on facing adversity.

The Prime stepped back and gestured the Erdant forward. It was the Matriarch of his Recognized's family group. She spoke with the regal bearing of her years. "As is tradition, the Conquering Hero will not be given a home without one to care for him and it. This is our offering. Take her as Iva or Eniva."

Take her as servant or mate.

Atric stepped forward, terrified that the veiled woman would not be his Recognized. His choice was to accept her veiled and as a servant or unveiled and as a mate. He hesitated, looking around through the crowd for his beloved, his Recognized, his promised one, and did not see her. He looked at the Elder before him, but found no clue as to who was under the veil. Just as the crowd was starting to look around, wondering what was wrong, the veiled woman whistled softly to him and Atric felt the life return to his numbed mind.

He whistled back to her, his Recognized, louder than he had intended, in their private way of speaking. They reached for each other as a flutter of laughter lifted itself across the crowd telling of what had just happened, and sharing the Conquering Hero's joy. With the removing of her veil, Atric finally set eyes upon Tamia after far too long, and resumed their courtship by grabbing her tight and holding her close while he kissed every inch of her face.

"Break that line, guardsmen! This is my ground and it's time to own it. You get me in there and do it now!"

That last bit was shouted into Guardsman Atric's ears through the comms so loudly, it felt as if the Senior Guardsman was standing at his back. It did the job it was supposed to do. Atric found himself screaming along with his fellow guardsmen in a charge he had not known he'd begun until he'd seen the reckless Ernic matching him stride for stride on his right and the beautiful Zatia on his left. Both were Erdants, part of his sub-unit. There were other Erdants in the unit. Along with a myriad of other races. The Imperial Guardsmen did not segregate its military unless absolutely necessary.

The three raced forward, firing weapons at anything that moved. They cleared the line ahead—cleared it well enough that the two sub-units flanking helped keep it clear as the rest of the ground pounders breached the line.

Atric shouted, "Line breached!"

"Good job, guardsmen, hold position and keep it clear. Fourth tier, move in and secure the target. No prisoners!"

As the fighting continued in that chaotic way that becomes part fire and part dance, he saw the light as it streaked toward them. Then, time slowed until each moment was a lifetime as Atric turned, screaming the word, "Incoming!" It was this act of turning and dropping—so very slowly—that saved his life while his sub-unit, his friends, died. Even as he reached for them, he was pulled away by unseen soldiers that either would not, or could not, listen to him.

He awoke to Tamia trilling at him, cooing in a soothing tone. She stood in the doorway of his room—soon to be *their* room when the proper rites had been observed—and stopped as she saw him. "You were thrashing… moaning. Crying out. I heard from my room."

Atric sat up and nodded. "It was those last moments."

"When they died?"

He nodded.

"It wasn't your fault. You…"

"It's not that." He wiped a hand over his smooth head, massaged his neck and was dismayed to feel his hand shaking, even pressed to his too-hot skin. "They took me away before I could get their *dusamez*. They wouldn't… I couldn't…"

Tamia broke all custom and hurried to his side. She hugged him close, their *dusamez* shimmering with their Recognition of each other. Atric clung to her, wondering how he was going to be able to fulfill the role of hero that everyone was so determined to put him in.

☥

"But, I'm not a hero, Joe."

Joe laughed and sat back in his chair. "Of course you are. You helped recapture a major asset in the war. All of Erdant loves you. I've never seen a ceremony like that. It was amazing. The speech, the songs, the gifts. One of the Honor Guard had to explain Tamia to me. I thought for a second… well, never mind what I thought. I was quickly corrected."

Atric shook his head. "I don't feel like a hero."

The other man shrugged and turned toward the computer screen. "Doesn't matter really. I had hoped to get you settled into your new duties as a recruiter here—I bet you do really well—but it seems we have four more honor award presentations to go for you. Nothing like the Welcoming Ceremony, of course. That was reserved for the Prime City. Lucky for us it was your home city…"

"It matters to me!"

The man that turned from the console was not Atric's new friend, Joe, but his boss, Senior Guardsman Landen. "No, it *doesn't* matter to you, Atric. It *can't* matter to you. You're a hero in the eyes of your home planet whether you like it or not." He stood up and came out from behind the desk to stand in front of Atric. Although he was a good head shorter than the Erdant, he seemed to fill the room. "You must be the hero your planet so desperately needs. You must be humble, charming, and the perfect Guardsman. The Guard needs more members and the Empire, needs Erdant's continuing support. You're a symbol of bravery, unity, and success. You must be the hero. You have no choice."

Unconsciously, Atric had assumed a formal military stance and listened. The automatic "Yes, Senior Guardsman" response was crisp and clear.

The two stood like that for a long moment—officer and subordinate—not equals and not friends. Then Guardsman Landen slumped back into Joe. "I'm sorry, Atric. I know you're uncomfortable. I know you feel like you led your fellows to their death. You—"

"It's not that."

Joe tilted his head in a question.

Atric unzipped the front of his informal uniform and pointed to the *dusamez* in the middle of the chest. "Do you know what this is?"

"It's the du-sa-mez."

"Yes. But do you know what it *is*?"

"It means 'core of the self'… but no, I don't know what it is."

Atric bowed his head. "It's important to us. When we die, it's retrieved for… the funerary rites."

"I'm sorry. I didn't know. I've never been allowed to attend one."

"And you never will." Realizing how harsh he sounded, Atric softened his tone. "The rites. They are our holiest ceremonies. Only Erdants are allowed. It is law."

Joe nodded. "I know. So, you're upset because you didn't retrieve Guardsmen Ernic and Zatia's *dusamez*."

Atric wanted to protest that it was so much more than that, but knew that Joe Landen, friend or superior officer, would never understand what he was saying. He was not Erdant. He did not understand the implications of the loss. Instead, Atric nodded.

Joe put a hand on Atric's arm. "I'm sorry. I sincerely am. We have their ident chits and their personal effects. They came on the ship with you. But, with the loss of these *dusamez*, it's even more important that you step up and be the hero that your people need you to be."

All Atric could do was nod the agreement his soul did not want to give.

Atric stepped through the gate to the Grove of Memories, pleased that he had obeyed Joe's insistence that he wear the honorary pendant marking him as the Hero. Its smooth, oblong sleekness, so much like the *dusamez*, afforded him privileges that no ordinary citizen of Erdant had. *Ah, but I'm not ordinary, am I? I'm a hero*, he thought, as bitterness and sorrow warred for attention.

Walking down the smooth stone pathway on the ground felt strange. When home, he lived in the trees—as did everyone else—except when taking the Mourner's Path to the Grove of Memories where, tomorrow, he would have to lead the families of Ernic and Zatia in mourning. Lead them in the *Rite of the Dusamez* and return the dead to the soil of Erdant. Only, there were no *dusamez* to return, and he had no idea what he would do.

"I was wondering when you would come, Hero." The ancient voice came from an even more ancient Erdant dressed in the Memorykeeper's robes. This Erdant was so old, his scarlet, yellow, and orange had all faded until his skin was almost a uniform dirty gray. There was a knowing tone in the words he spoke.

"Memorykeeper," Atric said as he gave the Memorykeeper his most humble crossed arm salute. "Please, call me Atric."

"Someday, you will lose your name, but for now, I will." The old Erdant stepped forward, his staff, more than ceremonial, bearing some of his weight. "I know why you've come."

Atric stood straight at this. He, himself, did not know why he was here. He whistled his query, low and polite. He was surprised when the Memorykeeper threw his head back and laughed.

"You are so like me," he said when his laughter subsided. "You truly are." Then he sobered. "You will understand soon."

"Why am I here?"

"Walk with me." It was a command, and the Memorykeeper did not stop to see if Atric obeyed. He turned and led the younger Erdant deeper into the grove. "In all my long life—and I am at least three times your elder, maybe four, I forget—there have only been two times the Welcoming of a Hero has been performed. The first time I remember because I was you. I was about your age and I was the Hero. Only, my 'Iva or Eniva' choice was to a female I had never met. I chose Iva. It worked out well enough. She never loved me and, well, I took this job soon after." He stopped and waved his hand in a dismissive gesture. "The point is, I returned home a hero but I also returned home alone."

Atric stopped walking and looked at him. "You left someone's *dusamez* behind?"

"Yes. No. I didn't want to. I had no choice. I was hurt, like you." He gestured to Atric's slow walk that almost hid his limp. "I was not awake to do the proper thing. My rescuers didn't know any better… and my brother's body, his *dusamez*, was left behind. And, as Hero, I was required to lead the mourning for him for my family."

"What did you do?"

"I came here and the old Memorykeeper showed me what I'm going to show you."

Atric looked ahead and saw a vaguely familiar light. It was a light he remembered from childhood. But, like a not-quite-remembered dream, he associated that light with sorrow, joy, and wonder. It was strangely soothing. As they approached, the Memorykeeper with his old Erdant walk and Atric with his young Erdant limp, Atric started to have flashes of memories about his grandfather—a man he had not thought of in years. Just flickering memories of the old Erdant tickling his chin and giving him sweetfruit.

This was the Well of Memories. This was where the dead were returned to the soil and their memories passed on to the rest of the planet. This was the holiest site in the Prime City.

Surrounded by trees of all sizes was a glade of lush grass that stood knee high. The stone path the pair of them walked continued into the glade and encircled a large depression in the ground. This depression was at least as wide as two Erdant and appeared as deep as one. Its sides were smooth dirt and it was filled with thousands upon thousands of *dusamez*. Each one flickered with faint bursts of light. Taken together as a whole, the *dusamez* within the Well of Memories seemed to be speaking to one another.

The Memorykeeper allowed Atric to stare, entranced by what he saw for a few moments before continuing the lapsed conversation. "I came to the Grove. I found the old Memorykeeper, who was not as old as I am now, and we talked. I was not the first to have friends die offworld, leaving the rest of us bereft of their *dusamez*. I would not be the last. He told me this, and taught me the lesson I will impart to you."

The Memorykeeper stood straight and began a cross between a chant and whistling song. The two sounds, melodic, beautiful, and poignant, caught at Atric's throat. His eyes widened as he saw the stone at the top of the Memorykeeper's staff glow. Before he could do more than marvel at this wonder, he was swept away by the memory.

It was a different planet; one filled with dry dust that served as a sea upon that world and a too-hot sun. The water was a hidden, precious thing. It was night with one full moon and one quarter moon. Four guardsmen sat around an all-purpose glowstone, eating rations and laughing with each other. Two of these guardsmen were Erdant. Two were humans.

"Sing us a song, Xent. A drinking song of your home planet."

Xent obliged by pulling out a small drum and beginning a raucous tune about the Elder's daughter and sweetfruit wine, that made them all laugh until one of the humans began to hiccup.

Atric was laughing when the memory let him go. As was the Memorykeeper. "That song got him into so much trouble at home, but it made us good friends on the Line."

"Your brother?"

"Yes."

"How?" Atric sobered and looked at the Memorykeeper with interest. "How has this memory of your brother survived? You were there. Those others were human."

"I kept the memory alive. I protect his memory—that one and many others—so that the memory of Xent will return to the soil when I die." He paused and looked Atric in the eye. "And that is how you will truly earn your title of Hero. You will keep Zatia and Ernic's memories alive until it is time for you to return to the soil and your *dusamez* is placed with the others. I will teach you how, and you will decide what to do with this knowledge."

The next day, Atric stood at the head of the Mourners' Path that surrounded the Well of Memories. On one side of the Well stood Ernic's family; on the other side stood Zatia's. Although the Memorykeeper was at his side, he was nervous. Until now, he had not spoken to a crowd in his role as Hero. But now, it was time to do what was right. He bowed his head and felt the Memorykeeper grip his shoulder, supporting him.

Atric raised his head. "I stand before you all as your Hero. I stand before you as a guardsman who returned home alone. I, and my fellows, accomplished our goal. But I failed to bring home the core of your kin, that which is to return to the soil and thus to all of us. I returned home, brokenhearted, feeling the failure despite the commendations and honors bestowed. I mourn as you mourn now. But hope is not lost, and neither are Ernic and Zatia."

He saw the looks of confusion and hope on their faces. Then he felt the Memorykeeper squeeze his shoulder and knew it was time to begin. He closed his eyes and began to chant and whistle, interweaving the two as he had been taught the day before. He felt the Memorykeeper's strength roll into him as the ancient Erdant added his song to Atric's.

The three stood together in a tight circle, laughing as one. Zatia was as beautiful as ever, even in her guardsman uniform, and Ernic had that smile that told the world he was on top. Atric completed the circle, holding the sweetfruit—battered and bruised—out to them. "Come on, let's get serious for a moment."

"All right, for one moment only," Ernic agreed.

Zatia accepted the sweetfruit, as was her due as eldest of the three, and said, "On this eve of battle, we eat of the tree and nourish our souls. We set out as one and will return victorious." She took a bite of the fruit and gave an appreciative whistle at its taste before passing it to Atric.

"We set out as one and will return victorious." *He also took a bite of the fruit and then passed it to Ernic.*

"We set out as one and will return victorious. From Erdant we come and to Erdant we will return. We eat of the tree and nourish our souls. If we should fall in battle, we will return to the soil and nourish Erdant." *Ernic took a bite of the sweetfruit.*

The three ended the Rite of Battle Ready *with a comingled solemn whistle. Then they looked at each other for a long moment before they all burst out laughing again. Zatia took the last of the sweetfruit from Ernic's hand and popped it into her mouth. Ernic tried to look wounded but failed as they all turned to gather their gear.*

As the memory and the song faded, Atric saw all of the mourners were smiling. It was a bittersweet thing. He raised his voice once more. "Though Ernic and Zatia's *dusamez* are gone, they and their memories are not. From now until the end of my days, I will earn my title of Hero as the guardian of their memories. All of you here can help me with this. Together we will remember Ernic and Zatia so that when we return to the soil, they will, too, and thus they will never be forgotten."

For the first time since he had arrived home and had the Hero's Honor bestowed upon him, Atric felt deep within his soul that he indeed could be the Hero that his people needed him to be. A calm contentment settled over his heart and allowed him to smile freely once more.

I LIKE THIS MOWRY STORY.

I thought it was about time for Eric to turn the tables on Joseph and give him a taste of his own medicine. I also thought it would be good for Eric and Joseph to come into conflict over something that wasn't trying to kill them. Joseph was getting a bit too high and mighty. He needed to be brought back to earth and to face his own flaws before he removed himself too far from his humanity. Not an easy thing to do to the Lion of God. This story also has the distinction of currently being the only story I've written that has its own challenge coin—something I need to remember to bring to Origins, Gen Con, and any other convention that Silence in the Library might attend. I don't want to be the one footing the drink bill.

THE TINKER'S MUSIC BOX
(A Mowry Story)

"It's my wife. She means everything to me. You've got to protect her when I'm gone," Patrick Smithson said as he caressed the music box sitting on the table between them. The table sat beneath the second story window of the inn room that belonged to the man Patrick was speaking so earnestly to: bounty hunter Eric Hamblin. The rest of the room was taken up by the single bed, a cedar chest, and a smaller table that held a wash basin and a pitcher of water. It was as private as a stranger could get in town.

Eric looked at the music box. It was a thing of beauty, with an inlaid ivory and rosewood case. It was about the size of a small breadbox, and its interior showed two brass cylinders—one smooth and one picked with a song. There were several switches on the inside, and a ratchet winding handle. All of the hardware was substantially gilded and told a tale of care, craftsmanship, and love. But to call it his wife was a bit unusual.

"Mr. Smithson…"

"Patrick, my boy," the old man interrupted with a smile. "I insist."

Eric nodded and started again, "Patrick… she is a beautiful music box, but I'm not a bank or a safe. Don't you think those would be better places for your treasure?"

"And lock my Clara up in the dark? No sir!" He shook his head with the air of a man who does not understand the stupidity in front of him.

"The music box, Clara, is a masterful…"

"Are you daft? Clara isn't the music box."

I think the old man is addle-brained, Joseph said in Eric's head. *I can't follow his words.*

Eric nodded to himself and to the spirit riding his body. The spirit in question was Joseph Lamb, Sheriff-cum-preacher, murdered by his own pistol, and now the Lion of God—protector of the innocent and exactor of God's vengeance—in one incorporeal package. He had chosen to sit this one out and let Eric make the decision.

Eric sat back and sighed. "You have the better of me. I don't understand."

Patrick gave Eric an earnest look. "I'm not just a tinker. I was a watchmaker. One of the best. But I discovered something… *invented* something marvelous. It's very complex and involves things you wouldn't understand." He patted the music box. "That was back east. I knew I had to come west to get away from people who knew I was working on something special. But there's little call for watchmakers out here in Arizona. Now tinkers, that's a different story."

"Yes, but what does all this have to do with your wife?" Eric shook his head. "For that matter, where is your wife? Don't you think she should have a say in this?"

The look of pride on Patrick's face scared Eric.

"Mr. Hamblin, Clara is *in* the music box."

Joseph's wordless surprise mirrored Eric's quiet question of, "Pardon?"

Patrick gently ran his fingertip over the picked music cylinder. "Clara, my love, this is her soul here. As she died of consumption, I drew her last breath into the music box with this." He touched a switch on the side of the cylinder.

Eric saw that the other cylinder had an identical switch, and did not know whether he should be impressed or horrified.

Joseph had no such qualms. *Blasphemy!* his voice rumbled in Eric's head.

Patrick, unaware of the silent criticism, continued. "Clara and I have been together like this for forty-two years. Forty-two happy years." The smile disappeared. "But now I'm dying and we have no children. I must find a way to protect her. I must."

Eric swallowed, his mouth dry. "What does Clara think of this?"

"Finding and hiring you was her idea," Patrick said.

"I can't believe you agreed to this." Joseph paced the room. "The very notion that a soul could be captured, imprisoned, in any clockwork is beyond the pale."

Eric, still sitting at the table, looking at the music box, smiled. "Beyond the pale? Seventeenth century poetry? You *are* upset." If Joseph had a body, Eric knew that the man's well-worn boots would be stomping out a temper tantrum on the hardwood floor. Instead, he paced in silent fury.

"Yes," Joseph nodded. "I am. That thing should be destroyed. If her soul is in it, it needs to continue on to its final resting place. Man was not meant to capture souls."

"How do you know destroying it won't destroy the soul?" Eric's voice was mild and curious. He had not seen Joseph this upset before—not even when the gun that was his body on this mortal plane was shot, actually damaging his spirit.

"It won't." His voice was short and final. "That woman's soul has been denied its final judging. She could have been tortured all these years. How are we to know?"

"That woman's soul could be just fine and she could be happy," Eric countered. "You're right… we can't know. And I'm not willing to possibly destroy a soul without knowing for sure."

"Perhaps someone would like to ask 'the woman'?" a woman's voice said. With neither fuss nor fanfare, there she was, sitting in the chair formerly occupied by her husband; a brunette with her long hair in a bun, wearing a cornflower blue walking outfit. "Perhaps 'the woman' would know a thing or two about the state of her soul or the home in which it resides."

Eric stood with his hand on the gun and frowned at her. "Clara Smithson?"

She nodded. "I am."

"You've been listening all this time?"

"Yes."

"Why haven't you made yourself known before now?" Joseph asked.

Clara gave an elegant shrug of her shoulders. "I had not been invited." Turning to Eric, she tilted her head. "I thought you would have asked to see me, meet me, at least. I am surprised you took him at his word. In truth, his words are addle-brained to the unknowing ear."

Eric looked between Clara and Joseph, his hand still on the gun. "You heard him."

Clara stood and walked to Eric, reaching out her empty hand to his armed one. "I did. And I can see him. There is no need for this." She pressed her hand down through his and trailed her fingers over the butt of the gun. "I am one woman with no weapons."

Eric felt a wisp of cold on and in his hand as her ghostly fingers slipped through his flesh.

"You are nothing," Joseph said abruptly. "You are the shadow of a soul and must be destroyed."

Eric and Clara looked at Joseph.

"She looks like a spirit to me," Eric said. "And she can see you."

"That doesn't matter. She has passed by her time in this mortal realm."

"As have you." Clara tilted her head. "Why do you fear me so?"

Eric realized that Clara was right. Joseph was afraid and reacting in anger. That was an unaccustomed emotion. He watched as Clara approached Joseph. For the first time, Eric watched the Lion of God retreat. Then he watched Joseph's face harden as the spirit stood his ground. Clara and he stood an arm's length from each other.

"You don't belong here," Joseph said.

"And you do?" Clara asked.

"I do. I have a purpose."

"Do you know for certain that I do not have a purpose as well?"

"I was given my purpose by God. I chose to become his avenging angel."

"I was given a choice of dying or remaining with my husband. I chose to stay by his side, as a good wife would."

"It's not the same," Joseph said, dismissing her.

Eric saw Joseph walk forward, intent on walking through her to make his point, but was shocked when their shoulders collided. He noted that Clara looked as shocked as Joseph did. "You can touch each other," Eric observed.

"That much is obvious," Clara said, returning to the table to stand by her husband's music box.

"You didn't expect it. You both thought that you would slide through each other. But you can touch each other," he repeated thoughtfully. "You knew," Eric said, turning to Joseph. "You knew that you could feel her."

Joseph shook his head. "No." He looked at his feet for a moment and then looked up again. "No, I didn't *know*, but I suspected. I wasn't sure until then."

"That's what you were afraid of. Why?" Eric asked.

Clara looked at Eric with hungry doe eyes. "I haven't felt anything for forty-two years. Not since I died. The sensation was… was…"

"Welcome…" Joseph murmured, more to himself than anyone else.

Eric looked between them. "He felt something a few months back. Pain. He was hurt. But now he has the chance to feel something more."

Joseph gave him a sharp look. "No. I will not. That is not my duty."

"Ah, but a man is not all duty. Perhaps Clara is here for another duty. To reward your service." Eric's voice was soft and tempting. Joseph stared at him, and for a moment Eric frowned at himself for having such a thought. But he felt compelled to continue despite the thought's unsavory nature. "Think of it. Why else would this music box be put in our path?"

Joseph's face was a thundercloud of conflicting emotions. "Blasphemy!"

"She could be your reward for good service. To ease your loneliness," Eric continued. "You think I can't feel it when you spirit-ride me? I can."

So intent on Joseph, Eric did not notice Clara shifting toward him until she reached out and yanked the 1851 Colt revolver from his gun belt. The engraved flames on its barrel seemed to flicker as she pointed it at Eric. "I will kill you both before I allow anyone to touch me without my permission."

Eric stepped away from Clara, toward Joseph. "Why didn't you warn me she'd be able to take your gun?"

"I didn't know, and I wasn't the one offering her up as a prize," Joseph said.

"Maybe I don't want to die," Clara continued over their surprise. "And maybe I don't want to be offered like a Calico Queen to the first man who comes by. I am a respectable married woman."

"Can she shoot the gun? How is she even holding it?" Eric asked, his hands raised.

"I don't know," Joseph admitted. "It is God's Will that fires the pistol." Then he looked at Eric. "I suppose we'll find out when she shoots you."

"Me?"

"You were the one offering her up to me like a whoremonger."

"Not seriously," Eric said. His face flushed with embarrassment as he looked at Clara. "I apologize if I upset you. I was only testing him. He's constantly testing me… my beliefs and morals. When I discovered how unsettled he was at his ability to feel you, your presence, I thought only to test him in the same way."

"You, Mr. Hamblin, are a cad, and I will not be used like this. I will not be offered up as a whore for some other spirit because we can sense each other. I do not care if it was a test. What if he had decided you were right? Dead or not, I am a respectable married woman and I will not have it!" Her voice rose with her anger.

Neither Eric nor Joseph had time to protest Clara's words before the door to their inn room broke in, followed by the even louder crash of the Colt revolver going off. Standing in the middle of the broken doorway was Patrick. He had one hand raised, wielding a large iron hammer, and the other hand clutched his chest where crimson blood spilled between his fingers. "Clara?" he asked, confused, before he dropped the hammer to the floor and sank to his knees.

Clara, also shocked and confused, dropped the Colt and rushed to her husband's side. "Patrick, oh, Patrick!" She reached for him, but her arms slid through his flesh as he shifted, falling on his back.

"Heard you yelling. Came to rescue you," Patrick wheezed.

She looked up at them. "Help him!"

"Your aim was true," Joseph said. He did not move from his spot, though he glanced out the broken door and saw that the entirety of the inn was showing a remarkable sense of self preservation and not coming to look at the ruckus.

"Just wanted to take care of you." Patrick's voice was fading and he lost his struggle to lift his hand up to his wife's face.

Eric hesitated a moment before reaching a decision and then crossed the room to the music box. He flipped the switch next to the smooth music cylinder and watched it turn. Then, he watched Patrick's face, watched him take his last few breaths as Clara sobbed in keening wails above her husband's body. When Eric looked back at the music cylinder, it was no longer smooth. He turned off the switch and contemplated the music box.

"What did you do?" Joseph asked.

When Eric looked at him, he saw the horror on his mentor's face.

"I did what I thought ought to be done. And maybe, if you weren't trying to be so high and mighty, you'd be trying to help that poor woman." Eric gestured at the sobbing spirit with his chin. "I can't touch her, but you can."

Eric took the blanket from the bed and covered Patrick's body. Joseph made no move towards Clara or Eric. He watched them with conflicted eyes.

"Shhh, Miss Clara. Shhh." Eric hunkered down and tried to look her in the face, trying to comfort her. "How long after your death did you know you were a spirit?"

She looked up at him, confused. "What do you mean?"

Speaking in tones reserved for frightened animals and hysterical children, Eric smiled at her and repeated, "How long after your death did you know you were a spirit?"

"Almost immediately. I no longer felt pain."

"I'm no longer in pain, my love." Patrick, looking younger and healthier, stood next to the music box. "I don't know why I didn't think to hire someone to draw my soul into the music box to be with you. It seems so obvious now." He nodded to Eric. "Young man, I owe you a debt."

Eric stood as Clara looked over her shoulder and saw Patrick. He opened his arms to her. With a whirl of skirts, she rose and ran to him. For the first time in decades, the two embraced, and this time her tears were tears of joy. Eric stepped over to Joseph's side. "Is it still blasphemy?" he asked.

As the ghosts disappeared, Joseph shook his head. "I don't know." They stood in silence for a moment longer before Joseph added, "I don't appreciate your idea of a test."

"Now you know how I feel when you do it to me," Eric said, "but you were tempted."

"Yes," Joseph agreed. "In life, as much as I tried to be a good man, I wasn't. I enjoyed life as much as any other man did. Without the temptations of the flesh, I can be the Lord's instrument. With her here, it would be much more difficult."

"What do we do now?"

Patrick answered the question before Joseph could. Once more, the spirits of the music box appeared without warning. Patrick and Clara stood side by side, her arm linked in his. "You must destroy the music box," Patrick said. "It is much too dangerous to have around. My invention is extraordinary and not something I want in the hands of evil men."

Clara glanced at Eric.

Patrick saw the disbelieving looks on Eric and Joseph's faces. "Clara and I have had a long talk. Time within the music box is different than here. It is possible that dangerous people from back east will come looking once news of my death reaches there."

"We could neglect to mention that you died," Eric said.

Clara shook her head and Patrick said, "We talked and we have decided. Now that we are reunited, it is time for both of us to continue on. We are ready."

"But, what if destroying the music box destroys the two of you?"

"Then that is what God wills," Clara said. "Man was never meant to live beyond this life."

Eric nodded, "How do I do it?"

"I'll tell you," Patrick said. "My tools are at my belt." He pointed to the blanket-covered body. "But, I think you should destroy it away from other people. Just to be certain no one else is hurt. The clockwork is special."

Joseph and Eric sat around the campfire with a thick smelting pot hung over hot, glowing coals. They were hunkered down at the base of a butte out of the wind; the Arizona desert was gusty around them, with dust devils whirling in and out of existence. As Eric took apart the music box piece by piece, he slowly added each wooden part to the fire to burn and each metal part to the pot to melt. He paused when he got to the cylinders containing Patrick and Clara's souls. "Why do you think He allowed it? Her shooting her husband?"

Joseph was slow in answering. Finally he said, "I think He was giving them what they wanted... to be reunited. We both know that revolver will not fire unless it's doing God's will."

Eric raised an eyebrow. "You don't think it was to punish him for the music box?"

Joseph shook his head. "No."

"I don't know why I started testing you. I'd never thought about testing you before. And you know me; I would never offer a woman up to another man as a prize. Not after what happened to my sister. The more I think about what I said, the angrier I get at myself."

"Maybe it wasn't you talking."

Eric put the cylinders to the side, unable to put them into the pot for melting. He unscrewed the bottom of the music box to look at the clockwork mechanism below and was startled at its complexity. The entire thing was a work of art. He really had no idea where to begin taking it apart. Then he remembered he was destroying the machine and used a small chisel to start prying gears and springs out, adding each to the pot of melting metal. "You think the Lord was using me to test you."

"I do."

"Why?"

Joseph shrugged. "I told you. I was once human, with a man's desires. Maybe He thought to tempt me with the pleasures of the flesh again."

Eric took the sideboard rosewood pieces off the case and added them to the fire. Using the chisel, he pried up more of the complex clockwork. "Or maybe He wanted to remind you what it was like to be human, with human emotions and needs."

Joseph frowned but said nothing.

"You're all fire and brimstone, and that's fine for those who deserve God's vengeance. But the Smithsons, they didn't deserve that. It was an old man trying to protect his wife's spirit when he was gone. Instead of offering that protection, you judged them." Eric, impatient with prying the last of the gears off the baseboard of the music box's remains, tossed the entire thing into the fire, sending a shower of sparks dancing into the noon sun.

"You're more than just the Lion of God, Joseph Lamb. You're a protector of the innocent as well. I think it's something you needed reminding of." Eric picked up the two cylinders and stared at them. "Maybe that's why all this happened."

Eric did not look at his mentor as he reluctantly put the two cylinders into the smelting pot. After a moment, the wind whipped up around the campsite, blowing sand into their faces. Eric covered his eyes with an arm until the unnatural wind died down and left with the sound of a sigh. Inside the pot of partially melted metal, the cylinders were gone.

Joseph's voice was soft. "I reckon you might be right. It's something I'm going to have to think about."

I BELIEVE THAT SCIENCE FICTION *writers really do pave the way for science. From time to time, I look at current technology and I extrapolate where I think it might go. This is one of those stories. It's not a nice story, and it's made all the more frightening to me by recent medical discoveries about "young" mouse blood revitalizing old mice. Suddenly, this story seems that much more plausible and I'm pretty sure that's not a good thing.*

THE BATHORY CLINIC DEAL

"I'm hungry." Lara's voice was small and sad.

Jackie tipped his head up. It was the normal state of things.

For once, it wasn't scalding hot out. The sun shone down on the cement steps, but the cool breeze kept Jackie and Lara from the usual afternoon roast. They watched people walk by in their bubble of a busy day, cocooned by personal technology feeding them music, news, political reports, and business dealings. Jackie sighed and wished he could afford the most basic education modules so he and Lara could learn online instead of going to the ever-underfunded, perennially out-of-touch, state-provided school.

Jackie saw that Lara wasn't watching the people passing. She was watching what they were holding—all of the packages of fast food and cups of fancy coffee. He knew her hunger was worse than normal. He checked his ever-present, beat-up backpack for his water bottle and saw it was mostly full. After taking a swallow, he offered it to Lara. "Here, drink this. The whole thing at once. It'll make you feel full. I can get more at Home."

When he said the word "Home" they both knew they weren't talking about a real home. It was the state-run dormitory where they could sleep in relative safety—which meant his little sister slept with him because of the predators among the other kids—and they could get one actual meal a day. It wasn't tasty, despite Cook's attempts otherwise, but it was filling, and they both ate as much as they could in that one sitting.

Lara did as she was told, gulping the tepid water.

"Think of apple juice." Jackie's voice was soft. He watched her close her eyes as she took another swallow, slower this time. "Sweet and tart."

"I can almost…"

"Shhh. Don't talk. Just think of apple juice and drink."

This time Lara did. She sighed with regret as she finished the bottle. "That was good."

Jackie took the bottle back and stuck it in his backpack. For a while the two of them sat in silence. There wasn't much to do, and loitering at Home wasn't encouraged. It only led to extra unpaid chores.

"I wish…" Lara stopped. She shook her head and slumped back down again.

Jackie grimaced. He hated that his sister was turning out just like him. He knew she was going to say something like, "I wish we had a library connection" or "I wish we could go to the park." But those things, like everything else they wished for, either cost money, were limited in hours, or were reserved for people with private citizen connections. Stuff they didn't have and couldn't afford.

He didn't like the droop of her mouth or the glassiness of her eyes. "Hey, c'mon. I've got something to tell you."

The curious tilt of her head filled him with love. The two of them began their "we've got to talk" saunter around the block, dodging shoppers, workers, and joggers. Out of habit—a bad one—Jackie's eyes picked out the most expensive things on the people they passed: feathered eyelashes, fiber optic mood hair, a woman with cat's eyes, an older man in a leather jacket with badly done implanted goggles, implanted jewels—not that you could tell if they were real or fake. One man waved his Smartie around like a baton.

What Jackie wouldn't give for an all-in-one smart device like that, or smart glasses. He'd never have to worry about a connection again. But that kind of thought wasn't getting him anywhere. Neither was the sudden urge to steal the damn thing. Besides, they might soon be able to afford such things—the low-end versions—for themselves. He turned his focus to Lara with an effort. She was watching him.

"I wasn't going to tell you…" He stopped at the clouds brewing in her expression. "Don't look at me like that. We agreed: some things I need to do on my own to help us."

Lara made a brave effort to smooth her face into neutral. "But you're going to tell me now?"

"Yes. I am." Jackie paused, unsure of how to say this. They turned the corner away from the downtown district toward Home. "I. Hmm." He shrugged. "I've been accepted to the Bathory Clinic."

Lara stared at him. Her mouth worked as dozens of questions crowded in her mind. All that came out was, "How?"

Trying to play it off like it was no big deal, Jackie shrugged. "I went in, got tested, got approved." What he didn't say was that he had skipped school to take a two-hour, extremely personal questionnaire, had had one hell of a physical that included a genetic scan, and then had had his blood drawn.

"But... Sue?"

His pretend girlfriend from last year. "A lie. To protect her from you-know-who."

Lara frowned, looking far too adult. "But... you're only fifteen!"

"And you're ten. What of it?"

"The law..."

"Was changed. They dropped the consent age for cosmetic procedures to fifteen back in February."

Lara's voice dropped into a tone reserved for conspiracies. "But... the *Bathory Clinic*."

And there was the rub. He had no snappy answer for her. Instead he looked away. "They pay well."

The Bathory Clinic was the pinnacle of plastic surgery, if you could call it that. It gave the old their youth back. No one really knew how it worked, but everyone knew it was stupidly expensive to get the procedure... and it required the blood of teenagers who met a stringent criteria that included that they be virgins. Other than that, the rest was just scuttlebutt on the street.

Of course, no one wanted to admit to being a Bathory Clinic client. The rich wanted to pretend they really were young. And no teenager wanted to admit to being a virgin. At least, not any of the guys Jackie knew. As for the girls, well, it was dangerous to admit either in the dorms. Too many wanted to take something from someone that they could never get back.

"How well?"

Lara's question pulled him back to the here and now. "I don't know yet. I'll know when I go in for my final... everything," he waved his hands to encompass all that he did and did not know, "... on Monday."

"Monday."

"Yeah."

"Wow."

"Yeah."

Lara thought about all this for a long time. Long enough that they were about to take the second turn when she finally asked, "Will you be okay?"

He squeezed her to him in a brief side-hug. "Yeah. I think so. I hope so." When she was quiet again for a long time, Jackie stopped them and turned her to him. "What's up?"

"What's going to happen to me?"

"Nothing we don't want. I won't leave you behind."

Again her brow furrowed. "What if I said I didn't want you to do it?"

"I guess I'd have to ask why not."

"Then I'd have to say that, one time when I was talking with Tanya, we talked about this and Tanya knew a guy who did it and... she said the Bathory Clinic stole his life."

Jackie sighed. This was one of the more popular rumors on the street. "Then I'd have to say that was probably just something Tanya heard from people who just wanted to talk."

"But, it was her cousin. They said he looked like a drug addict for months after each treatment, all skinny and yucky and stuff." Lara looked at the ground, her voice soft. "I'm scared for you."

He lifted her face to his. "It's going to be okay. If it was really dangerous, it wouldn't be legal, and they wouldn't let kids do it." When she looked unconvinced, he smiled with a lie. "And if it's bad, I won't do it again."

But Jackie knew that even if it was bad, he'd stay with it. Especially with the amount of money he'd heard the clinic paid. It would be enough to get him and Lara out of Home and into their own *real* home. With private bedrooms and everything. Besides, he was no stranger to pain.

They started walking again, in silence, enjoying each other's company. Also, Jackie knew that Lara needed time to think.

They passed a guy in the process of Elfinization. He had the pointed ears and the impossibly platinum hair, but his head was bandaged in that way that said he'd just recently undergone the surgical reconstruction to thin and elongate his face. Jackie wondered why the man would be out in public like that. Then he realized that, no matter what kind of mods you had done to you, life went on and a mod like Elfinization wasn't cheap. Most likely, the guy had a job to go to.

"Okay," Lara announced. "You can do it. But if it's bad, you stop after the first treatment."

"Thanks."

The Bathory Clinic public waiting room was just like every other medical place Jackie had been in, only nicer. Everything seemed cleaner. The chairs were plush and soft like suede. The front desk receptionist looked calm and poised, unlike the receptionist at the state-run medical facility all the kids at Home had to see once a year. There were even digital papers around where you could read the news or the latest tabloid.

Jackie swiped through images of movie stars on the red carpet in ridiculous clothing and mods. He stopped at a picture of his favorite actress, !Skylar!. She was almost completely unmodded; just a couple of tasteful gems around her eyes, accenting them and making them seem wider but not weird. Not like anime mods. As he studied her face, her beautiful, unlined eyes, he realized that she had been his favorite actress for as long as he could remember, and she hadn't changed at all.

A young man came into the clinic and Jackie gave him a double take as he went up to the receptionist. He was tall and too skinny, with a mop of brown hair that was styled to fall over one eye. His clothing screamed money: designer jeans, two-toned boots that were all the rage, a silk shirt, and smart glasses. Jackie had seen fake versions of all of these, and this kid wasn't wearing fakes. The smart glasses were top of the line and embellished with gold. They were amazing, to the point that Jackie almost missed the conversation between he and the receptionist.

"I'm sorry, Chaz, you don't have a session, you're too old."

Chaz shook his head. "Sorry, darlin', I'm not. There's been a mix-up in the records. I'm seventeen. It's right on my ID."

Jackie watched as the receptionist's polite smile tightened into a firm line of annoyance. He watched as her eyes flicked around the reception area to himself and a nervous-looking girl.

"Mister Daly, not only are you eighteen, but you failed your last physical. You are no longer a client of the Bathory Clinic." Her clipped tone could have scarred diamond. "It is time for you to leave before you are forcibly removed."

Chaz lowered his voice, but Jackie still caught every pleading word. "Please. I gotta have my session. I need it. You don't even have to pay me. I'll do it for free."

It sounded like a junkie pleading for just one hit to get him through until he got the money to pay what he owed.

Jackie swallowed hard as two large, uniformed men came in and grabbed Chaz by the arms. One spoke so quietly to the desperate kid that Jackie couldn't hear what was said. Whatever it was, Chaz calmed at once and nodded. "Yes. Shiny. Yes." The guards escorted Chaz to the back and that was that.

Again, it seemed like a junkie being promised that hit he needed, but first he had to do something for the dealer.

Both the other patient and Jackie must have looked horrified. The receptionist smiled. "I apologize for that. Sometimes people get in over their heads."

This platitude didn't make Jackie feel any better. He almost ran when the receptionist beckoned for him to come to the back with her. "They're ready for you."

The back hallways of the Bathory Clinic were even more plush and comfortable than the front reception area. Everything was decorated in a motif of burgundy, black, and gold, accented in white. The first time Jackie had come back here, he had been afraid to touch anything. He was still nervous about breaking the artwork, but had come to understand that this lush scenery was designed for the people used to it—the real clients of the clinic.

This time, he was left in a private sitting room filled with comfortable furniture, refreshments, and entertainment. Before the receptionist left, she pointed out the restroom down the hallway and assured him that the wait would not be much longer.

Jackie enjoyed a bit of the snacks, resisting the urge to sweep the whole plateful into his backpack to savor and share with Lara later. After pacing around the room, he poked his head out and looked around. There was no one in the hallway. More out of curiosity than a need to go, Jackie headed toward the restroom.

He stopped when he heard voices coming out of a room between he and his goal.

"You promise, Mannie? You promise I'll have another session soon? I can see wrinkles around my eyes."

The woman's voice sounded old and young at the same time—much like what Jackie remembered of his grandmother asking for more soup. He peeked into the room and saw a beautiful woman in a flirty dress that fell to the tops of her knees. In sky-high heels, she was taller than the older man she was with. Her wrists and fingers were covered in classic gold jewelry that twinkled as she stroked Mannie's graying hair. Jackie saw thin lines in them, indicating they were computer enhanced.

"Your laugh lines are lovely, Joy, but yes, I promise. It's just my turn now."

Mannie, his voice patient, turned enough for Jackie to see what looked to be a man in his late forties, maybe. You could never be sure once you knew someone was a Bathory Clinic client. He could be forty-eight. He could be one hundred and forty-eight. Right now, he had the soft look of a man who sat too much, ate too well, and indulged when the mood took him.

Jackie let out the breath he had not known he'd been holding. Mannie and Joy turned to look at him. Jackie froze, unsure of what to do. Mannie's soft face, the one that loved the woman he was with, turned hard and assessing as he looked Jackie up and down. Suddenly, Jackie knew he was not in the presence of a soft man.

"Is that him?" Joy's voice was awed and barely above a whisper.

Mannie raised a hand to quiet her as he continued to pin Jackie with his unflinching gaze. "Your name?"

"Jackie…"

"Is there a problem?" The voice came from behind Jackie, startling him.

As he whirled around to come face-to-face with one of the no-name, no-ID security guards who had escorted Chaz into the back hallways, Mannie spoke, his voice unconcerned. "This young man was just asking where the bathroom was."

Jackie nodded, his heart pounding so hard in his chest he thought he'd break a rib.

The guard looked between Jackie and Mannie for a moment. "This way," he said to Jackie. "Sir," he said to Mannie with a deferential nod.

Escorted to the restroom, Jackie found that he did have a sudden need to use the facilities and was thankful that everything seemed to be in the right place and worked in a standard way. Of course, the quality of the sink, the toilet, the towels—even the tiled floor—were so far beyond what he was used to—marble, granite, some stuff he couldn't identify—that if he had put too much thought into it, he wouldn't have been able to go. Not to mention, it was the all-time cleanest bathroom he'd ever used.

Jackie was not surprised to see the guard waiting for him when he was done. Without a word, the large man, not much more than a blur of "big" and "uniformed," escorted Jackie back to his waiting room. The guard left with a nod and was immediately replaced with a familiar face: Technician Costa.

Technician Costa was a hard-faced woman with kind gray eyes. The severe bun she wore did nothing to soften the sharp lines of her patrician nose and thin lips. Jackie liked her anyway. He liked the way she treated him like an adult.

"Sorry about the wait, Jack." She handed him a slim tablet and sat on one of the plush chairs. "There was a bit of a ruckus."

"Chaz?"

Jackie saw Technician Costa's mouth press into the same line of annoyance he had seen on the receptionist's face, and wondered if that was something that was trained into Bathory Clinic personnel.

"Yes, Chaz. I hope that little scene didn't dissuade you from becoming one of our clients. Erity said you looked unsettled."

"Erity?" Jackie flushed, not knowing who she was talking about.

"Erity Parker, the receptionist."

It was good to finally have a name for her. "Um, I was wondering. He said... Chaz... he said he wanted a session enough that the clinic wouldn't have to pay him for it."

"Oh. Oh, that." Technician Costa looked relieved. "Some of our clients find the sessions pleasurable. Most can handle it. A rare few... well... the Bathory Clinic will take care of him. We'll send him for counseling."

Her hushed voice shifted into something more professional and clipped. "But we're here to talk about you. This is the final consent form. I'm required to ask you each question in specific and you must answer each one completely. If you have any questions, we are to discuss each in full until you understand your rights and responsibilities. As before, this interview is being monitored and recorded. Shall we begin?"

Jackie, glancing over the digicontract on the table, nodded. "Yes."

Technician Costa leaned back in her chair and began. "What is your full name?"

"Jack Edward Sullivan."

Tap. Checkbox marked.

"Are you here at the Bathory Clinic of your own free will?"

Jackie remembered the day he and Lara were dropped off at Home by parents beaten down by a system designed to do just that. He had been ten, Lara five. His father had said, "I'm sorry." His mother had said, "Be good and protect your sister." Home had taken them in, fed them, clothed them, and sheltered them to the Federally-mandated standards required, and nothing more. There was no love, no care, no real desire to help. It was a just a necessary job. If that was not coercion, forcing him to fend for himself and his sister, he didn't know what was.

Even as the thought raced through his head, Jackie nodded. "Yes."

Tap. Checkbox marked.

"You will be paid the sum of $20,000 for this first session and every session afterward. This money may be paid out in $5,000 increments for the month of the session and the three off months afterward, or it may be paid out in a single lump sum. Choose one: monthly increments or a single payment at the time of your session."

Jackie did not speak. He could not wrap his mind around the concept of having that much money. It made him want to leap for joy and flee in terror. So many thoughts crowded in his head.

When Jackie did not answer, Technician Costa leaned forward. "Jack, may I make a suggestion?"

"Yes, Technician Costa."

"Call me Giada."

"Giada." Jackie's brain was numb.

"I'm going to suggest that you take the monthly increments. Most teenagers have parents they can turn to. We know that you're a ward of the State. This makes things more complicated because Home is not going to want to let you or Lara go. They'll lose funding for the two of you. It's a numbers game. If you take the monthly increments, you can manage your lives on a more reasonable level."

Giada tilted her head, looking at him. "Unofficially, since it's not on any of the medical forms you've signed or are going to sign, I will tell you that the Bathory Clinic has a transition specialist for cases like you. You're young, but just old enough to legally become your own person and take on the burden of caring for Lara. With the funds from the session, you'll have the means to do both. Our transitions person will help you set up a bank account and move you into one of the Bathory Clinic-owned apartments nearby. You'll pay rent but, unlike other places, you won't need to pass the credit check. We know where your money is coming from.

"However, you'll *officially* be on your own and no longer a ward of the State. That's why I'm recommending the monthly increments."

Jackie nodded, his brain still stunned by the amount of money. For a brief instant, he thought about reuniting with his parents and letting them deal with it all. He pushed that thought away. He'd told Lara they were dead. His parents had abandoned them. They could stay dead. "Monthly increments, please."

Tap. Checkbox marked.

"Do you understand that you are required to refrain from all sex?"

"Yes."

Tap.

"Do you understand that for a full thirty days leading up to your session you are to refrain from all drugs, including alcohol, unless prescribed by a Bathory Clinic physician, and must pass a Bathory Clinic physical the day before your session?"

Jackie nodded. He never had gotten into the drug and alcohol scene. Too easy to fall prey to someone who wanted power over you. "Yes."

Tap.

"Do you understand if you break the rules of this contract, or once you turn eighteen, that all Bathory Clinic benefits become null and void and you will no longer be a Bathory Clinic client?"

"Yes." He had seen the results of that already, but this was his only chance to get himself and his sister out of Home. To give them a chance at a real future.

Tap.

Giada smiled. "Good. Please sign here."

Jackie used the tip of his finger to sign the contract and stared into the onboard camera until it winked at him, indicating his picture had been taken.

Giada stood up, and Jackie followed suit. "So... now what?"

"Now, we get you ready for your first session."

"Okay."

She stopped him. "May I suggest that we have our transition specialist,

Alicia, go pick up Lara from school so they can gather all of your things from Home? We've picked out a nice two-bedroom apartment for you guys."

Jackie stared at her and then realized that he wouldn't be in any condition to get Lara from school. All of the literature he'd read said that he'd be very weak for the next couple of days. If all this was to happen now, that needed to be done first. "Oh. Right. Can I record a message for her for your specialist, for Alicia, to play? Lara won't come otherwise."

Giada smiled. "Smart kid. Of course. And don't worry; we're going to take good care of you both. You're important to us."

Jackie nodded, wondering just how much the super-rich paid to stay young… and how much he was going to wind up paying in the end.

Jackie looked around the surgical center. There were computer stations surrounding a comfortable-looking recliner chair. Everything was in muted beiges and whites. The only oddity was the fact that Giada's chair was on rails in the floor. Those rails circled the recliner.

"It doesn't look so… medical-ly."

"Medical-ly?" She did not look at him as she typed on the computer.

"You know. All of this?" He gestured to the room and the recliner.

Giada turned and smiled a professional's smile. "The less you see, the less you worry. We try to make the whole experience as pleasant as possible." She patted the recliner. "C'mon. In you go."

Jackie climbed into the chair and settled down. After a moment's stiffness, the recliner warmed and softened, conforming to Jackie's shape. It made him feel like he was floating.

"Good?" Giada tapped something on her tablet.

"Good."

"Okay, Jackie. The first thing we're going to do is immobilize your head…"

Panic welled. "Wait! Aren't you going to put me to sleep or numb me or anything?"

She tilted her head. "No. You're going to be awake. You won't really feel time passing and you won't be in pain. Believe me, no one has ever hated this experience. It's okay to be nervous, but it's time to get this done."

Jackie knew she was telling him to get himself together and earn that $20,000. His mouth was too dry to speak. He nodded and tried to relax.

Giada resumed her practiced setup. "First, we're going to immobilize your head. This is vital to the process. It's going to tickle."

Something came out of the chair behind Jackie's head and cold lines of metal slid down the sides of his head and neck, molding themselves to every curve and bump. It did tickle, and threw a pleasant shiver down his spine.

"This is for the visual stimulation. You can keep your eyes open or closed."

A strip of metal about two inches high wrapped itself around his face at eye level. Jackie guessed it to be about an inch out from his nose. Right now, it was just a shimmery piece of metal. He saw Giada moving around him in a fluid motion and realized she must be riding the chair on rails.

"Keep your breathing relaxed. This is for audio stimulation."

As she spoke, part of the head of the chair cupped itself around his head; again, not touching. Jackie remembered something in the literature about the music being pumped directly into his ears.

"This is the VIT collar. It's going to be a touch cold at first."

VIT. Vitae Infusion and Transfer. The cold metal sliding around his throat made him tense up again. The panic welled even as he tried to keep control.

"Wiggle your toes."

Jackie obeyed, wiggling his toes as hard as he could. Distantly, he felt Giada's hand on his arm and something pressed to his mouth. Something. A straw?

"Here's some water. You okay?"

He drank, sucking down deep swallows of the ice cold water. The delicious sensation of cold traveled down his throat and chest to pool in his stomach. As the chill warmed, Jackie realized he was still wiggling his toes and stopped.

"Better?"

Jackie tried to nod and failed. "Yes. Thanks."

"No problem. Now, here's where the fun comes."

Feeling like his head was floating and his arms tingled, Jackie smiled, realizing Giada had pulled a fast one on him. The water had been drugged in some way. It was the only explanation for the sensation.

"Now, I want you to start counting out loud, backward from ten to zero."

"Okay." He took a breath. "Ten… nine… eight…"

"Begin visual and auditory harmonization."

The metal band in front of his eyes glowed and pulsed with multiple colors as one of his favorite songs blossomed in the middle of his head.

"Seven… six… five…"

"Begin glandular stimulation."

Jackie felt the hair on the back of his neck rise and shivered again.

"Three… two…"

"Begin magnetic alteration of the subject's cerebral field."

Different emotions washed over him: fear, love, hate, desire, apathy, contentment, and a myriad of everything in-between. He clenched his fists in an effort to control what was happening and to relax into it, not sure if this was how it was supposed to be.

"One… zero…"

"Begin the VIT process."

There was momentary pain on both sides of his neck, exploding into the best wet dream Jackie had ever had. Falling into light, everything he had once thought "felt good" paled in comparison to this… whatever this was.

"And there you go. Enjoy."

Giada's words were a whisper of silk amidst the light, sound, and sensation of everything. For the next thirty seconds—or three thousand hours, he couldn't be sure—Jackie was lost in the best waking dream he had never had. His heart raced, his muscles clenched, and he gasped for air. It was like the best runner's high mixed with the shock of his first orgasm. There was nothing but the light and the music and the tingle of pleasure all over his body.

"Wake up, Jack. Wake up. Your session is done."

"Don't worry about that, Jack. All boys do that during their session."

"One leg at a time. Good. Now the other one."

"I'm Alicia."

"Just hold onto me. Slow steps."

"Let me have the bag. It's okay. Everyone's always woozy."

"Alicia, your transition specialist."

"Apartment 215. See? That's your apartment... okay, let's just get you inside."

"I've put your aftercare instructions on your smart glasses."

"No, you want to sleep now. Lara's fine."

"I'm Alicia. I'm going to be helping you."

"Just remember to put on your smart glasses and follow the instructions. All of them. Then call me when you're better."

Waking was a combination of half-confused memory and pain. Jackie refused to open his eyes until he had sorted out some of what he remembered. The one thing he could fasten on was "smart glasses." Apparently, he had smart glasses now—something he'd lusted after for ages.

Opening his eyes wasn't as bad as he thought it would be. Everything seemed dim and slightly out of focus. He blinked a couple of times and cleared his head. Looking around, wincing at the pain in his neck, he saw he was in an unadorned but comfortable room: bed, desk, entertainment system, computer, end table. Smart glasses on the end table.

Sitting up in a sudden motion because it was real, everything was real, Jackie gasped in pain as bolts of agony shot through his body. He felt like he'd run a marathon and then was beaten as a reward. Every single muscle hurt in that way that said "you overdid it in a bad way, man."

Trembling in the pain, Jackie sat there until he was able to think again.

Then, with a slow, careful motion, he reached for the smart glasses. They were almost too heavy to pick up. Only his desire for them kept him from dropping the smart glasses before he could put them on.

A brunette woman's face popped up. "Hello, I'm Alicia Stanton. I'm your transition specialist. I hope you aren't feeling too bad. I've been told by other clients that you should feel like you've been run over by a truck. In any case, welcome to your new home. I have Lara situated and I've hooked her up with an education module and a curriculum, but we can go over that later. Right now, the most important thing is for you to take care of yourself."

She gestured to the right and a list popped up. "These are your aftercare instructions. They include mandatory supplements which, I'm told, taste awful but will make you feel better almost immediately. Since you are now awake, I've been notified and will schedule an appointment to see you tomorrow. Don't worry, I'll meet you in your apartment."

There was a blip and the calendar appointment popped up. That was when Jackie realized that he'd been non-functional for almost a day and a half. Fear for Lara surged and he stood, staggering. He grabbed the cane that had been left helpfully nearby.

Moving as fast as he could in the baby steps his body could manage, he left the bedroom and was struck by the most delicious scent. Jackie stood, stupefied, trying to identify it. Unable to, but swearing it smelled like bread, he stumbled down the hallway onto a scene he had thought he could only dream of.

The hallway opened up on a single room broken out into several areas: the kitchen area with a breakfast bar separating it from dining area, and an entertainment area that was separated from the rest by a long, curving couch. Lara sat at the dining room table, working on something on her digipaper. From where he stood, Jackie thought it was a math problem. Lara had her "concentration face" on as she used her stylus to work the problem out.

Something in the kitchen binged. Lara looked up. She didn't even see him as she hurried into the kitchen to pull a loaf of bread out of the oven. An oven. A real one. Jackie saw that Lara felt safe and carefree for the first time in her life, and he knew the pain he felt right now was worth it.

"Careful," he said when she touched the loaf and gasped at the pain.

Lara grinned. "Jackie!" She crashed into him for a tight hug. He couldn't stop his cry of pain and Lara pulled back, looking him over. She gave him the kind of once-over only a ten year old can give. "You look awful. Are you okay?"

Not willing to take away her joy, he smiled and nodded. "Just sore. You've got to be careful with me for the next couple of days." Months, maybe, he did not say. He knew that the average recovery time was four to eight weeks. Sometimes as much as twelve. That was why sessions were allowed only three times a year, four months apart. "How you doing?"

"I've got an education module. Math and science. Real math, not that stupid baby math. And books. Real books, look!" She pointed to a shelf of real paper books. "And bread. I baked bread. Well, I took it out of the freezer and put it in the oven and baked it. But… we have food. Good food, and books, and I have my own bedroom!"

Jackie stared at the small shelf of real books, surprised beyond expectation. He had expected the basics: a nice, small place with a few things to make it comfortable. Instead, they had a palace, their own bedrooms, a real kitchen, and… paper books, a luxury that he had never even dreamed of.

While he was looking at their good fortune, his smart glasses binged, indicating he had a call. It was from Technician Costa. "Hello."

"Hello Jack. I've got some wonderful news. But first, how are you feeling?"

He glanced at Lara, who was puttering in the kitchen, getting out stuff for the bread. "Oh, you know. Sore."

"That's normal. Just make sure you take your supplements with food. It may be tiring but you have to do it."

"Yeah." He sat at the dining room table and saw the digital paper with a news subscription. "What's this good news?"

"You're almost a perfect genetic match for one of our platinum level clients, and their session with you went so well they'd like to sign you to an exclusive contract for a year."

He frowned, idly swiping through the news pages. "What's that mean?"

"Well, it means several things. You'll get paid $25,000 a session. You'll have four sessions a year. You need to abstain from all drugs and alcohol for the year. Also, you'll need to have monthly exams here at the Bathory Clinic."

"Four sessions. But…"

"Yes, I know. In the case of the VIP contract, you'll essentially be an employee of the clinic. We'll give you menus and keep you healthy."

"How much time do I have to think about this?" Jackie's eyes fell on an article in the paper and he zoomed in on it, reading the first paragraph. Then he zoomed in on the candid picture of the dead body.

"You need to give me a verbal contract on this call. Our platinum client is most eager. We'll get the necessary documents in a day or two."

Lara came over and plopped a plate with a piece of warm bread slathered in butter on the low table in front of him. She had her own large hunk of bread, bit into it messily, and grinned a butter-smeared smile at him.

Too afraid to say no and lose what he saw in front of him, the decision was already made. "Yes. I'll do it."

"I'm so glad to hear that. We'll talk soon. Now, I've got some paperwork to set up and give to Alicia when she comes to see you. Talk to you later."

"Yeah. Bye."

Lara pointed to the zoomed-in photo in the newspaper. "Who's this?"

"Just a guy I met once." Jackie swiped the picture of the dead body and article about the tragic drug overdose death of Chaz Daly out of view and promised *he* would keep control. *He* would do better. But even as Jackie bit into that piece of heaven known as fresh-baked bread, the taste of it was like ashes compared to the feeling of a Bathory Clinic session.

I WILL ALWAYS REMEMBER THIS
story for a couple of reasons—beyond the fact that it is one of the few weird west stories I've written that was not set in my Mowry universe. Though, in retrospect, it probably could fit in quite nicely.

First, the editor of Westward Weird, Kerrie Hughes, hated the first version of this story. Hated it to pieces and told me so in an e-mail. Then said, "let's talk." I figured she was going to tell me never to submit to her again. Obviously, that's not what happened. The main thing she wanted me to do was move the story from a train to a Wild West carnival. Of course I said yes. Then I asked why, what was she looking for? I got the details and rewrote the story—the same basic plotline, just set in the carnival—and turned it in. Obviously, Kerrie liked it much better.

Second, this was my third pro sale and qualified me from shifting my SFWA membership from Affiliate to Active. Getting that Active membership was one of my big career milestones and allowed me to trade up for better, more ambitious goals.

SHOWDOWN AT HIGH MOON

"There's never enough, is there?" Mena asked with a sigh as she watched the night sky.

"Of course there will be. We'll have what we need," Will said. He stopped counting the money from their latest coach robbery and shifted around the low campfire to sit next to the love of his life. "We'll get married, go west, and claim our homestead." He pointed across the plains. "Out there is our future. There's a farm just waiting for us to come get it. Just as soon as we've got the seed money, we'll go."

She smiled. "All right. Then the 'Star-crossed Bandits' can disappear into legend, never to be heard from again."

He gave her a peck on the cheek. "That's my girl. I'm going to make all our dreams come true."

Mena Scott. Will Brogan. Wanted for robbery. We would speak with you.

As Mena sat up with a jerk, her gun already in her hand and looking for a target, she saw that Will had woken up in the same manner. Both squinted at the flashes of bright light twinkling at the edge of their camp, confused as the rising sun pulled shadows from the surrounding land.

Will Brogan. Mena Scott. We would speak with you. We mean you no harm.

The voice, without inflection, reminded Will of a Chinaman learning to speak English by rote. Within the flashing lights he saw things hovering on the edge of the camp, but not the silhouette of a lawman as expected. He blinked again. The things looked like bejeweled metal tea cup saucers.

"Will, it's them." Mena gestured to the flying things. "They're talking."

"I see that." He raised his voice at them. "Speak to us about what? And would you stop flashing the light in our eyes?"

Immediately, scores upon scores of the flying things stopped hovering and landed on the ground. One of them, almost the size of a soup bowl but as flat as the rest, landed just inside the camp. Not quite sure of what to point her gun at, Mena lowered her weapon and looked at the thing next to her foot. It was silver, edged with flickering jewels on its rim and adorned with a bronze, maybe gold, top that had an engraving on it. The engraving was something she recognized. "A scarab," she murmured to Will.

The thing within their camp began to hover again. It slowly rose to eye level.

Scarab is an acceptable classification, Mena Scott. We would speak of hiring you for a job.

Mena and Will looked at each other. She nodded to him, letting him take the lead. He lowered his revolver. "Just Will and Mena, if you please. Hire. For what?"

Mena and Will, you are wanted for multiple robberies. You are not wanted for murder. We would have something stolen. We would not have humans killed.

"What do you want us to steal?"

In the dirt between them, the Scarab projected the image of a poster advertising a traveling carnival called "The Wild West and Mystical Wonders Show." While they watched, the poster changed to another, showing some of the wonders to be displayed. It featured a painted woman with black hair wearing a simple white linen dress, holding a staff. At the top of the staff was a disk that looked a lot like the Scarab before them, only bigger.

We would have you rescue our queen.

"What? The woman?"

No. Our queen. Held by the woman.

Will shook his head and wondered if he was crazy. "All right. I see her. Just the staff. Shouldn't be that hard. What's the pay?"

Gold.

Will swallowed. "How much gold?"

Enough for your needs. We have watched you. Listened to you. You will have enough.

Will frowned. It sounded too good to be true. "What's the catch? What aren't you telling us? Why can't *you* go in and get her?"

Our queen is a captive. Our enemy watches. He keeps her from the light. She is weak without the power of the sun.

"Enemy?"

A foul creature that can morph into other biological entities.

"Pardon?"

The enemy is a shapeshifter like the legend of werewolves. He does it on command. He is in control. He looks human now but he is not human. We are longstanding enemies. Will you help us, Mena and Will?

Mena gave a slight nod to Will who said, "We will, but you've got to tell us more about the enemy, this shapeshifter."

During the next few hours, Will and Mena prepared themselves as they heard the story of a longstanding feud between a race of small creatures made of "circuits and light" and a war-like race of beings that could take on the shape of things around them but were, by and large, "hostile biological entities." One of these creatures, dubbed Shifters by Mena, had managed to capture the Scarabs' queen and had kept her in the dark ever since. What he wanted? The Scarabs to cede Earth to the Shifters so they could immediately colonize it.

Despite not understanding all the Scarab told them, Mena and Will agreed that this Shifter was bad news and needed to be dealt with—starting with the rescue of the Scarab queen.

After setting the Scarabs to wait for them about a mile away from the Wild West show, the pair went on ahead, pretending to be a couple of locals just looking for a good time. The whole thing was less of a Wild West show and more of a carnival, with its emphasis on the "Mystical Wonders" part of the traveling venue. Still, there was a lot to see and do outside of the tents. Though, the tents with their private shows of extinct creatures, weird animals, weirder humans, and other such wonders were a definite draw.

As they walked arm in arm through the dusty show, they saw a couple of the locals trying their hand at target practice for a prize. Easy enough for anyone who had had real practice with a rifle, but not so much for an average man, with his girl looking on. Just down the way was a strong man daring a slender farm boy to "ring the bell," and another hawker shouted for people to toss rings around the bottle tops—three rings gets a prize. It was all good fun as the summer dust puffed around everyone's feet.

In one outdoor ring, a pretty woman—who would be mistaken for a jilly by the cut of her short dress in another time and place—was doing some fancy trick riding on a horse, while a very old, tired-looking cowboy performed trick shot after trick shot in the ring next door. The man looked like he could do his routine in his sleep, and Mena wasn't certain he was actually awake while she watched.

As they strolled deeper into the tent aisles of the carnival, barkers from food tents, knick-knack displays, and private shows vied for their attention. Will allowed Mena to drag him over to the tent showing "Wonders from Around the World." He paid their two nickels, as did several other couples, and they entered the darkness of the tent with anticipation.

There were four exhibits inside, each showcasing a different part of the world: a Zulu warrior of Africa, several Mongols of Asia, a serpent-tamer of India, and, of course, the Egyptian queen. The Zulu warrior was interesting mostly because neither Mena nor Will had seen a man with such black skin before. There was little doubt that he was an actor, but the man played his part well. If they had not been on a job, Mena would have spent more time looking at him. The Mongols were loud Chinamen, and the serpent-tamer was fascinating with his lunging snake. The exhibits were worth the nickel.

The Egyptian queen was stretched out on a chaise lounge and was beautiful. She looked regal, bored, and hot. There was an Egyptian warrior fanning her with a giant fan made of leaves. Mena smiled at this man. Clearly not Egyptian but still playing the part well, he was a good-looking man. While she strolled ever nearer to him, she let Will examine the queen, and more importantly, the object of their quest.

"Our Egyptian beauty is available for a private showing, should you have the appropriate offerings for her," the barker murmured to Will as soon as Mena was out of earshot. "Assuming the gentleman is available."

"The gentleman is, and his sister seems to have an eye for the warrior."

The barker leered, "The business between the warrior and your sister is theirs alone. My business is with our queen." He tilted his head back towards the woman on the lounge. Will saw that her gown was suddenly that much more revealing.

"How... what sort of offering does our queen take?"

"Five."

Will considered. "Five if you let this showing be in here." He allowed his eyes to follow the lines of her curves greedily.

"Your wish is our command. Come back at sunset." The barker paused. "And I'm certain your sister will find the warrior loitering nearby then." The two men grinned at each other.

Mena said nothing while she examined the Egyptian exhibit. But she used every bit of her feminine wiles to let the Egyptian warrior know she was much more interested in him than in what she was looking at. By the time Will retrieved her, and the barker was ushering them out, she knew she had her target snared.

"Come, sister-dear. We'll be back later. Sunset."

Mena glanced coquettishly at the warrior and smiled as she left arm in arm with Will.

⚘

They returned to the tent just as the barker was ushering the last of the customers through the exit. He grinned at them, watching Mena saunter off around the back of the tent to where her assignation loitered, and then waved Will into the entrance of the tent. While the rest of the exhibit workers had ducked out the back, Will saw that heavier curtains were drawn around the Egyptian exhibit, mostly obscuring what was inside.

He steeled himself to fight the Shifter if he had to, while pretending to be nothing more than an eager gentleman ready for a good time with the Egyptian queen.

The barker stepped in-between he and the curtain. "I'll be out front. You have an hour. I'll holler when you have fifteen minutes left." He held out his hand for the money. As Will paid him, he added, "It's always polite to tip our queen for her graciousness."

"We'll see how gracious she is," Will said, and stepped around him. He waited at the curtain until the barker left the tent.

"Do I have a supplicant?" a heavy feminine voice called.

Will opened the curtain and stepped into the Egyptian exhibit. "You do, my queen."

Before him, on the chaise lounge, the queen lay, posing for him—nothing revealed, but everything intimated. Then she sat up. "Join me."

All around her were the false artifacts of a sideshow exhibit. Stepping to her, he saw the chipped paint revealing wood instead of bronze and the hurried stitching in all of the fabric in the ground covering, the fur throws and even in the queen's costume. He took one offered hand and kissed her knuckles. He smiled at her laughter. "I have a gift for you, if you'll allow it."

"Of course," the queen said, enjoying her role, and obviously used to such gestures.

Will went to one knee before her, reached into his bag and brought out a small bottle. "It's perfume. I hope you like it." He opened it and offered it to her.

She accepted it, delight clear on her face, and took a delicate sniff. The look of delight changed to something more neutral "I… it's very interesting." She put on a brave smile and inhaled again. "I…" She blinked several times and collapsed. He caught her and the bottle before either hit the floor. After arranging her on the lounge, he waved the bottle under her nose a few more times to make sure she was out.

Will stowed the bottle away and stood. Looking down at the pretty woman, he smiled. "Guess ether works on Shifters, too." He turned to the thing that really mattered and approached it with caution.

The Scarab queen was still in her box, standing on top of a pole that was supposed to be part of a staff. He saw that the box was simple to close and, as part of her capture, was probably locked in the dark at all times. The shadows within made her silver and bronze finish dull, lifeless. Even the jewels on her rim looked like paste within the box. He walked around the staff, careful not to knock over any of the set pieces, looking for security, but found none.

Coming back around, he shrugged and reached into the box for her. The Scarab queen came free without resistance. In the scant light inside the tent, he saw the scarab etching on her bronze plate. It was that much more intricate and beautiful than the etchings on any of the other Scarabs he had seen.

"Let's get you home," he said to her before sliding her into his pouch and slipping out the back of the tent.

Mena walked with her Egyptian warrior, keeping her head down in pretend shyness. He had not bothered to change out of his costume and makeup. Other workers from the Wild West and Mystical Wonders Show gave them a knowing look. Such traveling shows did a brisk trade in the flesh of locals.

"What's your name?" she asked as they reached the back part of the show campground where the carts and wagons for the workers were. This part of the campground was quiet despite its festooned wagons that made a half-circle around a central fire pit. She could imagine the nightly gatherings that happened here.

"They call me Olaf. It's Norse."

"Norse? A Norse name for an Egyptian man?"

"I can be many things, my lovely." He stopped at a large wooden wagon painted with the bright colors of the Wild West show. He opened the door and invited her in.

Once inside, she saw that a couple of people lived in this wagon. She turned to say something to him but he was on her, hungry and passionate, kissing her, his hands exploring. After allowing him to paw her, kissing down her neck, she pulled away. "Whew… slow down there. I don't need to be taken like a conquest, yet. Let me freshen up."

He chuckled, low in his throat. It was almost a growl of amusement. He bowed his head and moved past her to sit on a bunk—his, presumably—while she shifted closer to the door. From her reticule, she pulled a damp handkerchief and dabbed at her throat. Then she turned, allowing him to see her dab at the cleft of her cleavage with it.

"I have a new perfume. Would you like to smell it?" She came close and offered it to him.

He smiled and took a deep whiff of the handkerchief. "It's pungent, but I like it. It will smell good on you." He pulled her closer.

Mena laughed, dabbing it up on her cleavage again before pulling it away from her face. She could feel the ether working on her, and that was not what she wanted. Playfully, she dabbed it on him—his throat, his face—and he breathed deep of the ether again, showing no signs of being affected by it. She was wondering if she was going to have to go through with her part of this little ruse when two things happened: a noise sounded from a jewel on the wall she had previously thought was just decoration, and that jewel sparkled and flickered with many colors, just like the jewels on the Scarabs.

She stepped back, realizing that she and Will had guessed wrong. The fake Egyptian queen wasn't the alien Shifter; the fake warrior was. And she was in deep trouble if she did not escape now. Mena turned and got two steps toward the wagon door before something hot, strong, and pulsing wrapped itself around her throat and lower half of her face. She tried to scream and grab for something to fight the creature, but to no avail. He was just too strong.

Forced to face him, she saw his eyes were pure black, and the thing that held her was one of his arms, elongated into a tentacle of boneless flesh. "So," he said. "This is your game. I assumed you were here to rob me like some whore with a bit of ether but you and your *brother* are so much more, aren't you?" He shook her for emphasis. "I was going to let him rob Jane while I ate you, but he's escaped with my prize, hasn't he? Well, not for long."

Mena tried to pull back in revulsion as she saw a lump rising up Olaf's throat. The Shifter opened its mouth to reveal a large, fat bug, black as his eyes and gleaming like oil. Without a word, the bug flew out one of the wagon windows. "I'll have my prize back and then I'll eat you and the man both."

With that, he picked up the forgotten handkerchief and loosened his hold on her just enough for him to use Mena's own weapon against her.

✦

Will arrived at the waiting Scarabs and horses. He was unhappy that he had not seen Mena trailing behind. The plan had been to drug both of the carnies and get out as quickly as possible. Mena's absence meant something was wrong. However, with the Scarabs hovering around him, waiting to see their queen, he could not leave them in suspense.

As soon as the queen was out of the dark bag, her jewels began to glow with a faint gold light. The larger Scarab, the one who had hired them, hovered nearby.

She is free, but she needs the sun.

"You've waited this long. Tomorrow's another day."

No. The situation is still dangerous.

Suddenly, the smaller Scarabs descended upon Will and the queen. As each one alighted upon her in Will's hands, her jewels glowed a little brighter, and the small Scarab fell away and all but crashed to the ground in an ill-controlled fall.

"What are they doing?"

They are powering her.

Will looked at the ground, now littered with small Scarab bodies. "Are they dead?" He could not keep the horror out of his voice. In the dying light of setting sun, the Scarab bodies once again looked like teacup saucers abandoned in the sand.

No. Dormant. They will power up with the sun. I ask that you take them with us.

"Sure. As soon as Mena gets here."

Then the queen hovered on her own, and the other Scarabs moved back. She made no sound, but the lead Scarab approached and the two of them hovered in tandem.

"What's happening?"

The Scarab queen answered. *I am now informed of all that has occurred during my captivity. I thank you for your assistance.*

"You're welcome." While the queen had the same uninflected voice as the other Scarabs, Will could tell a difference between them, and yes, the queen's voice did sound almost female. "I just want Mena to get back soon."

Mena Scott. She is your queen.

"Yes. She's the queen of my heart and—"

His words were cut off at the sudden flurry of the still-hovering Scarabs. They surrounded something in the distance coming closer. He hoped it was Mena, but by the time he could actually see what it was, he knew it was not his wife-to-be. "What is it?"

The fat black bug issued a series of ear-piercing sounds. Then it turned and flew away into the night, toward the faint lights of the now-closed Wild West show.

The queen, who had remained at Will's side during this, spoke. *The enemy has captured your queen.*

"Mena!" He could not keep the anger or fear out of his voice.

It is demanding a prisoner exchange in the largest tent on the campground when the moon is at its apex.

Will looked at the Scarab queen, knowing that rescuing her had also been rescuing the planet. But at this moment, he did not care. He would give the queen back to make sure his Mena was safe.

If the prisoner exchange does not occur, the human female, Mena Scott, will be eaten.

He looked at the hovering Scarabs, knowing he could not force them to give up their queen again. Scowling, he looked at the moon. It would be hours before it was at its highest point. "I'm not letting that thing hurt her." He turned to his horse and grabbed his holsters.

What will you do, Will Brogan?

"Fight."

We will fight with you.

He looked back at the queen and gave her a grateful nod. "Then let's plan."

Mena woke with the smells of horseshit and ether warring for attention. She turned her head and groaned. Ether left a nasty headache, one she recognized—you had to test a tool before you used it. She looked around. She was lying on her side in the dirt inside a large tent at the edge of the center ring. The scent of horseshit came from the shovel lying next to her, used to remove the pungent waste after any show with animals.

"You better hope they come soon. I'm hungry and I *will* eat you alive."

She saw Olaf standing in the center of the ring. At his feet were at least five score of those horrific black bugs. The light was coming from a couple of smokeless lanterns placed on either side of the ring. She sat with some effort, still woozy from the effects of the ether, compounded by the fact that her hands were tied.

As she shifted toward the shovel, Olaf turned around and advanced; the carpet of oily blackness moved with him. "You will lie on the ground and do nothing or I will kill you right now." His voice rose to a shout and she threw herself back to the ground, curling up there. She did not have to feign her fear. "When this is done, you'd better pray to your gods that I kill you quickly."

As she hid her face from his distorted features—elongated jaw, too-large eyes and clawed hands—the overpowering smell of shovel told her that she had reached her goal. She waited until the Shifter and his retinue returned to his spot in the center of the ring. Then she risked shifting her wrists onto the shovel's edge.

Will was surprised and a little unnerved at the complete silence of the showground. Whatever hold the Shifter had on these people, he made sure that they were all tucked away in their tents and wagons. He took a breath, readied himself with a revolver in one hand and his saddlebag in the other. He stepped through the front flap of the main tent.

Inside, it was twilight dark. In the center of the ring illuminated by lamplight, a man stood with a patch of blackness at his feet. All of the risers were still in place, as if a ghost audience watched what was about to unfold. As Will got closer to the ring and its meager light, he saw two things: there was something very wrong with the man, and the blackness at his feet was moving.

Then he saw Mena lying at the other end of the ring, behind the Shifter. He cocked his gun.

"She isn't hurt. Just scared," Olaf said. "Have you come to rescue your dear *sister*?"

Will saw her faint movement and his heart was glad. *Just let me get her out alive*, he prayed. "You demanded the exchange." He lifted up the saddlebag.

"Toss the queen here. It's fine if she bounces. She's made of stern stuff."

He did, and everything seemed to happen at once. As soon as the saddlebag hit the ground in the middle of the sea of black bugs, a dozen Scarabs exploded from it and started shooting bursts of light in all directions. As random as the bursts seemed, each one hit a cluster of bugs, some still on the ground and most flying. Every bug hit stopped moving, lying where it was or falling out of the air.

In the middle was the Scarab who had hired Mena and Scott. That Scarab flew at Olaf, firing light bursts, one after another. Through the haze of black wings and light bursts, Will aimed his revolver and fired two shots.

Both struck, but only one struck true, taking out one of the Shifter's eyes. The other one grazed his forehead.

"My turn," Olaf said, and whipped an impossibly long tentacle at Will. It would have struck if another Scarab hadn't thrown itself in the way of the weapon. Will dodged left and then right. Every tentacle that whipped out at him ended up with a Scarab embedded in it that then exploded like a small stick of dynamite.

The next two shots Will took were to Olaf's chest. These were accompanied by much larger bursts of light from the Scarab queen, who had come out from hiding. Olaf roared at the sight of her and turned his attacks that way, while shrugging off the wounds the bullets made in his flesh. More Scarabs sacrificed themselves to protect their queen, and Will knew he had only two shots left to hit the brain in the chest of the monster or to blind it. He decided to go for the kill and fired.

Both shots hit, but did nothing to slow the Shifter down.

The Shifter's tentacles captured the Scarab queen, and it roared again in triumph. By this time, it could barely be called a man. Opening its mouth to a prodigious size, it looked as if it were about to swallow the Scarab queen whole when it suddenly stilled, with its chest area pushed forward and a surprised look of real pain on its face. As its tentacles let go of the queen, it looked down with its remaining eye and saw the slim edge of metal poking out of its chest.

"My turn," Mena said and gave another hard thrust on the shovel she had used to penetrate the Shifter. Half of the shovel head came out the front of its chest. What was left of the creature's face collapsed in on itself, and the body fell over as Mena released the shovel. Will and Mena watched in disgust as the Shifter disintegrated into a noxious goo.

We need to leave, the queen said. She only had eight Scarabs left. All of them hovered in a protective pattern around her.

Mena ran to Will who kissed her once, hard and glad, before turning and leaving with the Scarabs.

As the sun rose over their small camp, the Scarabs that had sacrificed their energy for their queen, and those who had gone into battle began to glow in the morning's light. Soon they were hovering about the queen while Mena and Will sat close together.

"I'm sorry to see that your lead guy didn't make it," Will said.

He will be rebuilt. His core programming has been saved.

"Will we have to deal with any more Shifters?" Mena asked.

After a pause, the queen spoke. *I do not believe so. There are no records of other Shifters on this planet. We will investigate further as a matter of caution.*

They watched as the Scarabs formed up into orderly lines. The queen spoke again. *Will Brogan, lay your coat on the ground.*

Mena and Will looked at each other. She shrugged as Will pulled his duster from his saddle and laid it out on the ground with the lining toward the sky.

Mena Scott and Will Brogan, you were offered gold as payment for rescuing me. We do not have the gold we promised but we know where it is.

The queen then flashed a bright light onto the lining of the coat. When they blinked the spots out of their eyes, they saw that some sort of map had been drawn there.

There should be a sufficient amount of gold at this location for your needs. We thank you. If our paths cross again, may they be in good times.

With that, the Scarab queen rose high in the sky and moved faster than the eye could follow, toward the rising sun. The rest of the Scarabs followed, twinkling briefly before they disappeared.

"Well, I'll be… it's a treasure map." Will knelt to examine his coat.

"No one's going to believe this."

"They don't have to."

Mena smiled at him. "I guess another adventure or two can't hurt before we find our homestead."

Will stood and pulled her to him. "Not as long as I'm with you. That's homestead enough for me."

THIS IS AN ORIGINAL KEMBER EMPIRE *story, not previously published. This is for everyone who bought this collection. I wrote this as gender and race neutral as I could. The reader doesn't know the soldier's gender until almost the very last line of the story. The reader doesn't know the soldier's race— except for the one they decide to picture. I wanted to write a story that any soldier, or any soldier's loved one, could identify with. In this day and age of war, gender controversy, and discrimination, I wanted to tell a* human *story about a soldier missing home, a soldier doing their duty, a soldier dying in the line of fire. It is tangentially linked to "M.O.V.E." and comes later in the timeline.*

FOUND ON THE BODY OF A SOLDIER
(A Kember Empire Story)

[Transcript begins.]
5042.86.04 14:25

...and I don't want my last words to be "Tell my husband and my wife I love them." I want you both to know, right now, that I love you, and the kids, and the house, and our life together. I don't want you guys to doubt this for even one second of my time away.

Sorry to get maudlin. It's just something I've been thinking about. You know? Being deployed on the frontlines is hard. For us and for you. I'm not even sure why we got into a conversation about a guardsman's last words. I suppose because we're about to hit the hot war. I mean, I'm glad we're going. [Redacted] is a bad place to be. But, where we're going, I think it's going to be worse. I suspect we're going to be fighting in the middle of a charge.

Hard to do when you're on a spaceship. But I think once the flyboys are done with their run, me and my guardsman squad will be doing the grunt work of taking the capital city.

Don't mind me. I'm just complaining to complain, we all knew what I was signing up for.

[Knock on the door.]

"A word, Guardsman?"

"Uh, yes, Commander. Right away."

"My office."

"Yes, Commander."

[Closing of the door.]

Gotta go. Hope I'm not in trouble. Can't think of anything I've done to get the CO's attention. But you never know. I'd lose my head if it wasn't attached… or this recorder if it wasn't hanging around my neck along with my ID chit.

I'll finish this as soon as I can and then send it off to you. Love you lots.

5042.86.04 17:07

Hello again. You will *never* guess what the Commander needed. You remember Natara? My niece from Armanthe? Turns out she was on her M.O.V.E. on Space Station Killingsworth on the border of the Epiet system when the Epiets tried to expand into our territory by amassing a war fleet right there at the edge of the station's territory. It was an unsanctioned maneuver. We didn't react so well—as you might imagine.

But, get this. It was feint. The damn Epiets were using the war fleet as a distraction while a small sabotage ship got in and tried to poison Hydroponics. Somehow, I'm not sure how, and it sounds like Command doesn't know how, but Natara and another cadet were there and stopped it. They're going to give her a medal. Get that. Not even out of the Academy, and my niece has a medal.

The Commander got the word and realized that I'm the closest relative. There's half a chance that I'm going to be there for the ceremony. Assuming I live through this next skirmish. Which I should. Because I'm me and I'm that good.

That was the other thing the Commander mentioned to me. We're going into a communications blackout. Nothing in. Nothing out. Which means this communiqué home isn't going to be sent for a few days. Which means it'll be extra-long since I'll have a few more days before we're back on the grid.

Good night for now, my loves.

5042.86.06 24:26

We've arrived at our destination. It's classified and all that. So, no specific details. However, being a grunt on the frontlines brings with it a certain similarity everywhere you go. It always sucks. The accommodations are just as bad as usual: plastisteel, cold water, cots, and a Mess tent with barely eatable food. Just like home.

[Laughter.]

I jest. The food is pretty good. I suppose when you have to feed several thousand guardsmen fighting the old fashioned way—with overwhelming forces and bad attitudes—you need to keep them in fighting shape. Which means decent enough food. Everything else is lacking, of course. No real entertainment to speak of, unless you want to count gambling away latrine duty. It's a damn good thing I'm good at cards... which I have you two to thank for, of course.

To give you an idea of my day, now that the camp is set up, we follow a pretty strict routine. Up at too damn early, food, daily briefing, then duty mixed with patrols. The patrol schedule is the only thing that'll mix things up until the fighting starts. It's randomly assigned, and the patrol routes change daily. It keeps those watching us on edge.

And, yes, we're watched. How can we not be? We're set up just outside the capital city, getting ready to set the damn place on fire. Be a guardsman, travel to exotic places, meet new people and kill the shit out of them. I understand why we're doing what we're doing, but on the ground it's harder to get the overall perspective.

I mean, this city, its fucking gorgeous. All white stone and pillars. At least parts of it are. We're up high. Probably so we can bomb the hell out of those buildings. I'm sure the prettiest one, the one with gardens, is the palace. I hope, I really hope, that we leave it intact. It's got the look of age. But someone designed the city in concentric rings. You can see it from up high. Most of the rings are walking paths, but there are a couple of main vehicle streets.

Probably going to use them during the fighting.

Mostly, I hope that the leaders see us up here and decide it's better for the city and the people to surrender. There's no way they can win now.

But that's never what happens. Leaders don't care about people. They care about ideas. Ideas and personal principles.

And on that happy note, I've gotta go. Patrol duty with Certic. You remember him. Orange and red with the gem thing, uh, *dusamez,* in his chest and a face only a blind mother could love, but a heart as big as a battle cruiser. We volunteered for this patrol together because we're both masochistic. Or something. Actually, I just wanted an excuse to see the stars at night. You know how I like to look at foreign skies.

I love you all. Kiss the baby for me.

5042.86.07 11:01

Before I say anything else, per our family agreement, I am *fine*. A little bruised up but fine. I promise. I've gotten worse while roughhousing with the kids.

Last time I recorded something for you, I told you I was going on patrol with Guardsman 3rd Class Certic, The damn Erdant got himself killed. There wasn't anything I could do about it.

[Long pause.]

May the Empress bless Certic, but there was nothing honorable in the way he died. Nothing at all. We were on the end of our patrol and he saw something that interested him. I think it was a flower. I don't know. I wasn't paying that much attention to him. I was watching the valley, looking for danger. I didn't know it was right next to me until the explosive went off and I was thrown meters away.

Time's funny when you're panicked and your fellow soldier is screaming for help and those screams are getting weaker with each heartbeat. I don't even know how I got to his side, but I was there.

His blood was black. I never wanted to know that Erdant blood is black.

His legs and one arm were missing, but he was still alive. I called for help but I knew—*knew*—that he wasn't going to make it. He knew it, too. I held him, telling him it would be okay. That he didn't have permission to die. He grabbed my hand and pulled it to the gem thing in his chest. He made me promise to take it to his home world, to his Memorykeeper. He was so strong, he wouldn't let me pull my hand away from his chest and that bloody gem. He made me promise. So, I did.

He died in my arms, bleeding black blood everywhere, and that gem… that *dusamez* … came off in my hand.

That's how they found me, cradling Certic in my arms and holding his gem in my hand.

I've been debriefed and I'm required to speak to someone about this. The Guard Commander took the gem and promised me it would go home with his things. Told me I did as well as could be expected and that Certic's family would be especially grateful for the *dusamez*.

[Long pause.]

I know what I signed up for. I'm a soldier; a Guardsman of the Empress's Guard. I know why I'm fighting, why I'm risking my life. But, this was bad. Real bad. And I'm wondering why I'm still alive.

[Long pause.]

I just wish I knew what drew his attention so much that he missed the fact that it was a trap.

5042.86.08 15:36

This planet just gets worse and worse, loves. It makes me miss every last one of you all the more. The valley below has a weapon we've never seen before.

[Redacted: 351 words.]

We've got a way to combat it now, but it was a *bad* few hours.

It's been a hell of a couple of days. But, that's life in the military. No new deaths since yesterday. Later tonight we're going to have a small wake for Certic. The Mess gave us some fruit from his home world to eat in his remembrance. It's a small thing, but it's all we have right now: rituals and hope.

5042.86.08 23:44

Looks like we're in for a night mission. Don't know what. Just know I've been summoned. Guess we're going to go do what grunts do: kill the bad guy and save the day so the officers can take credit.

I just wish this communications quarantine was over. You guys are going to have a book by the time you get this comm. I suppose you could listen to each entry one day at a time. It would be almost like I was there.

Just wanted to say that I love you guys and I miss you.

5042.86.10 01:11

We've done what we needed to do for the moment and I'm exhausted. It's been a couple of days of pretty much non-stop fighting—the archaic kind of trench warfare mixed with building-to-building clearing.

So many prisoners of war. So many civilians. The civilians were released, of course, in an orderly fashion. The soldiers, the prisoners of war, are now in a modified lockup. They fought so hard, but once they became prisoners they just… stopped. Every last one of them—male, female, intersex—it didn't matter. It's a cultural thing. They even presented prisoner leaders… and prisoner sacrifices.

Sacrifices. Can you believe that? What kind of messed-up culture has built-in prisoner sacrifices? It makes me heartsick to know that they expect—*expect*—us to murder two percent of all prisoners automatically. Worse… it means they're going to murder two percent of our people they take as prisoners of war, and there's nothing we can do about it.

[Long pause.]

It makes sense in a sick sort of way, though. The price of war hurts. People die. I guess this is one way this planet keeps civil war at bay. Are you willing to sacrifice so many people? Is your cause so great?

It makes me wonder why they decided it was worth losing two percent of their world to attack Gamma IV. Was it a decision they did as a whole people or did—

[Sounds of an airstrike, explosions, and stone breaking.]

5042.86.10 02:59

I'm hit. I thought I got out. I thought I escaped. I'm hit. I love you Drellen. I love you Tamlyn. It's the Hour of the Wolf. I see the path. I… I love you. I love you. Never forget... never...

[Transcript ENDS.]

5042.87.09
From: Guard Commander Crusett
To: Group Family Seasarone

                Announcement of the Honored Dead

Dear Tamlyn and Drellen Seasarone,

We regret to inform you the Guardsman 2nd Class Lyric Seasarone was killed in battle at 0300 on the Morning of 5042.86.10 while an enemy force shelled the temporary military base stationed in the city of Bavury, on the plant Delta III in the Hephaestus System. Guardsman Seasarone died a hero, rescuing not only several squads of soldiers, but freeing prisoners of war who were trapped.

Attached to this *Announcement of the Honored Dead* is the transcript of Guardsman Seasarone's last intended communiqué. I regret that, due to the damaged device, and the classified nature of some of information in the communiqué, we are only able to provide a transcript of Guardsman Seasarone's last words to her family.

Sincerely,
Commander Eolian
Guard Commander Eolian
Infantry Commander, Hephaestus System

I'VE ALWAYS BEEN FASCINATED WITH
the space western and wondered if the early days of space colonization really will be like the Wild West, the land grabs from the days of yore, and the return to the attitudes of the past. I think the idea has merit. Thus, I set "Dust Angels" in a rough-and-tumble colony on the edge. At least, the historical parts of it. When I wrote this story for Beyond the Sun, *I wanted to explore the idea of a first contact situation where the aliens were so alien that they would seem monstrous, and communication would appear impossible. I think that's what will happen. I also believe that the breakthrough will be a painful accident but worth the cost. Humans are quick to judge, fight, and condemn.*

DUST ANGELS

Dac smiled a brave smile at Ken, then closed the stockroom door with a finality that reminded her that this room, this safe haven, could also be their tomb. She heard her husband riveting the boards in place as she turned and saw twelve sets of excited, terrified eyes watching her.

There should be more, she thought. Then shook her head of iron-gray hair. The rest would be hidden in other homes. She could not protect them all. However, looking at the children before her made her realize how frightened they were, and how much they needed her to provide a safe haven in the storm. "Look at you. Snuggled down like it was story time."

"We get a story, don't we, Dac? Momma promised."

That was Sho Whelan with his ginger hair and almond-shaped dark eyes. The youngest here at five.

Dac nodded. "Of course." She stepped through, weaving her way through the cluttered room of shelves and makeshift beds to the rocking chair that the children had automatically left empty. "But today's story will be special."

"Why?"

The rumble of something exploding too near for comfort silenced the room. Much of the excitement disappeared in the growing fear of what could happen. Dac turned in a flamboyant arc to get the children's attention back on her and sat.

"Because this story is true." Dac settled into the old rocking chair, a relic from another world, and put the pulse rifle to the side—within reach but a little out of the way. She held up her hand to forestall the next question bubbling up. The children were polite and well-mannered, but it was an extraordinary time, and tempers ran hot.

"When we came to New Montana on one of the first colony ships, our town was simply called 'Haven.' Nothing more. Nothing less." She watched Sho's face screw up in confusion and glanced to the other children. They knew where this was going. Every child over the age of five knew… and still they leaned forward, eyes bright.

"But…" Sho stopped himself and looked around at the other children, knowing that sometimes his questions upset them.

Dac smiled. "Why is the town called 'Angels Haven' now? That is what this story is about." She raised her gloved hand. "And how I got this."

Sho's eyes widened as he stared at That Which Should Never Be Mentioned.

"Are you ready?"

Again, something either hit the ground with tremendous force or landed too close for comfort. The ground rocked with a roaring sound from the north. Dac kept her face as neutral as possible and continued on without waiting for an answer. "This is the story of the Dust Angels and how they came to be. The first thing you need to know is that my name wasn't always Dac. It was Elsa…"

Haven, for all its hardship, was a godsend. The years on the colony ship had taken their toll. Far too many people died from illness in the close quarters. More became insane. We need fresh air and sunlight or we die. Just like all living things. Of course, I was born on the colony ship. I didn't see sunlight until we left the safety of our quarters. Mom being pregnant with me is what got my parents on the ship to begin with.

When we landed, New Montana was in the last stages of terraforming. Ships towing asteroids of ice were still months and months away. There was no Lake Degrasse or Lake Tyson. The polar icecaps were barely a blip on the screen. Those came later. When they did, it saved the planet from failure.

Did you know, once it was a crime to waste water of any type? It was sacred. First offense, imprisonment and hard labor. Second offense… exile.

We only had three ways to get it: a protected water table deep in the ground, the recyclers from the colony ship, and moisture farms. The protected water tasted the best. I was a little girl, just older than you, Sho, and my main chore was to collect water from the well. It was a cranky old thing with a pneumatic pump. I just had to make it work with a bit of sweat and quiet swearing. You know how stiff pumps get, even when they're powered.

Haven wasn't like it is now. There was no grass or trees or bushes. It was miles and miles of dirt, dust, and rock. I would see whirlwinds of dust called "dust devils" by my parents. I never really agreed with the term. They didn't look evil to me. They looked like the wind playing in the dirt. We don't get them anymore. Not since the lakes were created and integrated into the terraforming.

One day something fell from space. A meteorite, we thought. Not unheard-of and, despite the light in the sky, the explosion wasn't so bad. It didn't really hurt the buildings. Then again, plastisteel is awful hard to hurt. The thing it did do was break the recycler, from all the ground shaking.

This was somewhere between devastating and a catastrophe. Everyone had to ration water more than before. No showers. No washing dishes unless it was with third-use water. And, besides drinking water, the crops got the most of it. Or we would've starved. It was hard. The land was hot, hard, and thirsty. It made all of us like it.

Suddenly, water carrying was so much more important. I didn't realize how important until the Dust Angels came. We didn't know what they were… and they didn't know what we were.

My parents were worried about the water. That much was obvious even back then. Would we have enough for the animals? Would we have enough for the crops? Would we survive? Every colonist knows that a newly terraformed planet is a risk and a challenge. The rewards of land, space, a place to call your own, meant the danger of living on the edge for decades.

Things got worse when the animals began to die. My brother, Paul, found the first of the dead animals. You wouldn't think those big steers with their horns and bad tempers could die. They could. They did. I found out about it by overhearing my parents talk in hushed tones of terror.

Is there anything more interesting than something that frightens your parents? I see those looks. Of course not.

Danger or no, we all still had chores to do. My water carrying doubled. I was bringing all of the water in from the pump. Why the pump wasn't closer to the house, I didn't know. But at the time, if it hadn't been so far away, I probably wouldn't have found out what was killing the herd.

I first saw it while I was headed out for water. I thought it was a dust devil. A big one. But it didn't move with the wind. So, I followed it, watching. That's when I saw the eyes. They looked like glossy stones against the dirt. Then I saw it go to the grazing pasture. The herd ran from it, but one of the smaller females wasn't fast enough. The dust devil landed on her and next thing I knew, the cow was dead and the dust devil looked fainter… but redder.

It was tinged red with the cow's blood and every other fluid in her.

I dropped my buckets and ran home.

Lord help me, I told my parents what I'd seen. I didn't know what was going to happen. If I had… No. That's times past. That door can't ever be closed. My father grabbed his pulse rifle and my brother, Nels, came with him. I showed them where it happened. They sent me home with the water. I didn't stay home. I had to go get more water. Or so I told myself.

Really, I just wanted to see.

What I saw was my brother murdered before my eyes. What I saw was a dust devil become a blood devil, filled with my brother's lifeblood. What I felt was terror and sadness. I wanted to know why. So I followed it. I kept the water carrier with me. I thought I would be able to fend off the dust devil with those heavy buckets.

I followed that dust devil all the way back to where the meteor had struck. I watched it hover above the unfamiliar ball of metal and rock in a hole far shallower than I thought it should be. I didn't know what meteors looked like. I didn't know I was looking at a spaceship. Not at first.

But then I saw the dust devil rain blood down upon the ship and, while I watched, the rock melted away and the metal sphere healed itself and the dust devil became something more. A whirlwind of glittering wind. Things clicked over in my mind.

That's when it occurred to me that perhaps the dust devil wasn't a monster. Maybe it was an alien and it just needed water. Water was so precious. And I had two buckets with me. I gathered my courage to pick up one of the buckets from the harness and bring it over to the hole. I faced the heat of the earth, and my fear, and poured the water into the hole.

The alien sensed it and rushed over to the water, sucking it all up from the ground. While it rained water on the metal sphere, I hurried back to the other bucket and picked it up. When I turned around, the alien was there. Right there. I froze. I didn't know what else to do. I closed my eyes and waited to die.

Instead, the bucket got lighter. I opened my eyes and saw the alien was clear again. It was so pretty, and I was so young. I did what most children do: I tried to catch one of the sparkles. Instead the alien caught me; caught my hand; caught my mind. Because, as it had filled itself with the water in my bucket, its primary need was taken care of. Its secondary need came forward—the need to know the land.

While my brother was being killed, my father was searching the hills for the monster we knew was out there. That was how he found me. One hand holding a bucket. One hand stuck in an alien made of wind and jeweled eyes. I know this because I was seeing through the alien's eyes. I begged with all my heart for it to spare my father. I could feel its thoughts, so different from my own. But there was one thing that it understood—family.

Even as my father ran at it, futilely shooting it with the pulse rifle, it understood that there was more to this planet than it had first known. It had not seen us as sentient... or even living. The whole time my father railed at it, punching the wind, trying to free me from its grasp, the alien learned from me. It learned my fear and sorrow. It learned it had killed one of my family. It learned that we communicated in a different way than it did.

Then, as my father fell to his knees and begged the alien to spare my life, I felt the first touches of direct communication. The request to use my voice, because it had none. I agreed. I didn't know what else to do. I'll remember until my dying day what those first six words were: "Sorrow. Apologies. Mistake. Water needed. Please." I repeated this three times.

That was it. When the alien used my voice, my eyes glowed with its light. My father stopped his begging and listened. His only answer was to ask it to let me go. The alien did, finally understanding what Father wanted. When it did, it retreated to its ship. I fainted.

When I woke up, I was back at the house, in bed. My hand was bandaged up. I couldn't see or feel it. Not at first. Then I remembered what had happened. And I remembered so much more of what I understood from the alien. I knew I needed to tell my parents.

Half of Haven seemed to be in my house. They were all arguing about what to do. Most wanted to destroy the metal sphere. Father was of two minds. It had killed Nels, but it had let me go. When I came out of my room, they wanted to push me back in. I fought them. The aliens—the dust angels as I had started to think of them—needed our help. The dust angel was horrified at killing another sentient creature. It had not met one like us before.

It was Mother who made everyone listen to me. The alien had let me go. It hadn't hurt me that much. It had learned from me. The alien needed water, and then it would leave again.

But where to get the water? No one knew how much water it needed. And no one knew what would happen if it didn't get it. But we needed water to survive. It was a problem the colonists had never faced: a new alien species and a need for the same resource of water. No matter what happened, we were on our own.

While they were arguing, I slipped out of the house. I felt the dust angel calling to me. I thought enough ahead to bring out a pitcher of water with me. I was in the yard with the dust angel when my parents discovered me gone. We waited for the colonists to discover us out in the front yard. While we did, I tried to explain the problem with the water. How rare and precious it was. The dust angel seemed to understand and was still sorry about the death it had caused.

Once everyone found me and the dust angel, I let it use my voice again. There was a conversation, but this was a long time ago. Decades. Mostly I remember them talking about the water and how much was needed. Father asked about Nels, and the dust angel offered a life for a life. Its life in particular.

It wasn't a mistake that I had been generous with the dust angel to begin with. My parents refused to take the life of the dust angel. It's because of my parents' compassion that Angels Haven still stands. In the end, the colonists agreed to share the water. It would be tough on both sides, but it didn't need to be one or the other. No one had to die for the other to live. Resources could be shared, and that is the way we've lived ever since.

Dac's voice was soft as she told the tale of Angels Haven. She only raised it when she had to; when the fighting got too loud or when the bombardment came too close. New Montana was a fertile and valuable planet—one worth fighting for.

"Sho, bring me the water." She watched while the ginger-haired child did as she bid. He brought her the sealed pitcher. She accepted it with both hands, knowing that soon her left hand would be useless again, and put it on the box next to her. Watching the excitement rekindled in the children's eyes, she put her hand to the pouch on the long thong around her neck. It was something she never took off. The older kids knew what was coming.

"You know that in times of real danger… the kind of danger that we of Angels Haven cannot face alone, we go to ground. You've heard us speak of it. We did it when the UA came. We did again when the Corporation came. You weren't alive then, but you've heard tell of it."

Bright eyed and awed, Sho could only nod.

"Now, I'll show you why." Dac opened the beaded bag and poured a single clear gem from it. It was five centimeters in diameter and gleamed with an inner light that shimmered like ice crystals. "This came from the dust angel. After my parents refused to take its life, when it understood what my parents thought it was offering, it decided to stay and protect Haven from all comers. It gave itself to the planet because it took from the family, my family. It exchanged its life with its people to protect us. This is only one of the reasons we leave a bucket of water outside each night."

While she spoke, she let the beaded bag fall into her lap. Holding the gem in her good hand, Dac pulled the glove off her other hand, revealing the desiccated flesh. She held that hand up for everyone to see. She held it there for a moment, letting curious eyes drink in what had been hidden for so long. She knew it looked dead, mummified. The sight no longer horrified her. The glove was to protect her fragile skin.

"This is the hand I first touched the dust angel with. It didn't know what it was doing would hurt me. I didn't know what it was doing would allow us to communicate."

She looked at Sho. "Dac isn't a name. It's a title: Dust Angel Caller. With this hand, I can talk with our guardian." She paused and looked at each child in turn. "Eventually, someone will need to take my place. It is a small sacrifice for something so important to our community." She was pleased to see that more than half of the children, some her grandchildren, still looked her in the eye.

Dac put the gem into her withered hand and clenched her fingers around it. There was still pain, but it was better than the forthcoming numbness. She dipped her hand with the gem into the water and closed her eyes. When she pulled her hand out again, a small glittering whirlwind rose out of the gemstone.

Dac opened her eyes and light shone out. "The family heard my call. They come. They are here now. Heed. You are protected. The pact is upheld." She was vaguely aware of the gasps of surprise and awe from her charges.

Dac closed her hand and her eyes. "Thank you, dust angel. The pact is upheld." She put the gem back into the beaded bag as one of the older children took the empty pitcher before it fell from Dac's lap. Already the numbness spread through her hand. There was nothing she could do about it. Perhaps in a year she would have limited use of it again.

The silence of the storage room echoed the sudden silence outside. The dust angels were doing their work. Soon Ken would free them from this room and every sacrifice made would be worth it.

A light touch to her withered hand—felt more as a pressure than anything else—made Dac open her eyes. Sho was there, stroking her deadened flesh, looking curious. "Does it hurt?"

"Only for a little bit. Then it doesn't hurt at all. Not anymore." She spoke the lie with a smile, knowing one of the children listening would need to take her place soon.

LIVING IN THE PACIFIC NORTHWEST

with its mercurial, cloudy, rainy weather, it's easy to see the supernatural in the mist, darting through the back alleys of Seattle. The Fremont Troll has been an object of fascination for decades. The first time I saw it in person, Apocalypse Girl poked her head up and believed that it was a real spirit, bound into the concrete body of a troll under the Aurora Bridge. If you get the chance to come to Seattle, make sure you go to Fremont and visit the Fremont Troll.

He's a kind soul who appreciates the company.

THE LOVE OF A TROLL ON A MID-WINTER'S NIGHT

Stevie broke one of the cardinal rules of being an Ave Rat—show no fear or weakness. It was hard to look tough when you were trembling like a lamb in the cold of a Seattle winter night. Leather may look good, may turn knives away and blunt punches, but it did nothing for the biting wind that howled down University Avenue at three in the morning.

He was lucky, though. It wasn't snowing now, and most of the old snow had melted into dirty clumps in the gutters. That didn't stop it from being bone-chillingly cold. The rare lack of clouds made it colder. There was nothing to keep in the city's heat. Stevie huddled deeper into his scuffed jacket and thrift store scarf as he headed up the street past his favorite comic book store.

At this time of night, nothing was open and buses were rare. Still his feet took him toward the Wallingford Boys and Girls Club. He knew it wasn't open either, but there might be something worth eating in the trash at Bizarro's, the restaurant next door. He couldn't remember if they locked up their trash, though. The cold wouldn't let him think, and his belly was willing to chance it because he had to keep walking. To stop was death. And he had no other place to go.

Stevie grinned at himself at just how melodramatic that sounded in his head. "I'm not going to die." The words were supposed to come out tough and brave. They sounded like begging, to his numb ears. His brief good humor disappeared and he eyed the apartments and businesses on either side of him.

There was no welcome to be seen. No lights beyond the streetlamps. Despite the rows of buildings, he felt more alone than ever and hurried his pace back into familiar territory. None of his friends would talk to him after the fight with Joe; a fight he didn't want to think about. It was good to move fast. It warmed the blood and body. It promised success at the end of the journey.

But there was no success for Stevie. Not at the dark and cold Boys and Girls Club or Bizarro's—without an unlocked dumpster in sight. The lack of an accessible dumpster killed what was left of his hope. His stomach growled in protest, and tears stung his eyes. He rubbed the tears away with vicious swipes of his cold, shaking hands. He clenched them into fists, wanting to hit something, anything, but there was nothing safe to vent his despair on.

For a moment, Stevie didn't know what to do or where to go. He wandered until he met Stone Way and had his answer: he would go to his only real friend in this city. At least there, under the Aurora Bridge, there was a chance for warmth and to get out of the wind. Maybe there'd be others and they'd share their food. He might have to pay for it in one way or another, but sometimes you did what you had to do to survive.

The decision made, Stevie stopped looking up at the rare passing car, stopped looking for an opportunity that did not exist. It was a short mile to the Fremont Troll and he knew every step by heart. The right turn onto North 36th felt like the home stretch in a race against time.

Once he arrived, a quick walk up and around the Troll told him he was alone. Stevie sighed and stared up at the tall stone figure. Under its beard, he thought the Troll was smiling. Stevie was relieved to feel the relative heat of the area. He had been right. At least he'd be warm tonight. His stomach could deal with its hunger until the morning. He'd go begging for food then. Someone would feed him. Someone usually did. Even if it was one of the baristas out back of the coffee shop on 15th. Stale pastries were still sweet.

Sitting on the Troll's large right hand, he sighed. "I don't know what to do anymore. It's been tough lately. Too cold. Too hungry. Almost got sent to Juvie. Can't go home—and you know why not." He hung his head and lied to himself. "Not that I want to go home."

Most of the time, when he talked to the Troll, it was just mundane stuff. Not this heavy shit he was carrying around. The months on the Ave had hardened him, made him appreciate what was really important. This was his first winter in Seattle, and damned if he wanted to go through another one this unprepared.

"I had a fight with Joe. He said I took stuff from him… and maybe I did. But he didn't need it. Not like me." Stevie's words were a whisper of regret. Then his stomach grumbled loud, almost echoing under the bridge. "I'm just so fucking *hungry*."

The words out of his mouth broke the dam holding back his emotions. He buried his face in his hands and shook, muffling his sorrow, fear, and need. The creaking of rock brought Stevie back to himself. His hands stopped in mid-wipe as he saw what had made the noise: the fingers of the Troll's left hand had uncurled from their possessive grip on the VW Bug.

While Stevie watched, the door of the decades-old car swung open, inviting him in. Stevie looked up at the Troll's face and a saw a real smile where only stone had been before. The hubcap eye glistened with icy tears. The Troll nodded slowly in the direction of the car. Stevie saw that the Bug's interior was plush and warm-looking, and he smelled hot food.

Stevie rubbed his eyes and wondered if he was having the weirdest acid flashback ever. He could have sworn that he'd read the VW Bug had been filled in with cement to keep "bums" from sleeping inside it and "destroying the artwork." He shoved the thought away as he walked to the VW Bug, ducking under the Troll's outstretched fingers. Warmth and comfort radiated from the car's interior. He looked up at the Troll's face again. "For me?"

For you. For me. We need each other.

The voice in his head was a thousand years old. Stevie got into the car. The front seat bench was covered in a soft, warm, brown fur. As a cold wind chased him into the comfort, Stevie closed the car door and listened to the Troll's fingers curl about the vehicle once more. It was warm, cozy, and safe. Next to him was a stack of fast food from the local McDonald's: hamburgers, fries, hot apple pies, and a large soda.

"How?" Stevie asked as he crammed the food into his mouth.

The magic of a mid-winter's night.

Stevie had no response. Instead, he spent his time concentrating on filling his stomach until there was nothing left to eat or drink. When he was done, he gave a satisfied burp and gathered the trash into single bag. He moved that to the floorboard and lay on the bench. Part of him wondered how he was going to get out in the morning. Part of him wondered if this was the best dream in the world. Either way, he did not want it to stop. For the first time in a long time—and for the last time—Stevie went to sleep with a full belly.

Outside, the Troll cried tears of sorrow as he, too, was fed on a cold winter's night.

BIOGRAPHY

JENNIFER BROZEK is an award-winning editor, game designer, and author.

Winner of the Australian Shadows Award for best edited publication, Jennifer has edited fifteen anthologies, with more on the way. Author of *In a Gilded Light*, *The Lady of Seeking in the City of Waiting*, *Industry Talk*, and the *Karen Wilson Chronicles*, she has more than sixty published short stories, and is the Creative Director of Apocalypse Ink Productions.

A freelance author for numerous RPG companies, Jennifer is the winner of both the Origins and the ENnie awards. She is also the author of the YA *Battletech* novel, *The Nellus Academy Incident*.

When she is not writing her heart out, she is gallivanting around the Pacific Northwest in its wonderfully mercurial weather. Jennifer is an active member of SFWA, HWA, and IAMTW. Read more about her at www.jenniferbrozek.com or follow her on Twitter at @JenniferBrozek.

EVIL GIRLFRIEND MEDIA

WWW.EVILGIRLFRIENDMEDIA.COM

Look for the big red heart to find new favorites in the Sci-Fi, Fantasy and Horror genres!

ALSO AVAILABLE IN EBOOK AND PRINT:

The Heart-Shaped Emblor
by Alaina Ewing

Witches, Bitches & Stitches
A Three Little Words anthology

Roms, Bombs, & Zoms
A Three Little Words anthology

Stamps, Vamps, & Tramps
A Three Little Words anthology

Bless Your Mechanical Heart
An anthology

Made in the USA
Middletown, DE
25 September 2016